MW01003120

TheGreat Space

Book 6

Scrapyard Ship Series

Mark Wayne McGinnis

Copyright © 2014 by Mark Wayne McGinnis All rights reserved. No part of this publication may be reproduced, distributed, or transmitted in any form or by any means, including photocopying, recording, or other electronic or mechanical methods, without the prior written permission of the publisher, except in the case of brief quotations embodied in critical reviews and certain other noncommercial uses permitted by copyright law. For permission requests, write to the publisher, addressed "Attention: Permissions Coordinator," at the address below. This book is a work of fiction. Names, characters, places, and incidents either are products of the author's imagination or are used fictitiously. Any resemblance to actual persons, living or dead, events, or locales is entirely coincidental.

Cover design by:

Eren Arik

Edited by:

Lura Lee Genz

Mia Manns

Last Updated: June 21, 2024

Published by:

Avenstar Productions

• **ISBN-10** : 0990331490

• **ISBN-13** : 978-0990331490

www.markwaynemcginnis.com

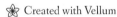 Created with Vellum

Prologue

"Captain, three Caldurian ships just appeared six hundred miles off our starboard bow," Gunny said. "It's crazy... they're just like..." Orion hesitated as she rechecked her station instruments.

"They're what, Gunny?"

"They're like us... they look like *The Lilly*. Three, I think newer versions, of *The Lilly*, Captain."

Jason looked up at the now refreshed view on the overhead wraparound display. The three ships were indeed nearly identical to *The Lilly*, but these ships had several minor differences: the slope of the bow, a broadening at the stern where a third drive had been incorporated, and they weren't matte black, like *The Lilly*. They were a blue-gray color.

"Cap, all three have weapons charging. They've deployed their plasma and rail cannons!"

Jason yelled, "Battle stations! McBride, phase-shift us the hell out of here... anywhere!"

All three Caldurian ships fired simultaneously.

The impact was enough to throw three crewmembers out of

their seats, and the overhead bridge lights flickered. "Shields are already down to twenty percent, Sir. Phase-shifting and propulsion is offline," the XO said.

"Weapon systems, Gunny?"

"Plasma cannons are offline... firing rails and missiles now."

Jason's mind reeled. He needed a way out of this, an idea, something, or they'd be destroyed within the next few seconds. Even now, in the midst of it, Jason wondered if he was dreaming. It seemed real, ultra-real... but then again, something was off.

"Hail them," Jason said, turning to Gordon on the Comms station.

"Shields down to five percent, Captain."

"More Caldurian ships coming out of another wormhole," Orion announced.

"No response from repeated hails, Sir," Seaman Gordon said.

Jason turned to see the arrival of the other ships. These were different, still had the hallmark look of Caldurian design, but were bulky, massive ships—he figured they were some kind of troop transport-type vessels. It was then that Jason saw it: on the other side of the wormhole, two Earth-like planets side by side. Actually, the unmistakable contours of North America meant one *was* Earth.

"Shields down!" Orion yelled.

The AI's deceptively calm voice filled the bridge...

Outer hull breach on levels two and four. Ship integrity lost... Abandon ship... Abandon ship... Abandon ship.

Jason's scream split the still silence of the Captain's quarters. With his heart still pounding, he sat up and realized where he was. His T-shirt—the sheets—were drenched with sweat. It was only a nightmare. He laid back and let his breathing return to normal. A nightmare with a new enemy... *God, it seemed so real.*

Chapter 1

They'd left the fringe of the Sol Solar System with the battered, war-torn fragments of what was once a Craing fleet, a graveyard of fifteen hundred warships, behind. Now they approached a lone Alliance warship that sat less than a mile off their bow in the distance.

Captain Stalls knew from sensor reports there was only a limited security force left behind onboard *The Cutlass*. Good, considering he had little in the way of an assault force himself. What he did have were the few dozen Craing who'd been marooned for nearly a year in space. So he'd need to get on and off *The Cutlass* as quickly as possible. But wasn't that what pirates, like him, were infamous for?

He watched the display and the bug-like warship, which was virtually identical to his three Craing cruisers—except this one was painted bright white and had red, white, and blue stars and stripes emblems prominently affixed at various locations around the ship's hull.

He smiled to himself as he contemplated Captain Reynolds's reaction when he learned of his daughter's abduction. From what Stalls understood from picked-up interstellar chatter, the Earth humans were already having a rough go of it. The Allied forces had been decimated in the past week; planets, hell, entire star systems had been annihilated.

Stalls felt Rup-Lor's presence behind him. There was something about the little Craing that annoyed him—even above the annoyance he felt for their race as a whole.

"Don't just hover there, what is it you want?"

"Captain, as ordered, I've assembled an assault team."

Stalls turned and looked down at his XO. "Where?"

"In hold number four, Captain."

"Fine. I'll be down shortly."

Rup-Lor hesitated, looking unsure of himself.

"What is it?"

"Sir, we've picked up Craing command communications. A formation of fifteen hundred warships is immobile near the sixth planet from the sun; humans call it Saturn. There are six breakaway ships, dreadnoughts, now nearing Mars. Sir, these are the black Vanguard ships. Planet killers."

Stalls had little sympathy for those on Earth, but this update certainly complicated things. He had a plan. Ultimately, he would rebuild his fleet and return home, but first and foremost, he would not let anything get in the way of his revenge on Captain Reynolds. Second, the thought of losing the Earth woman, Nan, was unthinkable. Added to that, he was also a humanoid. It was very evident the Craing were systematically eradicating the human race. The implications of that alone were sobering.

"Rup-Lor, go below. I'll join you shortly and assess the assault team."

"Yes, Captain."

Stalls sat down in the Captain's command chair and watched the little Craing officer leave the bridge. *That certainly changes things*, he thought. *Or does it?* In the event Captain

Reynolds survived the coming battle, which was feasible based on his past exploits, Stalls still wanted leverage over him. So the situation hadn't changed. He needed to grab the kid.

CAPTAIN STALLS ENTERED HOLD NUMBER FOUR wearing a newly cleaned dress shirt. As promised, Rup-Lor had assembled a Craing assault team. Thirty little warriors were standing in three rows of ten. Wearing Craing battlesuits and holding pulse weapons, the formation stood perfectly still before him. Stalls moved between the rows looking for something to criticize—perhaps eyes not locked forward, or improper posture, or anything. But the Craing formation was tip-top.

Stalls joined Rup-Lor standing before the group. "They look fine. You've reviewed with them the plan?"

"Yes. First, we'll approach from three different vectors. The attack will come fast, taking out *The Cutlass*'s drives; then we'll target the vessel's bridge. Next, with their shields down, we should have no problem breaching the hull and entering the ship at the three locations specified."

"And the objective?"

"To capture the young human female," Rup-Lor answered. "I will personally undertake that responsibility."

Stalls would far prefer to board the ship himself and lead the assault teams. But it came down to trust, and he didn't completely trust this crew not to hightail it away the second he was off ship—especially with the massive Craing fleet so close by.

"Five minutes, get your teams in position," Stalls said. He left the hold and made the long trek back through dark narrow corridors, up several flights of stairs, and arrived at the wider—better lit—primary level where the bridge was located. He entered the bridge and saw Drig sitting on the raised section of the bridge that contained the row of officers' chairs. Drig was now perched in the XO seat. Stalls sat down next to him, keeping his eyes on the display before him.

"Attack!"

"Go fish," Boomer said triumphantly.

Teardrop continued to look at its cards for several seconds, then down at the loosely stacked deck lying on the table between them. Boomer watched as the droid extended out its left articulating arm and, with surprising dexterity, plucked up one card after another and placed them into its right claw, among its ever-growing *handful* of cards.

Teardrop, an advanced Caldurian droid whose torso was teardrop-shaped, was Boomer's companion and protector. She was certain that without her loyal friend onboard this old, smelly Craing ship, she most certainly would have gone bonkers. As it was, she had enlisted the droid to play every game imaginable, from hide-and-seek, to hot-and-cold, to any number of card games, such as their current game of *Go Fish*.

With a metallic *clang,* her cabin hatch opened, and Petty Officer Miller entered. Boomer didn't look up, didn't acknowledge her presence.

"You know this isn't playtime, Boomer. I told you, one more hour of math." Miller strutted over to Boomer's small work desk and snatched up Boomer's tablet. Miller accessed the learning module and reviewed the day's assignments. "I guess you completed your assignments for today. But that doesn't mean play time. You could move forward and complete tomorrow's assignments."

Boomer continued looking at her cards. With her eyes only,

she looked up at Petty Officer Miller and raised her eyebrows. Miller brought her attention back to the tablet.

"Well, actually, it looks like you've moved ahead some." Miller continued to swipe the pages on the tablet. Her brow furrowed. "You've finished all the assignments?"

Boomer, back to playing her game, gestured toward her temple: "Remember? I have advanced nano-technology in my head. I completed all the assignments the first day you came onboard."

The Petty Officer made a disgusted face. "You're spending too much time with that robot. You need to interact more with your own kind. I want that thing out of here. Take a shower. You're starting to smell. Then we'll go to the mess and have some lunch."

Whoop Whoop Whoop...

The general quarters alarm blared into Boomer's small cabin, causing both Boomer and Petty Officer Miller to momentarily freeze. Teardrop transformed from playmate to combat droid in a nanosecond. It was up and moving to the hatch and taking a defensive position there.

"This vessel is being boarded by enemy combatants," the droid said.

Boomer got up, brushed past the Petty Officer, and disappeared down a short corridor into her bedroom cabin.

"Where are you going? You need to stay right here by my side, Boomer. You're my responsibility," Miller commanded.

Boomer returned, now wearing shoes; there was a small backpack draped over her shoulder. Hooked onto her belt was the gift from Woodrow, the light blue throwing knife.

"What do you think you're doing? Absolutely not. Take off that knife—"

The sound of a loud explosion interrupted Miller's words. *The Cutlass* violently jolted to the right, throwing both Boomer and the Petty Officer off balance and onto the deck. Before they could stand, two more equally jarring explosions happened in rapid succession.

The hatch opened. It was Petty Officer Woodrow. Armed with a pulse weapon and wearing a battlesuit with his helmet retracted, he gestured for Boomer and Miller to follow him.

Boomer felt an immediate sense of relief seeing that her highly capable self-defense instructor was there to protect her.

Miller held fast. "I'm responsible for this child. Tell me where you're taking us."

"You're responsible for tucking her in at night and making sure she eats her carrots. I'm here at the Captain's request and I'm responsible for keeping her alive at times like these. You're welcome to stay here, hide under the bed if you want, whatever, but she's coming with me."

Woodrow extended his hand and Boomer took it. Together, Woodrow and Boomer, with Teardrop close behind, took off down the corridor. Miller, several paces back, followed them. Turning the next bend, Woodrow and Boomer came face to face with an assault team of ten armed Craing.

Woodrow pushed Boomer to the deck with one hand while bringing up his pulse rifle with the other. Boomer looked back at Miller; as much as a meddling pain she could be, Boomer found herself worrying about her. Again, Woodrow pushed Boomer's head down. "Get down, damn it!"

Boomer screamed out as she watched Woodrow take four simultaneous plasma pulses to the head—he was dead before firing his first shot.

Teardrop, with its plasma cannon now protruding through a small compartment at the middle of its torso, was fully engaged —returning fire with short, precise bursts into the Craing assault team. Five of the Craing were already down. Miller was on her belly making her way across the deck over to Boomer.

Two more Craing went down, leaving the last two attempting to retreat the same way they'd come. Boomer, now at Woodrow's side, was hoping by some miracle he was still alive. He was not. It was then she felt Petty Officer Miller climb on top of her.

"Get off me! What are you doing?" Boomer yelled.

"Keep your head down! Don't move," Miller barked back.

Two more teams of ten Craing each suddenly appeared at both ends of the corridor. Teardrop continued to fire: first spinning in one direction, firing multiple bursts, then spinning in the other, and firing again. Boomer watched from below Miller's outstretched arms as Teardrop took continual plasma fire from both sides. Tears filled her eyes and blurred her vision.

"Stop! Stop hurting it! Please, stop!" She continued to scream until she felt her throat would give out. She couldn't move and couldn't reach for Woodrow's dropped pulse rifle that lay mere feet away. Miller's weight on her back was making it hard to breathe. She wondered if Petty Officer Miller was also dead.

Watching, Boomer saw Teardrop having trouble maintaining its ability to hover. Suddenly, the droid dropped to the deck. All the plasma fire around her stopped. Boomer continued to stare at the immobile silhouette of Teardrop, and then looked at Woodrow, lying by her side.

No one moved for several minutes. Then, in the distance, Boomer saw a lone figure walking her way. Tall, muscular, and with hair pulled back into a long ponytail, she knew exactly who he was.

Chapter 2

The distress call came in right as *The Lilly* phase-shifted out of *The Minian*'s hold.

Jason had just sat down in the command chair when Gunny Orion looked up, startled, from her console.

"Captain, I've got *The Cutlass* on comms, they've been attacked," Orion said, looking worried.

Having left *The Cutlass* only an hour earlier, Jason didn't see how. "Tell me my daughter..."

"I'm sorry, Captain. He says Boomer's been taken."

Jason was on his feet. "Who are you talking to? Put him on screen!"

A disheveled-looking officer appeared on a new video feed. He tried to sit up straighter when he realized he was being viewed. Jason recognized the officer. He was Commander Rick Casper.

"What the hell happened, Casper?"

"I'm not completely sure, Captain. Minutes after the convoy separated, we were attacked by three Craing cruisers. We only needed a few minutes to make repairs before we were going to join the convoy back on Earth. Our shields were down—"

"Where the hell's my daughter... where's Boomer, Casper!?"

The officer looked as if he was going to pass out. He gulped down several deep breaths and continued, "This was an organized strike. They seemed to know exactly where to find her. After taking out both the bridge and propulsion systems, they breached the hull in several locations, all near her cabin."

Jason said, "She was in the care of Petty Officer Woodrow—"

Casper was shaking his head. "No... He was killed fighting the Craing. The droid was fried as well. I'm sorry, Captain."

"And Petty Officer Miller?"

The Commander looked confused for a beat. "Um... well, she's currently not onboard. I assume she was taken, too. I wish I could tell you who exactly was responsible for this, Captain."

Jason held up a hand, "Hold on a second." He needed to think. *This certainly wasn't the work of the Craing. So who would do this?* "I may have an idea who's responsible. Stalls. Captain fucking Stalls."

Orion and Commander Rick Casper didn't disagree.

"What's the condition of *The Cutlass* and her crew, Commander?" Jason asked.

"All crewmen who were on the bridge, as well as in Engineering, are dead. More were killed as the three Craing teams entered the ship. All and all, we have thirty-five survivors, and half of them are injured."

So above and beyond Boomer being taken, one of the few ships he had was now badly damaged. Worse, most of the crew onboard had been killed. Hell... this small fleet of ships was needed to go up against the Craing. This seriously impacted their effectiveness. Just one more major setback at the hands of Captain Stalls.

13

"We'll be there in a few minutes. Have what remains of the crew prepare to abandon *The Cutlass*."

Jason signaled for Orion to cut the connection. "Helm, get us to *The Cutlass*," Jason ordered.

Sitting there, replaying the conversation in his head, he chided himself for not leaving a larger security contingent onboard. As the battered *Cutlass* appeared on the overhead display, Jason and the rest of the crew became quiet. The damage was far worse than Jason even imagined.

"Gunny, upload phase-shift coordinates to my HUD. XO, let Dira and her team know they should expect multiple injuries. Have Grimes ready *Perilous*; she can shuttle both crew and injured back to *The Lilly*. Let everyone know, we're leaving this area of space in ten minutes or less."

"Aye, Captain." Perkins took the command chair as soon as Jason moved toward the exit. Within several seconds, Jason could see he had the phase-shift coordinates for *The Cutlass*. He activated the phase-shift and in a flash was standing among the carnage of what must have been a devastating battle. No less than fifteen Craing combatants lay dead on the deck at one end of the corridor, and several more dead lay at the other end.

At the center of the carnage was the body of Petty Officer Woodrow. There were numerous scorch marks on his face and head. Had he activated his helmet, things might have turned out differently. One thing Jason couldn't take away from his fellow Navy SEAL, Woodrow had died protecting his daughter, and Jason would always be grateful to him for that.

Jason moved back toward Boomer's cabin, then walked forward again trying to piece together what had happened. It was obvious everyone onboard *The Cutlass* was taken by surprise. Woodrow would have been moving Boomer, and the others, to a more secure location on the ship. They were running —probably flat out. When they came around the corner, they were engaged by one of the Craing teams. Undoubtedly, Woodrow, or maybe Miller, would have pushed Boomer down flat on the deck. That split-second, a split-second Woodrow could have used to activate his helmet, was all the Craing needed to take him out.

Jason stood over Woodrow's body and noticed blood on the deck plates and adjoining bulkhead. Strange, since plasma fire actually cauterizes blood vessels. He'd never seen blood loss like this unless projectile weapons or knives were involved. Jason's heart skipped a beat. Boomer was a nut about knives lately. He knelt closer and inspected the deck and then the wall. It wasn't an arbitrary blood splatter. Was it... words? He had to tilt his head to read from the bottom of the wall up, but he saw it:

STALLS STOLE ME & MILLER

Realizing she must have cut herself fairly deeply to produce enough blood to leave this message, Jason had to fight back his rage. One thing was for sure: he'd get his daughter back and end Stalls' life, once and for all. As Jason continued to stare at the wall, another thought crossed his mind, a minor consolation. Stalls would most certainly have his hands full with Boomer.

JASON HAD WOODROW'S BODY, AS WELL AS Boomer's drone, collected and returned to *The Lilly*. Once Ricket was back from trying to bring *The Minian*'s battle-ravaged systems online, perhaps he could repair the drone. She'd come to love the thing and, it seemed, it loved her—if that was at all possible. He'd left Ricket, Granger, and Bristol onboard *The Minian*, which was now hidden within strewn space wreckage at the far end of the Solar System. Jason purposely tried not to overly think about Boomer being held captive in the hands of that pirate maniac. If he wanted to get her back, he'd have to rely more on smarts and cunning, instead of brute emotions.

The ship's AI made an announcement...

Captain on the bridge.

Jason entered the command center of *The Lilly*. It was a welcome sight to see a fully staffed bridge again. On their recent mission to the Craing worlds, where they'd absconded with *The Minian*, crews had been split between three ships—the now-destroyed *Her Majesty, The Lilly,* and *The Minian.*

The XO stood up from the command chair and waited for Jason to take his place.

"I am ready to relieve you, XO," Jason said.

"I am ready to be relieved, Sir."

"What's the status of the Craing fleet?"

"The bulk of the fleet is still stationary around Saturn, Captain."

"And the dreadnoughts?"

"Yes, there's six of them and they are holding steady near Mars. It's as if they're waiting for something."

Jason looked up at Perkins. "You looked tired, XO. You've been relieved, time to hit your bunk."

"Aye, Sir."

Ensign McBride waited for Perkins to leave the bridge before asking the one question Jason would be the most hard-pressed to answer. "Destination, Cap?"

Jason didn't answer. His eyes tracked the view of open space above as if he were scanning the heavens for an answer. Both his orders and his conscience were telling him to get back to Earth and defend her with all haste. Jason's first assumption was that Stalls would take his newly acquired warships, along with Boomer, back to his pirate world, or worlds.

But something wasn't sitting right with that logic. *Why take his daughter if he didn't want something in return?* Jason knew what that was. Sure, he wanted to kill Jason, but even more importantly, he wanted Nan. He'd want to trade Boomer for Nan. In all likelihood, Stalls was still close by. Watching and waiting.

"How long would it take us to return to Earth?"

"With a combination of wormhole travel and phase-shifting... once we're in close... minutes," Orion replied.

Just as he figured. *The Lilly* could be back in Earth's orbit in minutes to defend the planet if and when the Craing made a move toward Earth. Was that the best use of *The Lilly*'s resources under the present circumstances? Simply waiting around in Earth's high orbit? Jason didn't think so. He'd never liked playing defense. If they were going to thwart an attack, they—he—needed to take the initiative. *But how?*

"Captain, we're being hailed by a Craing vessel approximately twenty light-years from our current position," Seaman Gordon said. "He's identified himself as Captain Stalls."

Chapter 3

"I'll take it in my quarters," Jason replied. "Gunny, you've got the bridge." Jason stopped and turned back around. One by one, he made eye contact with everyone on the bridge. "I want his precise location. There's amazing Caldurian technology on this ship—figure out how to use it and find Stalls' ship. If you need help, contact Ricket as a last resort."

By the time Jason made it to his ready room, Captain Stalls' face was already on screen at the far end of the room. He smirked at the sight of Jason and offered him a condescending smile that made Jason want to reach through the screen and strangle him. Not giving the pirate the gratification of seeing a reaction, Jason sat down with a flat, deadpan expression on his face, and waited for Stalls to say something.

"It is so good to see you again, Captain Reynolds."

"Knock off the chit-chat, asshole. We both know why you've contacted me. What's it going to take to get my daughter back?"

Stalls gave an exaggerated expression of deep contemplation. "Hmm, that is the question of the day, isn't it? You know, she is such a lovely little girl. How old is she... eight? Nine? As a slave on one of the Polaris' moons, she would fetch a hefty sum. Of course, it's when she's older that she will really—"

"I asked you a question. Are you going to play games or have a real conversation here?"

"My, my, Jason. You're certainly serious today. All right, we'll get down to business. I have several demands. They are non-negotiable." Stalls hesitated, brushing away an imaginary piece of lint from the front of his ruffled shirt. "One... You will deliver Nan to me. She will come to me willingly, with the full understanding that she will ultimately be my wife, never to return to Earth. Two... You will deliver to me ten of your fully operational Craing warships. They can be a mix of heavy and light-cruisers." Stalls stopped again, tapping his pursed lips with an index finger in phony contemplation.

Jason watched the performance in silence, not letting Stalls' antics alter his passive expression. "Anything else?"

"Oh yes, there is one more thing: you, Captain Reynolds. As part of this negotiation, I require your life. Or, perhaps it would be more accurate to say, your death—a death by a means of my own choosing. Fulfill those demands, and little Boomer will be returned to Earth unharmed."

"You do know you're crazy, right? That you have a mental problem that could be treated with medication, or maybe even surgery?"

Stalls stared back with a bored expression, eventually holding up an open-faced palm. "I told you my demands were non-negotiable."

"I don't have ten warships to hand over to you. Don't forget it was you who just catastrophically damaged *The* Cutlass and killed or injured almost all of her crew. Understand, Earth may be attacked by a Craing fleet at any moment. Those warships could conceivably save thousands, millions, of lives on the surface..."

"That's hardly my problem."

"Here's what you get if my daughter is not returned today, right now: You get me dedicating my life to pursuing you—across the Universe if that's what it takes. I've beaten you down before and I'll beat you down again, and this time, before it's over, I'll be shoving your head up your ass. You'll be nothing more than a ponytail with two legs."

"Captain, I don't think you want to be making threats. Not with little Boomer's life at stake. I will contact you again in two hours. At that time you will either comply to my demands or watch as I slit her throat in front of you."

Jason fumed. He doubted Stalls would make good on his threat—give up his only bargaining chip—but was Jason willing to take that chance, with his daughter's life at stake? "Let me see her. I need to see that she's all right."

"She's fine. Unconscious from a plasma stun, but probably fine." Stalls gave a perfunctory shrug and the screen went black.

Jason heard a NanoCom tone—he was being hailed.

"Go for Captain."

Ricket said, "Captain, I've been contacted by *The Lilly*'s bridge... Orion, actually."

Jason sighed, and said, "I was hoping it wouldn't be necessary, considering the importance of what you're working on. With that said, does *The Lilly* have the necessary technology to find Stalls' ship?"

"No."

Jason's heart sank. The reality of what happened, was still happening, bore down on him.

"*The Lilly*'s technology—"

"I got it, Ricket. We can't track Stalls' ship."

"I was about to say, Captain, at the present time, *The Lilly* does not have the advanced technology required for such a task. But *The Minian* does."

Jason let a glimmer of hope enter his consciousness. "*The Minian* is a wreck. Have you repaired her to the point she can track Stalls' ship?"

"No, that is still hours, if not days, away. But I do know where that technology—something called the *probability matrix* —is located. My suggestion would be to extricate it and have it duplicated by *The Minian*'s phase-synthesizer, along with the necessary interface for *The Lilly*."

"That sounds promising, but it also sounds complicated. How long will all that take?"

"I can accomplish the task in a half hour, maybe less, Captain."

Jason didn't need to think about it. Not with Boomer's life hanging in the balance. "Do it!"

He cut the connection and stared down at the table before him. He knew what he had to do next and had purposely avoided. He hailed Seaman Gordon on the bridge.

"Seaman Gordon, Captain."

"Get me a comms channel to Earth. Track down Nan Reynolds and put her through to my ready room."

"Aye, Captain."

Jason looked up to see Billy entering the compartment. He was wearing his spacer's jumpsuit with the recently added, now standard issue, SuitPac device worn on his hip. No further need for the standard, bulky battlesuit configurations they'd worn before. Once activated, in less than three seconds the new Caldurian technology device would completely envelop the user in an advanced, segmented battlesuit.

Billy gestured toward a seat with raised eyebrows. Jason nodded.

"You know we're going to get her back, Cap. There's just no two ways about it," Billy offered up with more bravado than either of them totally believed.

"What I should be doing is beating a path back to Earth. Like right now. At the very least, be coming up with a plan to thwart an attack."

"Mind a little unsolicited advice?"

"I've got a feeling I'm going to get it anyway, so sure, lay it on me," Jason replied in a resigned tone.

"Don't let that bastard dictate the terms. He knows your emotions are involved and he's using them to beat you. You'll need to put them aside and do what you do best."

Jason waited for him to continue.

"It's thinking outside the damn box. Play your game, not his."

Jason knew he was right. If he were to have any chance of getting Boomer back, it would have to be by outsmarting the pirate. The truth was, he had no idea how he was going to get out of this one and still save his daughter. If it came to it, he'd give up his own life to save her.

The AI interrupted his thoughts.

The Seaman Gordon twins are standing outside your ready room, Captain.

Not everyone was granted unrestricted access to his quarters; Billy was one of the few. "Let them in," Jason ordered with a sigh.

Jason noticed Billy's bemused expression as the two red-haired identical twins awkwardly entered the ready room. Jason felt for the two Bridgecrew Seamen. With an identical mole evident on each twin's right cheek, everyone, including himself, had an impossible time telling one from the other. Typically, they didn't work the same shift, so using the same moniker —Seaman Gordon—sufficed just fine. It was when they were together, like now, that one needed to check name tags for the only identifying difference.

"Weren't one of you trying to locate Nan Reynolds for me?"

"Um. Yes, that was me, Sir. She's in a conference. I left instructions for her to contact you when she gets free."

"Fine. What can I do for you gentlemen?"

The twins looked at each other then, both talking at once, stopped, and the Gordon on the right spoke up, "Captain, we may have figured something out."

"How to find Stalls' ship? I already spoke to Ricket. He's on it."

"No, Sir. It's more of a communications thing. We've been working on a little side project, you know, on our own time. Anyway, we think we can decipher Craing communications. At least, those directed within close proximity of *The Lilly*."

That revelation got Jason's attention. "You think, or you actually can?"

Again they looked at each other. This time the other twin spoke up, "We most definitely can, Sir."

"Sit down... both of you. Tell me more."

"We've only intercepted one transmission, but it's a doozy. Neither of us speaks Terplin, but we think the gist of the message states that the acting Emperor lives. He's somehow survived the destruction of the Emperor's Palace. It seemed to be more of a general information type transmission... as opposed to specific orders to be put into action."

Both Jason and Billy glanced at each other. "Okay, I have one question: Since we can receive and decode messages, can we also transmit?"

"You mean, as if it had originated from another Craing ship, or otherwise?"

Jason nodded.

"I think so," they both answered at the same time.

Billy asked, "Can you block or disrupt their messages, their transmissions?"

"Theoretically we could. We'd need Ricket's help with that, though."

Jason hailed Ricket.

"Go for Ricket."

"I need you over here, Ricket. Something's come up."

In less than a minute, all heads quickly turned as Ricket entered the ready room holding a device of some sort, with multiple optical cables hanging from it.

"I was already onboard, Captain, on my way to install this into *Lilly*'s bridge," Ricket said.

"Seaman Gordon, tell Ricket what you told us."

Chapter 4

Jason listened as Ricket and the Gordon twins got deep into techy-weeds, far and above Jason's head. Billy had already excused himself and Jason was readying to leave when he saw Nan's face appear on the screen.

"Can you three take this conversation elsewhere?" Jason asked. Ricket and the two Gordons, seeing Nan on the screen, immediately stood and left the compartment.

"Jason. Are you all right? You look all right. But the message I received sounded so dire."

"Nan, there's no good way to tell you this." Jason paused to let her prepare for the bad news. "Boomer's been abducted."

Her face transformed from confusion to indignation. "What? How? Don't you dare tell me it's Stalls. I don't think I can handle that, Jason."

Jason didn't say anything. His expression must have said it all because her tears came with an inability to catch her breath. "Has he... Has he hurt her? Oh my God, Jason, has he hurt our baby?"

"No. She's absolutely fine," he answered, not really sure if that was true or not.

Nan's hands covered her face and eyes as if she were saying a private prayer. Wiping her cheeks, she caught her breath. "What does he want? He must want something to trade..."

She then came to the conclusion herself. "He wants me, right? He wants to trade her life for me being his... whatever."

"Among other things, yes."

"What other things? Tell me specifically what he's asked for."

"Ten of our Craing warships and my head on a platter."

She didn't need to think about it. "I'll go. Tell him I'll go and be his fucking concubine if he wants, but Boomer needs to be returned first—safe and sound."

"That's not an option. He'll never release her, Nan. That's not the way he's wired. Even you chained to his bed, and my head mounted on a wall, won't be enough for him. There's no honor with this guy. Boomer would inevitably be sold off to slavers, or worse. His hatred of me is that intense. Believe me on this."

"Then what do we do?"

"I have some time... a few hours. I'm developing a plan. I'll get her back and I'll deal with Stalls then, once and for all."

She closed her eyes and shook her head, still in disbelief. With concern in her eyes, she said, "No, I'll go to him... nothing's more important than getting her back safe." She started to tear up again.

"That simply isn't going to happen. Let me deal with Stalls... trust me, Nan. I'll get her back."

Eventually, she nodded, looking resigned to what Jason said. "On another subject, the Admiral's furious. Your convoy arrived but without *The Lilly*. The Craing are assembling, Jason. We need you."

"Nan, I think you know I'm not new to fighting the Craing. But six dreadnoughts and a fleet of fifteen hundred Craing warships are too much for us. Even if we had the Allied fleet fully intact, it would still be a slaughter. The only way we survive is by holding them off long enough to bring *The Minian* back into the fight. But that's going to take a day or two, at a minimum."

Jason reentered the bridge to find two consoles torn apart. In addition to Ricket and the two Gordons hard at work, doing whatever they were doing, Bristol was working there as well.

"I need to dump some additional code into the AI's core."

Jason wasn't quite sure whom Bristol was talking to until he saw the skinny, pimply-faced ex-pirate staring back at him.

"If you want to track where my brother is, get this *probability matrix* operational, I'll need your permission to modify systems-level code," Bristol said, first glancing over to Ricket, who had undoubtedly told him the same thing.

"Only under Ricket's direct supervision," Jason said.

"Well, he's working on the communications crap with the two Gordon *tards*."

"I won't tolerate that sort of talk on my bridge. I've warned you before, Seaman Bristol."

Ricket separated himself from working with the Gordons and moved to Bristol's side. "Captain, we'll need to update the AI core, or the new hardware won't be recognized. I've looked over his code. It's sound. Please understand, the upload will bring down all ship systems for a period of five minutes. Weapons, shields, life support... everything. There's plenty of air to breathe in that time, but we will lose gravity... it's a complete system reset."

Jason thought about that prospect—being totally defenseless for five minutes. That would leave both *The Minian* and *The*

Lilly sitting ducks. With the Craing, as well as Captain Stalls, somewhere out there in near space, that was unacceptable. "Gunny, roust our fighter pilots. I want every available pilot sitting in a fighter and ready to deploy within two minutes."

"Aye, Cap."

Bristol went back to work, burying his head inside a console.

"Ricket, keep a close eye on him. I don't need to remind you it's his brother Stalls, a fellow pirate, we're dealing with. I have no idea where Bristol's loyalties lie when it comes down to it."

Ricket didn't reply to that. "Captain, on a different subject, the Gordon twins have nearly completed their work on the communications equipment. It's really quite ingenious. With the reset of the core, we should be able to both receive and transmit Craing communications. Since it will be interfaced through the AI, all real-time translations will take place as well."

"Captain, thirty fighters are ready to deploy," Orion piped in.

"Go ahead and get them into space, Gunny."

Bristol looked up from the console at the same time the Gordon twins looked over to Jason, their thumbs pointing upward. Ricket looked at Bristol, who made an exaggerated, mocking, thumbs-up gesture as well.

"We're ready, Captain," Ricket said. "Both the new comms equipment, as well as new Caldurian tracking capability, are installed. We need to bring the ship's systems down now."

"Put me on ship-wide, Seaman Gordon."

"Aye, Captain."

"This is your Captain speaking. Over the next few minutes, all ship systems will be down. This is only temporary and nothing to be concerned with. Complete, halt, whatever you're doing and prepare for weightlessness until the ship's systems have been reinitialized. Captain out.

"Okay, Ricket, let's get it done."

Ricket entered a string of commands at his terminal and a moment later the bridge went dark. Almost immediately, dim backup lights came on. Everything went still and, as Ricket had said, gravity was now non-existent. Jason, seated in the command chair, clung to both armrests to keep himself from floating upward. Bristol, who hadn't grabbed on to anything, was already four feet off the ground and, with his legs out and his hands behind his head, was feigning being asleep.

The above three-hundred-and-sixty-degree wrap-around display was now disabled and the bridge seemed smaller, more confining. The bridgecrew, with the ship dead in space, either sat with their hands holding on to something, or floated above the deck, while the seconds ticked by.

Jason was being hailed.

"Go for Captain. What do you have, Lieutenant Wilson?"

"It's at the far reaches of our sensors, Cap; it's faint, but it looks like the signature of a Craing dreadnought. It's moving toward Mars."

"Thanks, Lieutenant, keep me posted on any other new developments."

Jason wondered if *The Lilly* being dark could actually be a good thing, but then remembered *The Lilly* was virtually impossible to detect anyway, by either long- or short-range sensors. His thoughts turned to the passing Craing ship... *Why send in another dreadnought?* It didn't make sense—another one was overkill. *Or was it?* Perhaps the planet-annihilation process required seven dreadnoughts, not six. The presence of the distant ship brought Earth's perilous situation to the forefront of his mind. He'd get back there the first moment he could.

Jason kept his eyes steady on Bristol as the last remaining seconds winded down. With a *clunk, The Lilly's* systems began to come back online.

Bristol, now hovering six feet off the ground, started to flail around. "A little help, please!" The words no sooner left his lips than the gravity generators kicked in and Bristol plummeted to the deck. He landed hard on his ass and bellowed a high-pitched *yelp* as he hit.

Jason stood. "Let's get these consoles closed up and the new equipment tested. A lot depends on what it will provide us."

Bristol slowly got to his feet, rubbing his hindquarters, and moved back to the console he'd been working at.

As things got battened down and the bridge returned to normal, Jason thought about his next move. He had to furnish Earth a reprieve from the all-too-imminent attack.

Seaman Jeffery Gordon approached. "Captain, the connections are complete. The next step will be testing the equipment."

"Let me ask you something, Seaman. I understand we're now able to intercept communications from Craing ships, and even from the Craing worlds. You also mentioned we'll be able to transmit. I want to transmit via a communications channel to both the Craing fleet, sitting off Saturn, as well as to the dreadnoughts parked near Mars. It's important we lead them to think this message originated from the Craing worlds."

"Absolutely, Captain. That's part of what we've engineered here. Celestial location markers accompany all Craing transmissions. We'll imbed the Terplin location, perhaps somewhere close to the Emperor's Palace, or what used to be the palace—we should be able to do that now."

Jason frowned. "This has to be one hundred percent believable. An audio transmission alone won't cut it ... Ricket, do you still have that Craing costume lying around... Emperor Quorp's?"

"No, Captain. But I can have an identical one replicated."

Jason continued to stare at Ricket. Days earlier, Ricket's

looks had been temporarily altered, via a MediPod, for his mission to Terplin and the Ion Station.

Ricket continued, "With the Emperor reported injured, it would fall on one of the high priest overlords, at least temporarily, to speak for the Emperor. Shall I have the garment made, Captain?"

"As soon as possible. You are going live in one hour."

Chapter 5

Boomer awoke on the floor in the dark. Disoriented, it took her several moments to come to. *Where am I? What happened?* Then she remembered the sounds of plasma fire; Petty Officer Woodrow pushing her to the deck, and then... his dead, staring eyes. Boomer's heart froze in her chest when she relived Teardrop being repeatedly shot at, then suddenly crashing to the deck, immobile.

Boomer tried to sit up and felt a spike of pain in her back. *That's right,* she thought, Stalls had shot her, or stunned her, while she was writing a message to her dad—a message in her own blood. She fingered her other hand where she'd cut herself and felt no pain—no sign of a wound. Her internal nanites had apparently repaired the injury so there wasn't even a scar. Her hands moved to her belt and her knife. It was gone. She felt something around her ankle. *I'm chained up like a dog.* It rattled as her fingers explored the bindings and long chain.

Something stirred to Boomer's right.

"Boomer? Are you there?"

"Is that you, Petty Officer Miller... Priscilla?"

"Yes. I'm here. Are you hurt, Boomer? Are you injured?"

"No, I'm fine. Where are you?"

She heard rustling and then, in the near darkness, saw movement. A hand touched her leg and then arms found her, engulfing her in a hug.

"I thought you were dead. We've been abducted, Boomer."

Boomer rolled her eyes, even though the effect was lost on Miller in the darkness. "I know that. It's Captain Stalls. The pirate. He's the one who took us."

There was silence for several beats before Miller spoke in a quiet, measured, voice. "I want you to follow my orders. We do whatever we're asked to do. If he says jump, we jump. We do nothing to upset him. It's all about survival until your father can rescue us. If he *can* rescue us. Do you understand?"

"Um... no way. I know Captain Stalls. You don't. He's a monster. He'll do bad things to us. He came close to killing me and my mom once before. So if you think I'm not going to fight back, you're crazy. Even if it gets me killed. I don't do the victim thing anymore."

Boomer heard Miller exhale a long, labored breath.

"I'm responsible for you. You're just a little girl. It's my job to protect you."

"No. *I'm* responsible for me. And I'm not so little anymore. Remember... I've been captured by the Craing, fought wild boars and saber tooth tigers, and even fought Captain Stalls. You do what you want. I know what I'm going to do."

They sat there in silence for a while. It was faint, but Boomer heard the words: "If you're sure about that, you'll need this."

Boomer heard more rusting and then felt Miller feeling for, and then finding her left hand. Something cold and hard was placed in it. Boomer knew what it was—her knife. "How did you..."

"During the fight on *The Cutlass*, while we were on the

floor, I took it from your belt. It's been hiding in my bra ever since. Keep it out of sight."

"I will, I promise," Boomer whispered back. "Thank you." She tucked it into a side pocket of her spacer's jumpsuit. The handle was a tad longer than the pocket and protruded out about an inch. She'd have to keep her hand over it or keep her hand in her pocket for it to stay hidden.

"I wonder where we are," Miller said.

"We're in a Craing warship, but not one of ours. Can't you smell it?"

She heard Miller inhale. "Oh, yeah... there's a slight burnt smell, like charcoal and something else... something foul."

"That's from their Sacellum... I'd know that smell anywhere ... it's from their cooking caldrons. What you smell is cooked flesh. It's part of the Craing custom... to eat the people they defeat in battle. So gross," Boomer said.

The implications of that were obviously not lost on Miller. They sat quietly for several long minutes when the silence was suddenly broken by a loud *clang* in the distance. A shaft of light appeared that progressively expanded out as a hatch door slowly opened. Someone stepped inside, revealing a tall silhouette against the bright light coming from behind him.

Boomer had zero doubt who the tall man was as he continued to stand there.

"What is he doing?" Miller whispered.

"Trying to scare us," Boomer whispered back. Sitting side by side, Boomer could hear Miller's heavier breathing and it was evident the scare was working. She too was scared, but Boomer remembered Woodrow's words... *Don't let fear of your adversary consume you; if you do, they've already won.*

More of the smoky air was wafting into their compartment from behind Stalls. Boomer tried to ignore him long enough to take a look around. The compartment was filled with metal tables and counters... everything metal. With the absence of light, everything looked gray. But she could make out odd-shaped things on top of the tables.

Stalls moved again—slowly making his way to a distant bulkhead where he stopped. When the overhead lights came on, both Boomer and Miller shielded their eyes from the brightness. What had been blackness and shades of gray was now a vivid kaleidoscope of colors. Both Boomer and Miller stared in horror at their surroundings. A macabre, horrific sight that brought bile to the back of Boomer's throat and sounds of gagging from Miller.

There were bodies everywhere—on tables, stacked two and three high against bulkheads—most of them in some form of dismemberment. Boomer recognized the headless upper torso of a rhino-warrior, lying atop one of the closest tables. Congealed, rust-colored blood was everywhere—on the tables, on the deck, and on the myriad of sharp, metal tools strewn about the compartment. Without a doubt, this was some kind of meat preparation room. So caught up in what lay about them, Boomer hadn't noticed Stalls coming to stand right in front of them.

"I know, it's really quite disgusting, isn't it? The Craing certainly have their peculiarities. I, for the life of me, will never get used to these people." Stalls gestured to the room around them. "Until recently, this area of the ship was open to the frigidness of space. What you're looking at is a perfectly preserved ship's galley where, over a year ago, the Craing crew were busy preparing for their next meal. All it took was a well-placed missile, most likely one fired from your father's ship, and their dinner plans were permanently canceled. I suppose one of these days we'll need to get this mess cleaned up. Perhaps a task suitable for crewmembers exhibiting unsatisfactory behavior, or maybe a job for newly arrived captives."

Boomer couldn't keep herself from making a disgusted face. "My father's going to kill you, you know."

Stalls raised his eyebrows while he considered her remark. "He's had more than a few opportunities to do just that, little girl, and you know what? I'm still here. I'm still alive and now I have something that is of great importance to him. No, I'm sorry to say, Mollie, the next time I see your father he will most certainly die a most uncomfortable death."

Boomer did not correct his use of her former name. There was no reason to let him know there were two Mollies now. She instinctively knew nothing good would come of sharing that information.

Boomer did not like the way Stalls was looking at Miller. Always the ever-present smile on his face. He patted his pant pockets until he found what he was looking for and retrieved a key. He lowered himself into a crouch, reached in, and unlocked the manacle on Miller's ankle. He gently opened it and let it noisily fall to the deck.

Stalls continued to let his hand rest on her leg while he watched her. "You're an attractive woman," he said, looking closer at the name tag on her spacer's jumpsuit. "Petty Officer Miller."

Boomer kicked out at Stalls with her free foot, missing his kneecap by inches. "Don't touch her. You stay away from us!" she yelled.

Stalls found that funny. He laughed out loud for several beats and then, in the next instant, turned serious. With surprising quickness, he reached out and grabbed Miller's ankle. She screamed, then pulled and thrashed to escape his grasp but was unable to break free. Stalls slowly stood, not releasing her ankle. He changed his grip around it, and then turned himself around and walked away, dragging the continually thrashing Miller behind him.

"Just do as he says, don't fight him," Miller yelled back, terrified.

"Let her go!" Boomer yelled after them. "Stop! Let her go!"

Boomer's words had no effect. He neither slowed nor sped up but continued to drag the whimpering Petty Officer out through the open hatchway. Once they were out of sight, Boomer heard what sounded like a slap and then the hatch slowly closed and clanged as the locking mechanism engaged.

Now alone in the Craing galley, Boomer tried her best to keep her fears at bay. She purposely averted her eyes from the dismembered bodies, the dried blood, and the sharp tools the Craing used to butcher the bodies. *Dad, where are you?* She tried several times to hail him via her NanoCom... nothing, no answer. It was then, while staring at the deck, Boomer noticed something. A key. Miller must have kicked it from Stalls' hand.

Chapter 6

Ot-Mul received the news he'd been waiting for: The replacement dreadnought would be joining them soon. Receiving the newest warship, fully equipped with the necessary weaponry to match that of other dreadnoughts in his Vanguard fleet of planet killers, had taken somewhat longer than he'd counted on. Actually, the delay should have been expected... there was more than a little disruption among the Craing fleets right now, having had much of their military hierarchy destroyed back at the Craing worlds.

Truth be told, Ot-Mul could not be more pleased—the lot of them were old gasbags, unable or unwilling to make the tough decisions. Now that he was acting Emperor, all that would change. He'd summon the nearby Craing fleet of fifteen hundred warships, now orbiting Saturn, to move in closer and provide an impenetrable outer ring defense, while his Vanguard ships moved into a higher orbit around Earth. Then he could proceed with the next stage of his plan, which had evolved over the last few sleepless hours.

Ot-Mul continued to lie in bed in his softly lit cabin. Knowing he had only minutes before he'd be rousted by one of the junior officers, he rubbed his tired eyes. Sleep had eluded him the past few nights and, for someone who never had problems sleeping before, it only underscored the momentous times they were living in. Soon, he would give the order to clear out all interstellar riffraff around the Craing worlds, and then *Operation Great Space* would commence. How many planets would cease to exist? How many lives would be snuffed out—hundreds of billions?

He felt his heart rate increase, his breathing quickening. He would be building a legacy, a pivotal point in time had come that would secure not only the Craing's, but his own, everlasting dominance throughout the Universe. But like all great military leaders did, one must adapt as strategic situations change. Destroying Earth before Captain Reynolds was properly dealt with would be a mistake—a mistake that could come back and bite him later. But it wasn't only the Earth Captain needing to be decisively dealt with; those two Caldurian vessels, *The Minian* and *The Lilly*, also needed to be captured, or destroyed, or additional attacks on the Craing worlds would surely continue.

Wasn't that what *The Great Space* was supposed to safeguard against? No, nothing was more important than corralling Earth, the Caldurian vessels, and Captain Reynolds. Total destruction of his beautiful blue planet could wait. Ot-Mul would be happy to do to Earth and the Allied forces what they'd done to his own worlds... *Wherever you are, Captain Reynolds, soon you'll be rushing back to protect your home, a home that will be in great jeopardy. You will see what it is like to witness your planet being strategically bombarded. An eye for an eye— your seat of government, a place called Washington, D.C., obliterated, in retaliation for what you did to the Emperor's Palace. We'll start there.*

The intercom chimed. It was time for Ot-Mul to return to

the bridge. An excited voice followed. "Chief Commander, we have an interstellar communication from Terplin."

"I'm on my way."

Ot-Mul joined four other officers on the raised platform at the back of the bridge. Each wore a silver, copper, or bronze-colored medallion proudly around his neck. By their expressions, something was definitely afoot. Ot-Mul sat in the command chair and brought his attention to the bridge display.

There, before him, was a young Craing dressed in a typical ceremonial robe and a tall, cone-shaped headdress. An overlord... and a high overlord, at that. As a whole, he never cared for any of the sanctimonious, pompous, priests. He'd make a point of lessening their involvement in government and military affairs as soon as he returned to Terplin.

"Chief Commander, I wish to inform you—"

Ot-Mul raised a hand, putting a halt to the Craing high overlord in mid-sentence.

"First of all, who are you? You do not look familiar to me. Second, I am to be addressed as my Lord or acting Emperor."

The high overlord looked stunned and unsure what to say or do next.

Ot-Mul's annoyance was growing by the second. "Speak, or I shall cut this connection."

The overlord nodded quickly and said, "Chief Commander, you can address me as High Overlord Cam. I am pleased to inform you that acting Emperor Lom has returned to the throne. Injured, still not one hundred percent, he is once again in command of the Craing people... the Craing military."

This time it was Ot-Mul who was at a loss for words. He glanced to the other officers only to see them return blank expressions toward him. The overlord was speaking again.

"Lord Lom regrets not being able to speak with you directly, but with the events of the last few days, I'm sure you can imagine the demands on his time. He has outlined your orders, which are to be carried out with all due haste."

"My orders?"

"Yes, our lord was quite explicit about them... You are to return to the Craing worlds at once. All fleets, including the Vanguard, will proceed to the nearest wormhole junction and return to Craing space within four days. This same message has already been delivered to fleet commanders situated around the sixth planet in the Sol system."

Ot-Mul was having a hard time grasping anything the overlord said. How had his good fortune changed so radically, so quickly? Lom's ability to make intelligent decisions must surely be compromised. Ot-Mul was well aware the overlord was waiting for his confirmation of the orders. Well, he could continue to wait.

Ot-Mul looked to the communications officer seated within the multiple rows of bridge stations. "Communications, please verify the originating location of this transmission."

The comms officer double-checked his readings and looked up. "My Lord, this transmission is coming from Calamine-Nu, Terplin. Two hundred miles from the Emperor's Palace."

"Is there a problem, Chief Commander?" the high overlord inquired with suspicion. "I have many more of these communications to deliver."

"I would request that the Vanguard fleet, at a minimum, be allowed to complete their original directive, to destroy planet Earth and the other planets within this system."

"No. You will return to Craing space immediately. As I'm sure you are aware, Lord Lom does not appreciate his orders being second-guessed. If you are not inclined to obey—"

Ot-Mul interjected, "We will prepare to leave this system

within the hour, High Overlord Cam. Please give my best regards to acting Emperor Lom."

Ot-Mul continued to stare at the display long after the smug overlord's image disappeared. The decisions Ot-Mul made now would impact the rest of his life and, quite possibly, change the fate of the Craing people.

The comms officer was speaking again. "Chief Commander, the rest of the fleet is leaving the system. The Vanguard dreadnoughts are requesting your orders."

And right then was the glimmer of hope he'd been waiting for. The individual captains of his Vanguard fleet, seven fully functional dreadnoughts, were waiting on his command. Doubtless, they too had been informed of the acting Emperor's orders.

"Tell them to stand by. New orders to come momentarily," Ot-Mul said.

So, it would come down to this... this moment. Would he comply and follow the orders of the obviously mentally compromised Lom, or take the initiative and do the unthinkable? *How badly do you want this?* he thought to himself. *Enough to risk everything? Yes.* His rightful place was on the throne. But he could not go it alone. He looked over to his fellow officers, "Are you with me?"

The four Craing officers remained expressionless. As if reconfirming an earlier-made decision, they glanced to one another and then, one by one said, "I am with you, my Lord."

Upon hearing those assenting words, Ot-Mul initiated a cue. He wasted no time. "Second in command, inform the Vanguard fleet commanders we are continuing on to Earth. Battle stations, I want their worldwide governmental seats of power, as well as their military and strategic targeting information, before we enter high orbit.

Chapter 7

Ricket removed the cone-shaped headdress from atop his head and turned to Jason. "Was that acceptable, Captain?"

Jason, seated at the other end of the ready room conference table, nodded. "That was quite a performance, Ricket. I guess we'll find out soon enough."

"Captain, if there's nothing else, I need to get back to *The Minian*."

Jason and Ricket left the ready room together. "Keep me informed of your progress," Jason said, as he headed off toward the bridge.

Jason entered the bridge, noting the logistical view of the Solar System and bright red icons that represented Craing vessels on the display before him.

Orion said, "Captain, the fleet's withdrawing. At least, the ships around Saturn are."

Jason sat and appraised the situation. Sure enough, the warships parked near Saturn were making rapid progress out of the solar system. He let out a sigh of relief and sat back in his seat.

He watched the other ships, the seven dreadnoughts sighted near Mars, and muttered, "Come on, follow the others..." As if hearing his comment, the dreadnoughts also started to move. But they weren't following in the direction of the departing fleet —they were headed directly toward Earth.

Seaman Gordon broke the silence: "Captain, Admiral Reynolds requests a private channel."

Jason stood. "Send it to my ready room, Seaman."

Twenty-five steps from the bridge, Jason reentered his ready room and sat down. Admiral Reynolds appeared on the display. Considering their grim situation, he looked better than expected. Shaved and wearing a fresh uniform, his father bore down on Jason with a cold stare.

"What the hell are you doing? There was nothing ambiguous about your orders... get back here to defend Earth."

"That was my intention. Things have changed since we last communicated."

The Admiral impatiently waited for Jason to continue.

"As I'm sure you've been informed, *The Cutlass* was attacked."

"Yes, I know all about that. And I know that Stalls has Boomer. I'm very sorry, Jason. My heart breaks for what that little girl must be going through. But *The Lilly*'s needed back here. Don't forget, that fleet of Craing dreadnoughts has atomized hundreds of planets and they're now on course for Earth. We're just lucky the rest of their fleet pulled up stakes and left."

"That was our doing. We've figured out how to receive and transmit Craing communications. We dressed Ricket up like an overlord and ordered the fleet back to Craing space."

The Admiral almost smiled. "Clever. Very clever. But for some reason, the Vanguard fleet wants nothing to do with those orders. Perhaps they didn't buy the act, or they've gone rogue, or who knows what?"

"What's the status of the Allied fleet?" Jason asked.

"I've just returned with what's left... four hundred and thirty-two warships. Normally, that might be enough to combat their seven ships. But these Vanguard dreadnoughts are on a whole different level than any of us have fought against in the past. Highly trained crews, not to mention the ships are equipped with massive plasma cannons. They're called planet killers for a reason. One direct hit from those guns and even heavy cruisers are quickly reduced to space dust."

"I've had good luck fighting dreadnoughts phase-shifting from the inside out," Jason interjected. "Big guns or not, they've little defense against our phase-shifting fighters, not to forget *The Lilly*. Look, I can be there in minutes. Better if they're surprised anyway. From our estimates, the dreadnoughts are moving slowly and won't reach Earth for at least an hour. I need that time to deal with Stalls and his deadline."

"Deadline?"

"Before he says he'll kill Boomer."

"We're playing with fire here. The defense of a planet, our planet," the Admiral said, rubbing his forehead and looking away. He loved the girls and was obviously torn on what to do. "Promise me you'll come as soon as called," he said.

"We're closely watching the situation. The priority, of course, is to protect Earth. I just need a little time to save my daughter."

The Admiral nodded almost imperceptibly and cut the connection.

JASON KNEW HE HAD VERY LITTLE TIME LEFT TO deal with Stalls. His father was right; he was, in a sense, prioritizing Boomer's life above the fate of an entire world... but what else could he do? Leave his daughter in what would unquestionably be an unforgiving, extremely dire, existence? No. He'd often rolled the dice anti to what wise convention called for and, once again, he needed the gods of fate to rule in his favor.

There'd been too many interruptions getting *The Minian* even minimally repaired, but Jason needed to interrupt again Ricket, Bristol, or Granger. None of *The Lilly*'s bridgecrew had a clue how to operate the newly installed Caldurian tracking technology. This time it was Granger, along with Sergeant Toby Jackson, his ever-present guard, who'd been called to *The Lilly*'s bridge.

"What exactly do you want to accomplish, Captain?"

"I need to track down a Craing warship, or multiple warships, that have moved outside of sensor range," Jason told him.

Granger moved over to an open station and sat down. His fingers flew over the input device and, within seconds, the logistical display altered and contracted in, revealing a much-expanded portion of surrounding space—represented in muted, grayed-out symbols and icons. "What you're looking at now," Granger said, while continuing to tap away, "is actual space and probable space. The grayed-out areas are only best guesses, based on probabilities... not only from this reality but influences taken from the Multiverse as well. Based on the last incoming communications from Stalls, you can see his location was approximately twenty-five light-years away... here in this area," he said, gesturing toward the logistical feed displayed above.

"That was hours ago. He may have... most likely has... moved far from that location," Orion interjected.

Granger smiled, "And here's what's amazing about this technology." Granger tapped again and another, similar feed appeared on the display. There were multiple overlays now, each symbol and icon fluctuating... sometimes flickering off, and then reappearing at the same location; other times, the positions slightly changed. Granger turned in his seat to face Jason. "We've had this discussion before, Captain... I want to stress again that when dealing with the Multiverse and other planes of existence, what you consider reality is misleading. Reality is quite fluid, altered by such things as intention and other subjective, always fluctuating, concepts. What you're looking at is a best guess... a live construct of possibilities. I have it set to show only the most probable, but multiple probabilities can be displayed easily enough. As you can see, according to the *probability matrix*, it places the position of Stalls' three warships to now be twenty-five light-years into this area of space."

Jason stared at the fluctuating gray icons and felt a glimmer of hope. Quietly, he said, "Hold on. I'm coming for you, Boomer." Jason turned to Orion: "You got this... how to work this thing?"

"I think so. Enough so that I can hail Granger with questions, if necessary," she replied.

"Thank you, Granger. You can return to *The Minian*."

Granger stood, heading out of the bridge, then stopped. "Captain, I know that we've had our differences in the past, but I want you to know I'll do whatever I can to help you free your daughter."

Jason nodded and watched Sergeant Jackson and Granger leave the bridge.

"Seaman Gordon, please inform Ricket on *The Minian*, as well as Commander Douglas on *The Determined*, that we're leaving. Provide them with our guesstimated coordinates of Stalls' ship in case we run into a problem. When you're ready, call up the interchange and request a wormhole. Ensign McBride, move us on out of here."

"Aye, Captain."

As *The Lilly* separated from *The Determined* and *The Minian*, Jason noticed the outside hull of *The Minian* was undergoing a confluence of activity. Multiple repair droids had been activated and were now hard at work making repairs. A hopeful sign.

It took several minutes to reach the mouth of the wormhole. Seaman Gordon excitedly said, "Captain, we're receiving an interstellar communications hail... it's Captain Stalls, Sir."

"Don't answer him," Jason ordered.

Keeping his eyes on the logistical display provided by the *probability matrix* Jason saw that Stalls' ships had moved, but not significantly enough for them to alter outpoint wormhole coordinates. *The Lilly* entered the wormhole and then, just as quickly, exited the mouth at the other end.

The *probability matrix* feed updated with no significant alterations. "Get in close, Helm, but stay outside their sensor range."

"Aye, Captain."

Jason kept his eyes on the three Craing warship icons. "I'm coming for you, Stalls."

Chapter 8

Boomer unlocked the manacle and let it drop to the deck. She rubbed the red and raw abrasion on her ankle and stood up. She took another look around her disgusting surroundings and held back tears. It would be so easy to let the fear envelop her. *Come on,* she thought to herself, *I'm only nine years old! Seriously, how many nine-year-olds go through this kind of thing?*

She eyed the hatch across the room but before she could take her first step, the overhead lights flickered once, twice, before everything went totally black. As she stood in the silence, her other senses came alive—most prominently, her sense of smell. Old blood, rotting flesh, and that ever-present charcoal smell filled her nostrils. With hands outstretched, Boomer moved in the direction, her best guess, of where the hatch would be.

The floor was slick in places, sticky in others. She had a rough idea where the closest table was holding the carved-up rhino-warrior. She closed her eyes and tried to picture the rest of the kitchen galley in her mind.

There were at least three more tables to pass in front of her, a virtual obstacle course she'd need to traverse. After four steps Boomer exhaled in relief; she'd passed the rhino-warrior's remains. Another two steps and she stepped on something thick and squishy. She'd been so concerned with what was above the decking she'd forgotten to be mindful of what was strewn about beneath her, on the deck flooring.

The thick, squishy thing slid out from beneath her foot and, before Boomer could catch her balance, she lost her footing and went sprawling backward. She landed hard on her backside. After first determining she wasn't hurt, she noticed the smell. On the deck it was even worse. She retched, trying to breathe only through her mouth. Using both hands, she pushed off the deck as a slick, sticky Jell-O-like substance squished through her fingers. Worse, she felt something trickling down her cheek and swiped at it.

Oh my God, what's on my face! Between more retching and doing her best to hold back sobs, Boomer managed to get back to her feet. She wiped first her palms and then the back of her hands on her jumpsuit.

Four more steps and she walked into the first of the three tables. Reflexively, her hands came down on the surface, where she encountered cold hard metal. She used the flat vertical edge to guide her hand around the table and then kept on walking. Four more hesitant steps and she reached the next table. Whatever was lying atop this table was all dried out; at her mere touch, it disintegrated, like a sunbaked sandcastle at the beach.

Again, she wiped her hands and did her best to only use the table's edge to navigate forward. *Two down and one to go!* This was beyond awful, Boomer thought to herself, but she was almost through the maze. This time she anticipated the location of the third table. Purposely, she avoided the top surface, letting her hands move directly to the table's edge. Then she heard the sound.

Boomer stopped and listened, turning her head this way and that, trying to decipher the direction from which the noise had originated. There it was again... a rustling sort of sound. One thing was definite ... she wasn't alone. "Hello?"

Silence.

In the totally oppressive blackness, Boomer thought she sensed movement off to her left. Were her eyes playing tricks on her?

Her increasing heart rhythm pounded in her chest—in her ears—to the point trying to listen for anything else was futile. Boomer took another step and then another. Startled, Boomer froze in place. The table was moving, a rocking motion. Before she could pull away, a hand grabbed her wrist. Boomer screamed into the darkness—a scream like none other in the history of all screams across the Universe. She used her free hand to pull back her captive arm.

"Let me go! Get away from me!"

"Boomer, it's me... Priscilla." Her voice was weak and there was something else. There was sadness in her tone.

"Petty Officer Miller?"

"Yes, it's me. Stop screaming, Boomer."

"How did you... I didn't hear you come back in." Boomer used her hands to feel around the top of the table and then touched Miller's legs; patting her, she realized her clothes weren't right. They were undone, open in places. Miller pushed her hands away.

"It's okay, Boomer. Just don't—"

"What did he do to you?" At that moment all fear evaporated. Anger and rage had turned the room's blackness into vivid red. Boomer wasn't exactly sure what Stalls had done to Miller but she knew it was invasive... something horrible.

"I'm going to kill him!" Boomer took a deep breath and screamed out, "I'm going to kill you, Stalls!"

The laughter was deep and menacing. Boomer turned toward the sound.

Miller's voice came up from the table. Weakly, she said, "Careful, Boomer... he can see us; he's wearing some kind of NVD."

"A what?"

"A night vision device." Miller's voice was slurred and barely audible.

Boomer had her back to the rustling sound behind her, where she knew Stalls was watching them. She understood this was all about him getting even with her father. He was torturing them. Stalls' hatred seemed to fill the room. She'd heard it in his laughter. She gave Miller's arm a gentle squeeze and stepped away from the table. Again, she closed her eyes and called up the teachings she'd learned from Petty Officer Woodrow.

She heard his voice in her head... *you need to calm your nerves, slow your breathing.* She could do that. How many times had she practiced these types of scenarios with him? Even the total darkness was familiar. Stalls was now moving closer. Boomer heard his approaching footfalls. What happened next came naturally, from countless practiced repetitions.

She pulled the knife from her pocket as she spun to her left. The knife felt familiar in her hand as she clasped the blade firmly between her fingers. Woodrow had explained the principle—how using her body's centrifugal power, combined with the uncoiling sweep of her arm, would provide tremendous force ... terms she didn't fully understand. But she didn't need to think further about what had become as natural a movement to her as walking or running.

By the time Boomer spun around, releasing the knife at just the right moment, she already knew its intended trajectory would be right on. *Practiced confidence,* Woodrow had called it. There, in the split second it took for her to hear that all-too-familiar *thump* sound ... the sound of a knife driving home into its intended target ... Boomer was anything but still. She went low and headed for the only escape. She didn't want to leave Miller, but she figured if he survived the attack, the best thing she could do would be to draw him away.

By the sounds of his gasp and subsequent scream, Stalls wasn't dead. He was injured, but definitely not dead. Zombie-like, with her arms outstretched before her, Boomer ran full out in the opposite direction. She silently prayed she was moving in the right direction, toward the hatch. She careened into something hard, her head hitting a metal surface, and she fell down to the deck. She wondered if she'd lost consciousness. How much time had elapsed, with Stalls alive in the room, somewhere near?

Crawling, Boomer reached into the darkness with an outstretched hand. Totally disoriented, she had no idea which direction was which ... where was the hatch? Where was Stalls? In a half crawl, half reaching out motion, her fingertips grazed something. Something fleshy. She gasped. *Had she just touched Stalls' face? Was he there, in front of her?*

"You little bitch. I'm going to slit your throat. I'm going to make you suffer."

Stalls' voice was raspy and coming from behind her but getting closer. He was still a threat. The good news was he was obviously in pain. He was also on the other side of the room. With that knowledge, Boomer continued to reach out in front. She discovered she'd come across a stack of bodies.

Her hand landed fully on the face of whatever it was—not human, not rhino-warrior. A face having multiple mouths and at least five or six eyes. She recalled having seen these bodies earlier when the lights were still on. She needed to move. The hatch wasn't even near here. *Crap! Oh God, where was it? Oh yeah, over there, to the right.* She had to move her feet and run.

The sound of Stalls' voice changed everything. She was beyond scared. Boomer was certain she had just moments to live. Running now, it was just a matter of seconds before she would careen into another table ... more bodies. The instant her hands touched its surface she knew she'd reached the hatch. Having spent significant time onboard other vessels, she also knew how the latching mechanism worked. If it was locked, she knew her fate would be sealed. But with a quick turn of the inset mechanism the hatch opened.

Going from the pitch-blackness of the galley into the bright lights of the corridor beyond made seeing a problem. But she heard the sound of running feet. With a quick glance over her shoulder, she saw Stalls appear out of the darkness. In a split-second she took him in. Yes, her knife had found its mark. The area of his upper left chest was a bloody mess. He also had something on his forehead... that NVD thing Miller was talking about. There was another thing Boomer noticed before closing the hatch: Miller, half-dressed, was crawling off the table.

Using both hands, Boomer slammed the hatch shut. There was a way to lock these things, but Boomer had never needed to do so. She inspected the inset ratchet-type mechanism. *Okay, to open it you turn the thing to the right. So how do you lock it?*

Stalls was now at the hatch. Boomer saw the mechanism start to turn and she used both hands, all her strength, to turn the handle back in the opposite direction. Something clicked. Now nothing moved. *I've done it!* Boomer thought. The hatch was locked. Boomer took two tentative steps backward. Was that pounding she was hearing from the other side? Tears filled her eyes. She'd just locked Miller inside with that monster.

Chapter 9

Jason figured Boomer should now be well within range. He used his NanoCom to hail her.

"Stalls is chasing me!" she excitedly whispered in rapid short breaths.

"We're close, sweetie. Tell me what's happening. Has he hurt you?"

"No, I'm okay. But he hurt Petty Officer Miller."

"Is she still alive?"

"I think so. I had to leave her in the ship's galley."

"That's okay. We'll get her out of there. Right now, you need to tell me exactly where you are."

"I'm on one of the lower decks, looking for a place to hide. Where have you been, Dad?"

"I'm sorry, Boomer... it took us a while to find you. You sound out of breath. What's going on?"

"I'm still running. Stalls is really, really mad. I threw a knife at him and I hurt him."

"Wait... you threw... Seriously?"

"He's a bad man," she said defensively.

"You did the right thing and you're right, he's a bad man.

Listen. Find a good place to hide and keep out of sight. I'll find you."

"Okay, I will. And we need to help Petty Officer Miller, too."

"Don't worry, I'm coming."

Jason cut the connection and realized everyone on the bridge was staring at him. Having heard only his side of the conversation, they were anxiously waiting to hear what was going on.

"Gunny, can you determine which of the three ships Boomer is on?"

"Already have her location pinpointed, Cap. She's on that middle ship, in the aft section of deck two."

There was a schematic of a heavy cruiser on the display, showing multiple life icons. As the Gunny indicated, Boomer's bright green icon was on the move on deck two, at the rear of the ship. There were approximately thirty other icons onboard; most were either on the bridge or in the engineering sections. There was also another green icon several decks higher, mid-ship, which was probably Miller's life icon.

"Cap, the other two warships have the same comparably minimal crew members," Orion added.

Jason, now on his feet and looking at the ship's schematic, saw Billy enter the bridge.

"A little birdie told me there might be an opportunity for a little whoop-ass," Billy said, looking at the diagram on the display.

"Put together three small teams. Plan to phase-shift shuttles onboard each of the Craing ships and take control of their bridges. We want those ships, as well as their crew, left intact, Billy."

"And what are *you* planning on doing during all this?" Billy asked.

"You'll hold your attack until I give the order. I need to take care of Stalls."

"By yourself? I don't think that's a goo—"

"It's not open for discussion, Billy," Jason interrupted. "If I don't surprise Stalls, he could kill Boomer out of pure spite."

Seaman Gordon had two fingers up to his ear and his voice was elevated—he looked scared. "Yes, Sir... right away, Sir," Gordon said to whoever he was speaking to on his comms channel.

"What is it, Gordon?" Jason asked, already moving toward the exit.

"Two incoming hails, Sir. That was Admiral Reynolds. He says the Vanguard fleet will enter Earth's orbit within ninety minutes. He told me to tell you, his words, *get your damn Captain's ass back here, now!*"

"And the second hail?"

"It's Captain Stalls. He's still waiting to talk to you."

Jason looked to Billy. "Remember, your three teams are to wait for my command before you go... Orion, roust the XO from his beauty sleep and call down to the flight deck. I want *Pacesetter* prepped and ready for flight by the time I get down there." Jason turned to the comms station. "Seaman Gordon, go ahead, forward Captain Stalls to my NanoCom."

Jason left the bridge and ran for the nearest DeckPort. En route, he triggered the SuitPac device at his belt and felt the hardened battlesuit expand and take shape around his body. The helmet was the last segment to take shape. He took in the HUD information and saw that Gunny had already pre-loaded phase-shift coordinates for *Pacesetter*, as well as for the Craing warship's schematics. He found Boomer's life icon... she'd moved up from deck level two to level three. She also wasn't moving.

Jason entered the flight deck to find two hotshot fighter pilots, Lieutenants Miller and Grimes, waiting for him.

Grimes spoke up first. "Let me pilot you in, Sir."

"Billy will need three shuttle pilots—you can pilot one of those."

Ten more sleepy-eyed pilots entered the flight deck, each in one stage, or another, of suiting-up.

"We're more than covered in that regard, Captain." Grimes handed him a multi-gun, which he took, checking both its power levels and settings via his own HUD.

"Fine, let's hurry up," Jason said, not losing a step on his way toward the dark red, already powered up, two-seater *Pacesetter* fighter idling in the center of the flight deck. Jason climbed the inset ladder and stowed his multi-gun within the fighter's storage locker when he noticed that Grimes had already activated her own SuitPac and was waiting for him to get out of her way. *Smart-ass...* she passed Jason her multi-gun to stow. He hurried into the rear cockpit position, while Grimes took the forward seat.

"I have the ship's layout and your daughter's most current location, Captain," Grimes said. "There's a hold area on that level, no more than fifty yards from her icon."

Jason saw the hold area she was talking about. It was smaller than he liked and even though it was the closest, he'd purposely discounted it for that reason. "That's a tight fit, Lieutenant."

"Not for me, Sir."

"Let's do it."

"We'll need three separate phase-shifts getting there, Sir."

"We're wasting time, Grimes! Let's move it along."

The weight of the situation, everything happening, was making him impatient and irritable. Earth was soon to be literally surrounded by seven planet-killing dreadnoughts, yet here Jason was, planning to conduct a difficult excursion elsewhere.

Yes, it was to save his daughter. But he knew his priorities were ridiculously out of line; the fate of one little girl shouldn't outweigh the plight of billions. His mind went to Mollie and Nan, and then to the unborn son Nan carried in her womb.

The bright lights and increasing sound of whirling-up drive engines on the flight deck disappeared. There were three consecutive flashes, once out in open space, before *Pacesetter* settled within the dark confines of the Craing warship's third-level hold.

Jason studied his HUD. The two green icons were now virtually right next to each other. Stalls had found his daughter. Jason hailed her.

"Boomer! Captain Stalls is very close to you."

What Jason got in response was a NanoText message. Boomer's physiology was still being recognized as Mollie...

Crew Mollie Reynolds:

Dad! He's got me. Where are you?

Capt. Jason Reynolds:

I'm here onboard, close by.

Grimes had already initiated the raising of *Pacesetter*'s canopy. He gave her a couple of quick pats on her shoulder and scurried out of the cockpit, heading down the ladder. "Stay with *Pacesetter* unless you hear otherwise."

He retrieved his multi-gun and made his way down to the deck.

Capt. Jason Reynolds:

Boomer. I'm coming... what's he doing now?

Crew Mollie Reynolds:

He's standing at one of the ship's intercom panels. He's talking to someone. Dad, he has a knife to my neck.

Capt. Jason Reynolds:

Just stay still. I'll be there in a few seconds.

Crew Mollie Reynolds:
Wait... you're here? Like right now?
Capt. Jason Reynolds:
Yep. Like right now.

Jason glanced at his HUD readout. Earlier, while in *Pacesetter*, he'd set a mission countdown timer for ninety minutes—a quarter of that had now ticked by—he calculated he still had time to take care of Stalls and get back to Earth—well before the Vanguard fleet arrived.

Jason figured now would be a good time to open the channel to Stalls. "Captain Stalls, this is Captain Reynolds. I apologize for the wait. But getting all your demands met has taken me longer than I figured on."

"I warned you, Reynolds. Unfortunately, I'm already holding a blade to your daughter's throat. I was trying to decide: do I slit her neck from right to left, or should I slice it left to right... being ambidextrous, it makes either one an option. What do you think I should do?"

"So, more of your game playing. Don't you tire of it, Stalls?" Jason asked, sounding cool and collected while in reality, he was having a hard time keeping the mental vision of his little girl's throat being cut out of his mind.

Jason heard him exhale. "Do you have everything I requested? The ships... my beautiful Nan, and you, ready to lay down your life?"

Jason didn't answer right away. Instead, he phase-shifted onto level three. He'd purposely placed himself at an intersecting corridor that put him out of sight from where his HUD indicated Stalls was still positioned, in front of an intercom.

"Nan is en route. As for the ten warships, they'll be here within the hour," Jason lied.

"That wasn't our agreement, Reynolds!"

"Two hours was always an impossible timeframe. Just be content everything is going your way. You're getting what you want. The good news for you is... I'm here alone."

Jason couldn't chance Stalls making good on his promise to cut Boomer's throat. He retracted his SuitPac, placed his multi-gun on the deck, and walked around the corner with his hands held high. Stalls stood thirty paces away, leaning against a bulk-head with the edge of a knife pointed at the middle of Boomer's neck.

His other hand held a plasma pistol. Startled, Stalls looked toward Jason as he advanced. He looked confused at first, then angry. He brought up his pistol and pointed it toward Jason's head. "Stop right there."

Jason did as he was told and raised his hands. "I see you've had a little accident. Cut yourself shaving, or did that nine-year-old girl get the best of you?"

Stalls looked down at his bloodied shirt. "I assure you it looks far worse than it is."

"Uh huh... sure." Jason watched Boomer's face. She was doing all she could to stay brave. But she was terrified. Her eyes were pleading with Jason to save her. "This is between you and me, Stalls. You can see I'm unarmed. If you want me to make good on your demands, you'll have to let my daughter go... right now... this second."

Stalls smiled and looked down at Boomer. He tilted his head, as if getting a better perspective, then repositioned his knife to where it hovered just millimeters above her carotid artery. Jason slowly moved his hands over his SuitPac device but realized in the time it would take him to trigger the device, accessing its integrated weapons system, two to three seconds would pass, minimum, and Boomer would be dead.

Stalls' arm jerked. Jason's heart stopped in his chest as he watched his daughter fall to the deck. He continued to watch in suspended horror only to realize she wasn't bleeding. She reached for her neck as if feeling for blood.

"Move away from him, Boomer! Hurry! Do it now."

Boomer crab-walked backward away from Stalls and then got to her feet.

Stalls held up his pistol, first pointing at Jason and then at Boomer. Boomer slowly moved over to Jason. He reached an arm around her and pushed her behind him. He'd taken the SuitPac device from his belt and, as discreetly as possible, placed it into her palm.

Stalls continued to point his weapon at Boomer. "The little bitch stays right there. I get what was promised before she goes free."

Capt. Jason Reynolds:
Boomer, put that thing on your belt. Then squeeze the two small tabs.
Crew Mollie Reynolds:
What is it?
Capt. Jason Reynolds:
Put it on your belt and squeeze the tabs inward at the same time.

Before Jason had completed the NanoText, her SuitPac segments were already expanding outward to cover her body. Boomer took a step to the side, showing her newly outfitted self to Stalls. His expression seemed perplexed.

"By the way, Stalls, I lied," Jason said, "those ten ships you demanded... they're not coming. Nan... she's still twenty-five light-years away. Oh, and one more piece of news—within the next few minutes your three ships will be boarded by my teams. You've pretty much lost everything."

Jason knew the easiest thing for Stalls to do would be to fire a plasma bolt into his forehead and be done with it. With his SuitPac already in use, Jason wasn't sure what his next move should be. He counted on Stalls wanting the kind of revenge that came with him using his fists first... and now, by the crazed, enraged look Jason saw in his eyes, that's exactly what was coming.

Like a charging bull, Stalls sprang forward. A yell of frustration emanated from deep within his core. "I'm going to rip your head off!"

Jason took in the pirate's contorted face and, in a flash, remembered all the pain the man had caused. How many fellow crewmembers had lost their lives at his hands? For God's sake, he'd actually killed Nan. Jason recalled the grief Boomer had undergone, as she stood broken-hearted at her mother's funeral. And now... what torturous things had Stalls done to Petty Officer Miller? Was she even still alive?

Jason darted forward, coming in low, and met Stalls' advance head-on. As the two collided, Stalls was ready for him and swung the butt of the plasma pistol down on the crown of Jason's head. Pain blazed as Jason fought to stay conscious. When the second blow hit him precisely in the same spot as the first, his knees began to buckle...

Chapter 10

J ason's nanites were already working overtime repairing what he figured must be a fractured skull. He'd underestimated Stalls' first move. Fortunately, by the time the crazed pirate was bringing the butt of his pistol down for a third strike, a strike that would undoubtedly lead to Jason's early demise, Jason still had enough wits to bring his left arm up to block the blow. Still unsteady on his feet, Jason staggered backward. But what surprised Jason next was Boomer.

She went at Stalls like a crazed animal. She charged forward, first punching, then kicking at him. The battlesuit's micro-servos enhanced every blow and she was hurting him. By the time Stalls managed to bring up his plasma pistol, he was down on one knee. He fired directly into her visor and didn't let up. Boomer staggered backward as Stalls regained his feet and pursued her.

Jason watched, knowing the advanced battlesuit she had on was nearly impervious to anything Stalls might try to do to her. And though Boomer would dislike the sensation that came from being blasted in her suit's visor, repeatedly thrown backward, she was safe from actual harm. In the meantime, Jason was getting some needed seconds to recover from the strikes he'd taken to his head.

Jason figured Stalls' plasma pistol's power pack should be just about spent. He'd fired hundreds of pulses at Boomer, with no effect. She was now standing, both hands on hips, defiantly looking up at Stalls with an expression Jason recognized as one he'd often made himself.

Finally, Stalls' pistol fired its last pulse and died. Angrily, he threw it at Boomer and rushed toward her. Jason was there to stop him, hitting him hard in the jaw with an uppercut.

"I've got this, Boomer," Jason said, getting in between the two. Stalls took an unsteady step backward, and then another, until his back was against the bulkhead. He lashed out with the knife clutched in his other hand. The blade sliced through the air, missing Jason's ear by a fraction of an inch. Stalls used that same momentum to spin away from the bulkhead. Jason followed him as he ran down the corridor, toward the intersection, where Jason's multi-gun lay against the bulkhead around the next bend.

Both men were now running full out. Jason, seeing Stalls near the turn, stretched out his arms and dove toward Stalls' legs. He was sure he had him but felt the smooth fabric of the pirate's dress slacks slip through his fingers. It was only by pure chance the back of Stalls' heel lifted at the right instant for Jason to make a grab for it. The heel, too, slipped through his fingers but it was enough to stumble the fleeing pirate. Both men went sprawling to the deck in a tangle of arms and legs.

As Jason got to his knees, Stalls delivered a kick to Jason's solar plexus that doubled him over, making him gasp for air. Jason saw movement from the corner of his eye—a quick reflection of light gleamed off Stalls' blade. Now, both on their knees, Jason intuitively blocked out with his left arm, striking Stalls' knife hand at the wrist. The knife flew from his grasp and skittered across the deck.

Momentarily hesitating, the men stared at each other, and Jason glimpsed a flash of fear in Stalls' eyes—perhaps a realization he was about to die. Jason jabbed hard with his left fist, nearly flattening the cartilage in Stalls' nose. As blood spurted high in a wide arc, Jason followed through, using all his strength, with a haymaker powering into Stalls' left cheek.

As Stalls went flying downward on the deck, Jason got to his feet and retrieved the knife. He first held it in his open palm, before grabbing the handle so tightly in his fist his knuckles turned white. It was now time. Stalls' wrath of killing would finally come to an end. Jason felt no remorse for him. He'd killed men for less. The only difference here was the satisfaction he'd get from doing so. He turned to look down at Stalls sprawled awkwardly below him. He was coming around, trying to heave himself onto an elbow.

Jason took three steps and lowered himself down on one knee, pushing the bloodied pirate back down with his left hand. Slowly, Jason brought the knife up over his head, stared down at Stalls' chest, picturing his beating heart, inhaled and—

"Dad, stop!"

But Jason was already driving the knife down with everything he had, using all his strength, until the blade was driven down to its hilt. Silence. Nearly a minute passed before Jason let go of the knife and raised to face his daughter. She stood at the end of the corridor with her eyes locked on Stalls' inert body. It was then that she spied the knife's handle protruding out from an open grate in the deck, no more than an inch from his head.

Stalls' eyes were leveled on Jason, the condescending smile back on his lips. "I would have killed you," he rasped. "Someday I will."

Jason brought two fingers up to his ear and hailed Billy.

"Go for Billy."

"Billy, it's a *Go*... time to take all three ships. Move fast... we need to be on our way within the next few minutes. Also, I need a security team here, at my coordinates."

"You let the dog live—didn't you?"

Jason didn't answer.

THERE WAS NO RESISTANCE FROM THE CRAING crew. Billy's teams moved, making synchronized phase-shift incursions. Security teams of ten men each were now stationed on all three ships, and two additional armed combatants were placed on each ship's bridge.

As Boomer led the way back to where she'd last seen Petty Officer Miller, Jason continued to take care of critical mission strategy and other ship business. He realized he'd need to assign new commanders to all three ships. He hailed his brother, whom he'd noticed had become somewhat listless, directionless, since the destruction of his first large ship command, *Her Majesty*.

"Go for Brian."

"Brian, I was wondering if you could do me... the Alliance another favor?"

"Are you serious? I think I'm all out of favors this week, Jason."

"That's fine. You don't work for me; it's up to you."

"What were you going to ask, just out of curiosity?"

"I've got three Craing cruisers that we'll be bringing into the Alliance. One of them, a heavy cruiser, is in excellent shape... but we'll get one of the fighter pilots to take command of her—"

"You offering me a ship? One of those big cruisers?"

"I don't want to force you into anything."

"No, I want it!"

Jason cut the connection and noticed Boomer had neared a hatch. The locking mechanism appeared to be blown out as if someone had used a plasma weapon on it from inside. Boomer, still wearing Jason's battlesuit, swung the hatch open and entered a large, brightly lit, compartment.

"This is the kitchen galley. It's really gross in here, Dad."

That's an understatement, Jason thought to himself. Bodies of God knew what species were stacked against bulkheads, like cords of wood. Metal tables, the kind you'd expect to see in a morgue used for autopsies, were strewn with cadavers as well. Jason held back his gag reflex as the overpowering smell of decomposing flesh filled his nostrils.

"She's over there!" Boomer said, running toward the back of the galley.

Jason followed but wasn't at first sure what he was looking at. Then he realized it was Miller. She was lying on the deck, balled up in a fetal position. Jason ran, reaching her in four long strides.

Miller's clothes were ripped and splattered with blood. She was facing the bulkhead, her hair covering her face.

"Let me in here, Boomer. Stand back." Jason carefully brushed Miller's hair away but stopped when he saw the damage. Black and blue bruises covered most of her face. Her lips were split and blood trickled from both corners of her mouth. Her chest, equally bruised, was exposed. Jason could see she was alive, her lungs filling with air in slow deep breaths. He pulled her torn spacer's jumpsuit together and saw Miller bring a hand up to hold the torn fabric in place. Her eyelids, two swollen slits, opened and watched him.

"Where's Stalls?" she whispered.

"He's been dealt with. You're safe. You're going to be fine."

Jason straightened up and hailed Dira.

"Jason! Are you all right? How's Boomer?"

He had to smile; she'd never quite conformed to following proper military communication protocol. "Boomer's fine. Petty Officer Miller is injured and requires your attention. She's pretty badly beaten up. I'm not sure if I should move her—"

"No. Don't move her until I can assess her condition. I'm on my way."

Chapter 11

W ith Captain Stalls locked securely within *The Lilly*'s brig, Petty Officer Miller spending needed time recuperating within a MediPod, and the three Craing cruisers outfitted with minimal security and officer crews, Jason was ready to move the lot back to Earth to defend against the quickly approaching Vanguard fleet of dreadnoughts. His only remaining task was to check in with Ricket for an update on *The Minian*'s condition.

"Captain, much of the hull reconstruction has been completed. The ship's repair drones, co-mingling with the ship's outer hull, self-repairing nanites, have accomplished the rebuilding. Your first priority directive to have weapons systems and shields up and running is now complete. Granger, Bristol, and I are spending most of our time getting *The Minian*'s drive and navigation systems fully operational. I believe we are close to completing that task also."

"Ricket, that's amazing. I'm not sure how you've accomplished so much in such a short amount of time, but I'm thrilled. As I'm sure the Admiral will be, too. What's your best-guess timeframe for being ready for space travel?"

"Minimum... five days... max, maybe seven," Ricket responded.

"Seven! That's about six days longer than I'd hoped to hear. We'll keep *The Determined* by you. The second you have nav and propulsion systems up and running, I want to know. There's a good chance *The Minian* will be the deciding factor defending Earth, as well as all other planetary systems throughout the sector."

"I understand, Captain. But I wouldn't underestimate the capabilities of *The Lilly* herself. Over the past year, much of the same technological advances you find on *The Minian* have been integrated into *The Lilly*. I would suggest you take Bristol with you. He's aware of the technology and can think on his feet if required."

"He's also impossible to work with. But I see your point. We're leaving this area of space now and will wormhole close to you, before moving on to Earth. Have him ready to phase-shift onboard."

"Yes, Captain."

THE LILLY EMERGED FROM THE MOUTH OF THE interchange wormhole thirty thousand miles out from Earth's upper orbit. Ships were everywhere. Already at battle stations, Jason waited for Orion's tactical assessment of the situation.

"This is what's left of the Allied fleet, Captain: four hundred and thirty-two warships... some in Earth's upper orbit, others positioned farther out in space."

"And the Vanguard fleet, Gunny?" Jason asked, looking from the ever-picturesque sight of Earth to the numerous nearby warships, now occupying local space. Visioning Earth again never got old.

"They appear to be stationary, approximately six million miles out, Cap."

"Captain, incoming hail from *The Catchfire*," Seaman Gordon on comms interjected. "The Admiral's onboard and they're en route to converge on the moon at stipulated coordinates."

"Thank you, Seaman. Helm, change course to the newly-supplied lunar coordinates."

Jason saw Seaman Gordon shaking his head. "What is it, Seaman?"

"Now that we can pick up Craing communications, and I can actually understand what's being said..." Gordon stopped mid-sentence as if he were listening to something on his comms. "Captain, I think they know."

"Know that we're here?"

"No, well, yes. They know *The Lilly*'s here. Apparently, there are several small Craing corvettes in local space whose sole purpose is to spy on our comings and goings. But they also know about our ruse... getting their fleet to return back to the Craing worlds." Gordon, with two fingers up to his right ear, was quietly listening again. "Yes, Sir, they definitely know. Not only is that same fleet, which they call Fleet 9, en route back here, several other fleets are also returning: Fleet 173, and Fleet 25—that's close to five thousand warships total."

"Damn!" Jason exclaimed under his breath. He knew it was inevitable but had hoped for more time. "Gunny, can you pick out the two corvettes Seaman Gordon is referring to?"

"I'll do it," Bristol said, entering the bridge with a sour expression on his face. "I'm betting she's clueless on how to use the new *probability matrix* tech, anyway."

Orion swung around, looking ready to tell Bristol where he could stick it, but caught herself when she saw Jason's raised palm. She got the message... *don't, it's just not worth it.*

Bristol found an open station and immediately went to work, taking a seat between Gordon and Orion. He suddenly rolled his chair sideways until he was practically on top of Seaman Gordon. "You might want to watch what I'm doing here, Gordon. I'll even go extra slow for you." Bristol rapidly entered information at his console, pointed to something on the small holo-display, and then tapped at the keys some more. "See? Don't forget to show this to your twin. I definitely have no intention of getting this close to either of you again." Bristol turned toward Jason and pointed to a newly added segment on the overhead display. "There's your hidden corvettes. Stealthy little ships... wouldn't even show up under standard sensor readings."

Jason saw two faint icons—just outside, and on opposite sides, of Earth's higher orbit. "Gunny, can you get a lock on those two ships?"

"No problem, Cap."

"Do it."

Jason watched the display as two newly added missile icons came into view and quickly made their way across open space. First one, and then the other icon several seconds later converged on the two Craing vessels.

"Both Craing corvettes destroyed, Captain."

Ensign McBride said, "Captain, we'll be at the lunar coordinates within five minutes."

"Very well, Ensign," Jason answered.

Bristol rose and stood beside the command chair. "Captain, I request permission to see my brother."

"Captain Stalls is in serious trouble."

Bristol shrugged one shoulder. "Hey, I realize he's a maniac. But he's still my brother. I should see him... even if it's for the last time."

Jason brought his full attention over to Bristol and assessed the skinny, irreverent young man standing next to him. "I can't let you see or talk to him unsupervised."

"How about if Dira escorts me?"

Jason reluctantly nodded. "Only if and when her schedule allows. There will be no physical contact. Five minutes, no longer."

Bristol looked as if he was about to object, then set his mouth into a thin straight line. He left the bridge without saying another word. Jason knew he was giving Bristol far too much slack—not only for his shitty attitude but also the lack of respect he showed both him and the other officers on the bridge.

The overhead display changed to a view of the moon. *The Lilly* navigated to its dark side and quickly descended to the lunar surface. Piloting *The Lilly* down, less than two hundred feet above the surface, McBride slowed, then brought the ship close to a white, freshly painted, U.S. light-cruiser.

A small shuttle left the Admiral's ship and made its way into *The Lilly*'s open flight deck. "Please inform the Admiral I'm waiting for him in my ready room," Jason said.

JASON NO SOONER SAT DOWN, WHEN HIS FATHER entered the ready room.

"Jason, stay seated. We've a lot to go over."

"Good to see you too, Dad," Jason said with a wry grin.

"How's Boomer? That was quite an ordeal she just went through, from what I've heard."

"Remarkably well. She's a little warrior," Jason said.

The Admiral smiled. "She'll definitely be someone to contend with when she gets older."

"She already is. But I think sometimes we—I—forget she's just a little girl. She's been through so much... At least she'll be happy to hear her droid, Teardrop, has been repaired.

"So, where are we at with the coming Craing onslaught?"

"We're waiting. Your latest intel... about the three Craing fleets en route toward Earth... has made a serious situation seem more impossible. Even with *The Minian* and *The Lilly*, I don't see a way out of this, Jason."

"Why bring five thousand warships into Earth space if their only intention is to destroy her?" Jason asked. "It doesn't fit."

The Admiral leaned back in his chair and continued to stare at one of the wall-mounted displays sited on the far side of the table. Eventually, he took an exaggerated long breath and let it out, saying, "Fuck if I know, son."

"My guess would be that it's looking more like a conquering force engagement, one geared toward inhabiting... capturing the planet. Not blowing it up into space dust. I might be wrong, though."

"No... I've had similar thoughts. Something has changed." The Admiral got up from his chair. "You got something to drink around here?"

Jason gestured toward a sideboard table. The Admiral opened a cabinet door, found the half-full bottle of whisky, grabbed two glass tumblers, and poured. Reseated, the Admiral clicked his glass against Jason's, and both men drained their glasses. Jason poured two more fingers worth into each glass.

"What's happening on Earth, Dad?"

"Well, they're scrambling. Washington is a ghost town. The President's been moved below ground. The Vice-President is constantly in the air, on Air Force Two. The majority of the cabinet is with the President; others are en route to Cheyenne Mountain... the NORAD and USNORTHCOM Alternate Command Center. It's pretty much been asleep for the last decade, but there are few safer locations on the planet." The Admiral took another swig and continued, "Jason, under my orders, both Nan and Mollie are en route there now."

Chapter 12

Ot-Mul had to give the Earth Captain his due. Deciphering Craing communication protocols was something no one, at least to his knowledge, had ever done before. But it was that bogus overlord performance that brought an amused smile to Ot-Mul's lips. To think that he and others within the fleet were so convincingly duped served to demonstrate humankind's resourcefulness.

Although many of the communications coming in from Terplin had been intercepted—or out-and-out blocked—enough of them had gotten through recently. Now to paint a better, more accurate picture of what the real situation actually was back on the homeworlds. Most important to him was the news that acting Emperor Lom had, in fact, subsequently died from his wounds, inflicted during the strategic missile attack.

With his appointment to become Emperor only a technicality now, Ot-Mul had never felt better about things. Although he'd never admit it, he was almost grateful to Captain Reynolds and that amazing ship of his.

So, what to do about Earth? He would not be giving the order to destroy the planet... at least not today. With her bright blue oceans and temperate green continents, he'd rarely seen a more beautiful gem of a world. He could see why late Emperor Quorp had been so enamored with it. Terplin was an unspectacular, dreary world that did not befit Ot-Mul's new stature.

Directives for *The Great Space* would continue. But for now, this Star System would stay intact. Hell, if it could be cleansed of its human vermin population, Ot-Mul could not think of a better place to establish a new throne of Craing power. The problem before him was to destroy Earth's populace, without destroying her beautiful landscape.

Ot-Mul continued to sit upon the *dulp-dulp*, the Craing equivalent of a toilet and bidet all in one. He let his mind wander back in time to another far less interesting planet. *Sandora? Tandora? No...* Gandora, *that's it!*

Ot-Mul triggered the button on the nearby intercom panel. "I need you to check our containment cells."

The second-in-command officer waited for more, then asked, "What exactly are you looking for, my Lord?"

"Five years back we came across a most distasteful creature. You were with me there, on a planet called Gandora, or something like that. The planet's surface was infested with these creatures... dark brown, multiple appendages; the things crawled around but could stand up straight as well."

"I'm sorry, my Lord, that's not sounding familiar to me—"

"Well, think harder... They're hunters like I've never seen, and they move with lightning-fast speed. They spit something to incapacitate their prey, then wrap them up in a cocoon."

"Oh, yes. Now I remember. You're right... very unpleasant creatures. They breed like those nasty alien insects... *skatch* flies. If we do have any, they'd definitely be isolated from one another."

"Check and see," Ot-Mul commanded, and cut the connection. He finished his business on the *dulp-dulp* and headed over to the shower. He stepped in and let the hot water envelop around him. His mind continued to ponder what his next move would be. He rinsed the tuft of hair at the top of his head before turning off the water and standing beneath the warm, overhead dry-blowers. The intercom was chiming.

"Yes, go ahead, second."

"We have twenty-two of those molt weevils onboard, my Lord. Eight males and fourteen females."

"What's their typical incubation period?"

"Once they've mated... they give birth the same day. Each litter contains no less than five thousand offspring."

That brought another smile to Ot-Mul's lips. "Here's the thing. I don't want those creatures living forever. Be worse than the humans. Can you inject them with something—perhaps something that cuts down their lifespan and their offspring's, lifespan?"

"Ingenious, my Lord. Certainly, the molt weevils will be of a sufficient quantity in a few short days to have searched out every human on the planet. And you're right, they incapacitate their quarry, wrapping it up in some kind of cocoon, for later feeding of their offspring."

"Fine... whatever. Just as long as all the molt weevils die off within the first few days."

"That shouldn't be a problem, my Lord. Shall I proceed, then?"

"Yes, I want that planet teeming with these little killers as soon as possible."

NAN CONTINUED TO PROVIDE NEWS NETWORK interviews until she and Mollie were directly ordered by the President to move to a protective site... Cheyenne Mountain. Nan knew things were far worse than the average person on the street was aware. Even with constant reassurances that the Allied fleet was now circling Earth, and would protect the planet from any alien onslaught, the general populace was quickly moving toward mass hysteria. Every available space-worthy warship had recently been deployed to upper space to bolster Earth's defenses. The only option for traveling to DIA in Colorado was to fly commercial.

Up ahead, through the throngs of people, Nan saw two federal DoD agents waiting for them as they disembarked from the plane. Both Nan and Mollie had carry-on suitcases in tow. Mollie was having trouble with her suitcase. It repeatedly flipped around backward.

"Stupid thing's not rolling right!"

"Just give it to me. You take mine," Nan said. As soon as they swapped bags, sure enough, Mollie's bag began to awkwardly flip around backward as Nan tried to pull it.

Mollie giggled, "I told you that thing's a piece of—"

"I don't want to hear it," Nan answered irritably.

"Ms. Reynolds, Mollie, I'm Special Agent Reese; this is Special Agent Clark."

Nan shook hands, first with the nice-looking black agent, and then with the serious, plain-faced woman.

Agent Reese said, "If you will follow us, we have a car waiting nearby."

Nan and Mollie followed closely behind the two agents, nearly getting separated in the frantic, nearly hysterical, crowd. As eyes turned in Nan's direction, inevitably there was recognition, often followed by finger-pointing. She had one of the most public and recognizable faces in all government.

Nan had a hard time keeping track of the two agents while also monitoring what was happening on the numerous high-mounted TVs around the airport. "Can you hold up?"

Both agents stopped, neither looking pleased. They turned

to see what Nan was looking at. Up on the monitor a *Breaking News* graphic took up the bottom portion of the screen. Above it, an animated diagram, depicting Earth in the center, showed three massive fleets approaching Earth from separate directions in space. Seven boxy-looking warships were moving into Earth's orbit.

"Oh my God. They're already here!"

"Who's here, Mom?"

"The Vanguard dreadnoughts," Nan said, having a difficult time taking her eyes off the screen. She felt her cell phone vibrate in her breast pocket. Caller ID showed **White House**. "Hello, this is Nan Reynolds."

After a series of clicks, President Ross's voice was on the line: "Nan, I'm glad I caught you."

"Yes, Mr. President. We just landed and are en route to our car."

"Nan, you need to do whatever it takes to get to the safety of Cheyenne Mountain. In some ways, you're even more important than I am. In the coming days, if any of us live through this... the American people, hell, the world, will need reassurance from someone they trust. Get to the mountain, Nan. At all costs, just get there."

The line went dead. The TVs on the walls went black. The overhead lights flickered off. Moving fast, Agent Clark had Nan by the elbow—Reese scooped Mollie up in his arms.

"Hey, my bag!" Mollie yelled, looking back over the tall agent's shoulder. Reese was talking in an elevated voice. It was then Nan noticed he had the telltale curly-q wire at the back of his left ear.

Reese said, "Yes, Sir. But those were assets we were counting on... We'll improvise. Yes, we're en route now."

"What's going on, Special Agent Reese?" Nan asked.

The four of them made an abrupt left into an *Airport Employee Only* set of doors.

"Incoming," Reese said. "Something's dropping from space... we're being invaded."

Men and women in various airport uniforms rushed by. Clark had her creds out and held up in front of her. No one seemed to care or even notice.

Nan let that sink in and then wondered if this could be it... the end of the world. Nan looked toward Mollie and then, instinctively, looked toward the small windows on a set of double doors. She saw a patch of bright blue sky. "Okay... So where are we going?" she asked, more persistently this time.

"We need to requisition a new vehicle," Agent Reese said.

"I thought you had a car."

"It's no longer there, ma'am."

Chapter 13

The seven dreadnoughts moved into formation around Earth with stunning speed. Jason and the Admiral stood together on the bridge and watched with horror as thirty or more U.S. warships came under immediate fire. It took only a single plasma blast from one of the dreadnoughts to atomize an Allied vessel.

"Admiral, at this rate those dreadnoughts will take out the entire Allied fleet."

"I know that!" the Admiral barked. "What would you have me do?"

"Have them back off. At least until we figure out how to disable those big guns of theirs." Jason wasn't sure how well *The Lilly* would fare against those guns, and he didn't want to find out the hard way.

Pacing the length of the bridge, the Admiral, two fingers up to his ear, was engaged in a heated discussion. From the one-sided conversation that Jason could hear, his father actually had multiple conversations going on with separate fleet commanders.

A logistical display segment provided a sobering view of the situation. Three massive Craing fleets were en route from three different directions and looked to be no more than twenty-four hours out. The seven Vanguard dreadnoughts were now in high orbit around Earth. Periodically, a bright amber vector line, depicting plasma bolts, meant, beyond any doubt, another Allied warship had ceased to exist.

Finally, the Allied ships were backing off. Jason studied the screen, then turned to Orion. "Talk to me about those dreadnoughts, Gunny. Other than those guns, are they any different from what we've gone up against in the past?"

"I'm afraid so, Captain," she replied. "We've come across dreadnoughts with beefed-up defenses before. But these Vanguard ships are far more protected... more robust, with nearly twice the hull plating we're used to seeing. Their internal defenses are formidable as well, as if they were designed especially for defense against a phase-shift incurs—"

The Admiral interrupted the conversation, "What does that look like? How do they defend against that?"

Orion added a new segment to the wrap-around display showing an internal schematic view of a Vanguard ship. "These dreadnoughts no longer employ the same open main corridor. It was a tight fit before, but there was sufficient space to phase-shift *The Lilly* into. Now, though, the open corridor is closed off into multiple levels and is segmented.

It still runs the length of the ship, close to a mile long, but everything is far more compartmentalized. They also have more plasma guns in use. Not too different from their new, external big guns, these are strategically mounted within the ship. They've gone out of their way to ward off any ship, such as *The Lilly*, or even smaller fighters, attempting to phase-shift into that corridor."

The Admiral, having disconnected from his conversations,

stood with his hands on his hips. "What's the status on *The Minian?*"

"Last we checked, she was still unable to move under her own power. We can always go get her, using *The Lilly* as we did back at the Craing worlds..."

"And be without either ship here? I don't think so." The Admiral snorted dismissively.

"Captain, I was wrong. One of the seven dreadnoughts is different," Orion said, adding a new segment to the overhead display. Jason saw that, unlike the six uniformly black Vanguard warships, this dreadnought looked fairly typical. The feed changed to a schematic view. "See? It has the standard configuration with the open main corridor."

"Finally, we get a break!" the Admiral said.

The screen zoomed in. "The ship's been retrofitted with the same gargantuan plasma cannon, and maybe some additional plating, but that's definitely not a Vanguard ship."

Jason's mind was already at work on a plan. If they were going to attempt taking that dreadnought they'd have to do it faster, stealthier, than the way they'd conducted their past incursions.

"We have activity, Captain," Orion said.

Jason's eyes had already caught movement on the adjacent feed. Both he and his father took a step closer.

"What the hell are those?" the Admiral said.

"Drones. Non-piloted," Orion said. "But this is weird... they're teeming with life. Individual life signs for multi-thousands of organisms."

"What kind of organisms?"

"The AI has a match." Orion leaned in closer to her console and the small holo-display in front of her. She made a disgusted face. "Molt weevils. A lot of legs and really deadly."

Jason continued to watch as one hundred or more small

drones appeared from one of the Vanguard ships and, in single file, moved directly toward Earth below. "Target those drones... take them out... all of them!" Jason commanded.

Jason had no sooner given the command when more drones were released from the other dreadnoughts. One by one the drones were eliminated, downed by *The Lilly*'s multiple plasma cannons. Orion shook her head.

"What is it?"

"We took care of all the drones within our line of sight, nearly six hundred drones in total. But on the far side of the planet... that hidden dreadnought's drones have made it all the way down to the surface. I'm sorry, Captain."

Jason continued to watch his home planet slowly revolve on its axis. Seeing the continents of Europe and Asia before him, he knew which continents lay on the other side.

The Admiral spoke up first: "You're telling me one hundred of those drones... drones teeming with some kind of alien life... just landed in North America?"

"Yes, Sir," Orion said.

"First thing's first, Admiral. We need to deal with these dreadnoughts before we divert our attention, and before the other fleets arrive." Jason returned his attention to the only non-Vanguard dreadnought. "Where's Bristol?"

"I DON'T HAVE A LOT OF TIME, BRISTOL. I'm not real sure why you chose me to escort you to see your brother," Dira said.

Bristol shrugged, but the truth was Dira was the only person on *The Lilly* who was ever nice to him. Maybe nice was too strong a word... She was accepting of him. Actually, Bristol wasn't sure why he wanted to see his brother. It wasn't like they had a strong sibling bond or anything. But when it came right down to it, who else in his life really cared or mattered? If for no other reason, Bristol just wanted to say goodbye to his brother. Say goodbye to a past way of life.

He had to take an extra step to keep up with Dira's longer strides. He looked down at those long legs of hers... legs that had become the focused attention of so many men onboard the ship. He just didn't get it. As they rounded the next intersection, they made their way down the same corridor where the ship's brig was located.

An on-guard SEAL brought his multi-gun up. Recognizing Dira, he relaxed. "Five minutes, no more," he said to Bristol, and let them pass through the now-open hatch.

Another guard acknowledged them as they stepped into the circular brig compartment. There were four identical, brightly lit holding cells, each containing a bunk, a toilet, and a sink. The brig's only inhabitant was at the far side of the room. Captain Stalls, wearing bright red overalls, stared out from behind a light-blue force field.

Dira held back, placing a hand on Bristol's shoulder. "Go ahead. You don't have a lot of time."

Bristol continued on alone toward his brother. Seeing him ahead, dressed in brightly colored overalls, his long hair hanging free, Bristol felt more sympathy for him than he thought possible.

"Well, well, if it isn't the little traitor."

Bristol stopped in his tracks and took in Stalls' smug face.

"It's not like I had much of a choice," Bristol said defensively.

"There's always a choice, little brother. Just like you have a choice now to still be a traitor or to get me out of here. That is unless family doesn't mean anything to you anymore."

"You're the only family I have left—"

"Actually, that's not entirely true. Remember... you and I are only half-brothers. Someday, if I survive long enough, we'll talk about your other brother."

"I would have known about another brother. Nice try, bro, but I knew every derelict pirate around—no other brother," Bristol replied dismissively.

Stalls shrugged. "I don't care if you believe me or not. Just remember where you were born. I never said he was a pirate... why would he be? Your mother wasn't one."

Stalls did have a point. Bristol had no memory of his mother. He'd been an infant when his father, another colossal misfit of a pirate, had absconded with him after one of his many pillaging and plundering treks across the sector.

"Time's up," the SEAL said.

"Without me, you'll never know, Bristol. Don't you want to know who your mother and your brother are? You're smart, little brother; get me out of here and I'll take you to them myself. I promise."

Chapter 14

Reese, far larger and more imposing-looking than his partner, was now out front and had just plowed through two swinging aluminum doors. He'd drawn his weapon and was doing an effective job clearing a path through more frightened-looking airport personnel.

Running to keep up, Nan held Mollie's hand but could feel her trying to wriggle it free. "Stop doing that, Mollie!"

"Why is everybody running? What's happening?"

"Just keep up. We can ask questions later." Nan wondered the same thing. *What had happened in the past few minutes to ratchet up mass hysteria to this level?*

They were mid-way through the airport's vast baggage handling infrastructure, with multiple layers of yellow and blue conveyor belt systems. With only backup emergency lighting present, this non-public access area, with its exaggerated long shadows, looked more than a little creepy. Mollie was no longer trying to extricate her hand from Nan's. In fact, her grip was almost too tight.

Reese yelled, "This way!" and darted to the left. Nan and Mollie changed direction and ran after him while Agent Clark brought up the rear. There was sunlight in the distance, and the sound of jet engines was getting significantly louder as they approached DIA's expansive formation of gates, runways, and taxiways.

As they cleared the building structure, Mollie brought her hands up to cover her ears. But what made Nan stop dead in her tracks was not what was on the ground, but above in the air. Ten or more low-flying commercial jets were circling the airport— needing a place to land. But that wasn't possible. The runways and taxiways were a congested mess.

Apparently, several large aircraft had attempted to maneuver themselves out of the way, only to become stuck: half on and half off the concrete. Numerous pushback tractors were at various stages of hitching up to stranded planes, but even Nan could see the futility of that process. Moving any one of the marooned jets would be possible only if there was sufficient open space about to move it *to*—which clearly there was not.

Reese was on the run again and Clark was yelling above the whine of jet engines, "Move it! That way."

An assorted array of airport emergency vehicles was clustered near the main runway ahead. As many as ten fire engine pump trucks, and even more ambulances, were idling—their red and blue revolving lights flashing. Nan felt Mollie tugging on her hand and looked down at her.

"I'm scared, Mom."

Nan could barely hear her daughter's voice above the din from the surrounding whirling jets. Their hair was being tousled as if they were standing in hurricane winds. Nan bent down and picked Mollie up and realized there was no way she would be able to run with her. Reese was back at her side and, seeing her expression, took Mollie from her in one arm and headed off toward the EMT vehicles located on the other side of the taxiway.

They passed beneath the belly of a red and blue Southwest 737. Reese slowed and turned toward Nan and gestured for her to keep away from the massive jet engines. *I think I figured that one out on my own,* she thought, but simply nodded and continued after the big DoD agent. Mollie had her arms tightly wrapped around his neck, her head buried in his chest. The first of the emergency vehicles was a large fire truck, with a big water cannon mounted on top. A worried-looking man wearing a fire helmet looked down as they passed below him.

He was yelling something and shaking his head. His outstretched arm, a finger pointing in the direction of the main airport structure, made it clear he was not happy with them being there. They passed two smaller utility trucks before Reese put Mollie down next to Nan and motioned, with two upturned palms, for them to hold here.

He had his creds out in one hand and his handgun in the other. He approached the driver's side door of an ambulance. Then came drowned out shouting back and forth as the vehicle's driver and Reese got more and more animated. Eventually, Reese held up his weapon and, with two commanding jerks, gestured for the EMT tech to get out of the vehicle. The door opened and with two raised arms the driver got out.

Clark ushered both Nan and Mollie forward from behind. As the EMT tech saw their approach, he did a double-take. Recognition crossed his features when he saw Nan. He then nodded and quickly moved around to open the back doors of the vehicle. Nan helped Mollie into the ambulance and then followed. Clark closed and secured the back doors and after several moments joined Reese in the front cab. Nan and Mollie had no sooner found a place to sit down than the ambulance turned and accelerated back toward the airport.

In less than a minute they slowed again. Nan ducked her head down enough to see through a small oval window, giving her a view into the forward cab and out the front windshield. A ten-foot gate at the outer perimeter of the runway stood before them. She heard Reese yelling something and then the gates, first one side and then the other, opened wide. Reese wasted no time and gunned the engine. Both Nan and Mollie held on tight as the ambulance proceeded to make numerous, quick left and right turns.

"What do you see, Mom?"

"I'm just watching the road ahead. There are lots of cars. A traffic jam."

"Are we going to get stuck here?"

"I don't know, sweetie. Maybe."

Nan saw Clark reach up and toggle a switch. *Whoop-whoop-whoop*—a Siren blared outside. From what Nan could see of the road ahead—an endless line of immobile cars—there was no way to move another ten feet, let alone drive the ninety miles to Colorado Springs, where Cheyenne Mountain was located. Reese coaxed the ambulance off the airport access road and onto a just-wide-enough shoulder and kept the vehicle moving.

Mollie was on her feet and staring out one of the two back windows. Nan looked out the other. Most people were outside their cars—some sitting on their hoods, others standing together; perhaps trying to come up with a plan to get back to their homes... back to their families. Nan was being hailed via her internal NanoCom.

From all her time onboard *The Lilly*, she answered with the standard crew comms protocol, "Go for Nan."

"Nan, how are you and Mollie holding up?"

"Jason! Thank God. I forget I have this thing in my head. We're fine... in Denver. Two agents are escorting us to Colorado Springs. Government personnel are being distributed around the country and sent below ground where possible. Our destination is Cheyenne Mountain. Where are you? What is happening in space?"

"I'm with my father on *The Lilly*. I wish I had positive news for you, but Earth has been surrounded by seven dreadnoughts. What's worse for those in the Western Hemisphere, and there in North America, drones have been deployed. We're not sure what that means exactly... perhaps a foreign life form."

"Life form? What the hell does that mean? Life form different than Craing?"

"Yes. Most definitely different than Craing. It may be an organism... something called a molt weevil."

Nan's attention was drawn to a commotion out the back window, off to the side. A circle of twenty to thirty people stood in a wide arc around something that must be one of the drones Jason was referring to. Spherical in shape, with raised, angular plates around its circumference, the drone looked menacing. Abruptly the crowd jumped backward, then began to run away. A woman grabbed her young daughter into her arms. Even at some distance, Nan saw the terror on her face.

Multiple plates around the sphere opened. Nan leaned forward and squinted her eyes. Mollie turned back and looked at her mother with a questioning look. *Things* with legs, lots of legs, were moving... more like crawling... out of the drone. There was a constant progression of them... *God, how many of them are there?* Nan wondered.

"Nan, what is it? What's wrong?" Jason asked.

Chapter 15

It took them close to six hours to make it to the outskirts of Colorado Springs. As bad as the gridlock had been earlier, it was worse here. Even the I-25 emergency vehicle lane was totally blocked.

Mollie was fast asleep on the ambulance gurney and Nan was dozing on the bench seat at her side. When the two back doors opened, they both bolted upright.

"What is it? What's happening?" Nan asked, looking over Reese's shoulder to the jammed up highway behind him.

"This is as far as we go in this thing."

"Far as we go? Are we close?"

"Not particularly. I'm guessing ten miles," he replied in a matter-of-fact tone.

Mollie was on her feet and wiping the sleep from her eyes. "Mom, I have to..." She looked at Agent Reese and flushed.

Nan nodded and gestured for Reese to give them a moment. Understanding, he nodded and closed the doors. Nan heard him from outside: "We really need to get moving."

Nan looked around the confined space, not seeing anything

that would suffice. She opened several side cabinets, eventually pulling out a plastic basin, which she held out to Mollie.

"No way! I'm supposed to pee into that thing?"

"That or you can hold it."

Mollie narrowed her eyes and tightly constricted her mouth into an expression that said *I really hate you right now.* Nan handed her the basin and followed it with a small box of tissues. "You'll need this too."

Mollie grabbed both. She tilted her head and raised her eyebrows.

"Oh, sorry." Nan smiled and turned around. Outside the window, she saw people running. Then there was distant yelling and screaming coming from further down I-25.

"I'm done," Mollie said. "What's with all the screaming out there?"

Both back doors crashed open. "We have to go... right now!" Reese urged. He leaned in and grabbed Mollie, threw her over one shoulder, and then helped Nan jump down from the back of the ambulance.

"What is it?" Nan asked. Clark was at her side and not so gently coaxing her to move faster. Reese and Mollie were weaving between the four lanes of parked cars while dodging a steady stream of people running north on I-25. "Where's everyone going?" Nan asked Clark over her shoulder.

"There's another one of those drones south of here, on the highway."

Nan squeezed between the back bumper of a VW Jetta and the hood of a beat-up minivan. She stepped up onto the Jetta's bumper and looked south. There it was, no more than a few hundred yards further down the highway. There was something else—dark *things* moving about.

"Move it! Ms. Reynolds," Clark barked from behind.

Nan didn't need additional prompting. She'd glimpsed

enough of what was coming in their direction to be more than a little afraid. Had her eyes played tricks on her or were there hundreds, if not thousands of those dark crawly things, the same things she'd seen earlier at the airport?

Screams of terror that were now far too close brought a shiver down Nan's spine. Up ahead, Reese had just cleared the highway and, with Mollie still draped over one shoulder, was running full out and down an embankment. Nan reached the last lane of cars. Too close to wedge between them, she climbed up onto the hood of a small Mazda Miata and felt the thin steel dent beneath her feet. Another glance to her left and she saw something that brought her to a complete stop.

Three car lengths away was one of the crawly critters. About the size of a standard clothes dryer, it had six octopus-like appendages and a formless torso and head. There were eyes, and what she guessed was a mouth, but also a ring of tubular protrusions that flopped about as the thing moved. What held Nan transfixed to the point she couldn't move was the vision of a middle-aged woman held tightly within two of the beast's appendages. Only her head was still fully visible because the rest of her body was being wrapped up into *something*.

Her body was spinning round and round as a *mucous-like* substance sprayed from the ring of tubes… layers upon layers of it were coating every inch of her body. Eyes wide and her mouth agape in a perpetual scream, Nan watched horrified as the two of them locked eyes. Then the woman's head, too, was completely encased. The cocoon process completed, the wrapped-up woman was flung onto the bed of an old pickup truck.

"Move it!" Clark screamed, with panic in her voice. But her words were cut off abruptly as she ran face-first into a misty spray of something. Immediately, she was vaulted into the air, grabbed by the same damn creature. How it had moved so quickly, with such speed... Nan was having a hard time comprehending.

Clark looked to be paralyzed with fear and, like the other woman, her open eyes were wide and desperate, her hands held out in front of her like rigid claws. The beast used its other appendages to start the spinning process. At this distance, Nan could hear the wet sloshing sound as the secretion process began covering Clark's body. Spinning-spinning-spinning around, Clark's form rotated. By the time the female agent was halfway immersed into a cocoon, Nan pulled herself free from her terrified paralysis.

Ready to flee, Nan noticed Clark's handgun on the pavement below. Without thinking, she jumped from the Mazda's hood and scooped up the gun. Six feet separated Nan from the preoccupied beast. She raised the semiautomatic pistol, aimed, and squeezed the trigger... nothing.

Nan found the safety switch, changed the setting, and tried again. The recoil caused her to nearly drop the gun. The creature screeched—a high, relentless, terrifying sound that caused Nan's knees to nearly buckle. Clark, the lower portion of her face web-covered, was lying on the pavement face up. The creature was flailing, all six of its legs probing at a gaping hole in the middle of its torso. Shit-colored secretions seeped from the wound—a wound the creature was attempting to cover with the same mucus substance it had used to make Clark's cocoon. Nan squeezed the trigger again and again until the clip was empty, and the gun's breach locked open.

Three more creatures arrived in the brief span it took Nan to kill one of them. Clark's cocooned body was up again in the air, held in the tentacles of another beast, and was being spun around. The dead creature was also in the air, quickly being spun into a much larger cocoon by two other creatures.

Slowly at first, Nan backed away. When she felt the hot

metal of the Miata hit the back of her legs, she spun around, climbed onto its hood, and was up and over the sports car with all the speed she could muster. In two strides she was heading down the same embankment she'd seen Reese fleeing down earlier. *Where the hell did he go?* Where was Mollie?

Gunfire erupted from up ahead—somewhere over the grassy knoll she was now halfway up. Out of breath, she almost didn't hear the distant scream. It was Mollie! Nan's mind flashed to the image of Mollie, captured, spun into a cocoon; her little face nearly covered, her eyes pleading... help me, Mommy.

Nan crested the knoll and saw more creatures in the distance. A large building occupied a city block just ahead. High above it was a sign reading *CATERPILLAR*.

She heard Mollie's screams again and then saw her. A hundred yards away, atop the building, Mollie stood with her arms waving above her head, signaling to Nan.

Nan ran toward the building with everything she had. The creatures looked to be circling around the building and hadn't noticed her yet. She watched them as they scurried about and saw how quickly they moved. Unlike an octopus that slithered around on all its appendages, these things could stand upright on any two of them and run like a person. As she approached, she slowed and crouched down into the tall chaparral grasses.

The entrance to the building was close to her, but there were several beasts running back and forth in front of its large plate-glass windows. A black pickup truck emerged from the back of the building. Moving fast, it headed directly for Nan. Standing in the bed of the truck was Reese, and he appeared to be holding a rifle. Someone was driving the pickup, but the sun's reflection on the windshield made it impossible to see who it was. Nan saw Reese's gunfire before hearing its retort come a half-second later.

Two of the creatures, one on each side of the truck, were in fast pursuit. As fast as the truck was speeding, the creatures were faster. Reese fired several shots at his pursuers and missed. As one of them moved forward on the left side of the truck, Reese finally hit his target. In a tangle of legs, the creature rolled and flopped to a stop. Before Reese could turn and bring his aim to the other creature, it was already attacking from the right side of the truck.

Less than twenty yards away, Nan could now see the driver. One hand was on the steering wheel as the other aimed a pistol toward the passenger window. The creature leapt and grabbed onto the cab. Two arms reached across the windshield, while other arms found purchase above and below the pickup's cab. The man fired three times before the creature fell away onto the ground. The truck braked to a stop right in front of Nan.

"Get in!" Reese and the other man yelled simultaneously.

Chapter 16

Bristol arrived in the Captain's ready room and found Orion, Billy, the Admiral, and Jason in mid-discussion.

"Take a seat, Bristol," Jason said.

Bristol did as he was told. Jason slid a SuitPac device across the table where it came to rest before him.

"Yeah, I've seen these before."

"More than a few of us are still alive because of that thing. The significance of this technology means we can protect our assault teams, make them more effective, and create more opportunities to slip past the Craing where we can gain an advantage. That's the plan, anyway."

"Okay, I still don't know why I'm sitting here."

"Apparently, there's a whole lot about them we're unaware of. According to *The Lilly*'s AI, once expanded, these body-conforming battlesuits have far more capabilities than any of us thought."

"Like what?"

"For one thing, propulsion," Orion interjected. "These suits are, for lack of a better term, miniature fighters."

"Cool," he said, flipping over the little cigarette pack-sized device in his fingers. "So what do you need from me?"

Jason answered, "*The Lilly*'s database has only cursory tech specs on these things. We need you to figure out their available propulsion technology and show us how to use it."

"And do it within the next twenty minutes," Admiral Reynolds added.

"Twenty minutes?"

"Now nineteen minutes," the Admiral replied, stone-faced.

"I'll need Ricket's lab, up on 4B."

"Get going, Bristol. We'll check up with you a bit later," Jason said.

Bristol stood and hurried out of the room.

"You sure we can trust him not to booby-trap the damn things?" the Admiral asked to no one in particular. "He did just spend a few minutes down in the brig with his brother."

"Bristol is a royal pain in the ass. But he's gotten us out of more than a few tight spots over the last few months. We don't have much choice, anyway... we're out of options and out of time," Jason said.

"So back to the plan, Cap. We get from here to the dreadnought without being detected. We're on the bridge, surprising the crap out of them. What then?" Billy asked.

"We first ensure that the other dreadnoughts, especially the command ship, have no clue we've boarded the ship. Once there, it'll take some time to enter the specific coordinates of each of the other dreadnoughts' main cannons."

Orion said, "There are fairly consistent video communications going on between each of those ships. That's a problem. A big problem. Any disruption, such as our blocking their video feeds, will alert Craing command that something's amiss."

"So... what do we do?" Billy asked.

Jason smiled, "We swap out the key players. As we speak,

Gaddy is down in the hold with the Craing bridgecrew from Captain Stalls' pirated Craing ship. She is explaining to them, in no uncertain terms, that they will be replacing the current crew onboard a specific ship and they will be expected to carry out our orders, to the T."

"And you just believe they will? That they won't alert the others?"

"Fear is a wonderful motivator. Right now, down in the hold with Gaddy, is our old friend Traveler. He can be highly convincing, actually terrifying when he wants to be. Also keep in mind these same crewmembers, their fleet, were defeated one year ago by a single ship. They've been disgraced. They all know they'd be beheaded just as soon as they return to Terplin. Between the potential wrath of Traveler, and a beheading certainty on Terplin, I think we're more than safe in that regard," Jason said.

"Now, it's very important that our actions be coordinated, timed perfectly," Orion said. "Four of the Vanguard ships' main guns will be targeted, those within our boarded dreadnought's line-of-sight. But two dreadnoughts won't be. Those two need to be dealt with directly by *The Lilly*."

"Back to the replaced Craing bridgecrew. What will we do with them?" Billy asked.

"From what we've observed there are several areas outside the viewing range of any of the bridge cameras. The overtaken crewmembers will be held there. The first to infiltrate the bridge will be Gaddy and the replacement Craing crew. Immediately, the AI's security alerts will be dealt with, allowing the rest of our boarding party to come onboard. They'll need to stay outside the field of view of the cameras."

· · ·

It was closer to forty minutes before Bristol returned to the ready room. He entered wearing a new battlesuit.

"You're late," Jason said.

"There's a lot more to these suits than I figured," Bristol said. "Most of my time was spent updating *The Lilly*'s phase-synthesizer to manufacture these things... the way *The Minian* can."

"Fine. Break it down for us, Bristol."

"First of all, yes, they have their own integrated propulsion system... not unlike that found on *The Minian*'s fighters. I've modified the menu system. Now there's a whole range of settings under the heading of *Propulsion*. There's a lot I still don't know... didn't have time to dink around with. But the propulsion aspects are now accessible and fairly straightforward to operate. I suggest we all go somewhere open, perhaps the flight deck, to practice."

Bristol handed out twelve freshly manufactured SuitPacs—first to Jason, Orion, Rizzo, and Billy. Then Gaddy received hers, followed by seven of Captain Stalls' Craing ex-crewmembers.

Gaddy said, "Captain, these three, NaNang, Drig, and Rup-Lor, seem to be the most familiar with Craing bridge duties. I'd suggest that once onboard we allow them to disable AI security measures and assist Orion with weapons-targeting."

"Very good, Gaddy." Jason triggered his own SuitPac and waited the two to three seconds it took for it to expand outward and cover his body. All the others, including the Craing, followed suit. "Okay, Bristol... front and center. Show us how it's done."

Bristol joined Jason at the front of the group. "Um... well, I guess I'll show you a few things I just learned. I'm no expert. Keep in mind the suit had an anti-gravity aspect to it that wouldn't do you good in space. Remember, these are propulsion characteristics we're talking about."

Jason watched as Bristol took several strides away and then hesitated, probably accessing his own HUD menu. The first thing to catch Jason's attention was the slight sound of rushing air. Then bright blue flames were emitted from multiple thrusters on his suit: two slits along his chest; his outer shoulders; his wrists and upper thighs; his upper and lower back; and on the soles of his integrated boots.

Bristol rose into the air and hovered for several seconds. "If you take a look at your HUDs, you'll see I've added a secondary video feed. What you're seeing is my HUD. These are my settings... watch what I do on my HUD as I maneuver around." With that, Bristol rose higher in the air, turned 180 degrees, and flipped himself sideways, so he was now horizontal with the deck. He increased his backward thrust. With his arms stretched forward, in a Superman pose, he flew forward—slowly at first, then picking up speed, until he was jetting around the flight deck.

Jason was about to tell Bristol to slow it down when he careened straight into a repair drone. Both fell to the deck in a tumble of arms and legs. Bristol got back up, seemingly unharmed. The drone stayed where it lay, unmoving.

"Like I said, I'm not an expert at this or anything. Why that fucking thing's hovering around during an important presentation..." He cut himself short.

"Don't worry about it, Bristol. Why don't you take some time and get us familiar with the controls and HUD menu settings? We'll break into groups of three. Time's an issue so no more than five minutes of instruction per group."

Chapter 17

They'd all made it safely into the modern, gargantuan-sized, Caterpillar building. Nan was only now starting to get her breathing back in check. She glanced up and saw that Reese was staring at her accusingly.

"Please tell me what happened to my partner?" Reese asked.

"How could you ask such a stupid question? Those things... the things Jason called molt weevils... they cocooned her," Nan retorted, incredulous.

"Yes, I gathered that. I'm looking for specific details. What exactly did they do to Agent Clark?"

Nan shook her head and thought back to the recent events on I-25. "We were crossing the highway. She was two steps behind me. In the distance we saw a woman being wrapped up... she was terrified. Both Clark and I stopped. I wanted to help, but what could I do? By the time we were on the move again, the alien thing jumped over a car, right next to Clark. It grabbed her up and just like the other woman she was being spun around and covered with that stuff, whatever it is."

"Did you see her die?"

Nan stared back at Reese for several beats. "No. Not actually die. But..."

"So there's a good chance she's still alive, inside that cocoon. All those people may still be alive. Right?"

"I don't know. Do I look like a scientist to you? What I can tell you is I picked up Clark's gun. I killed the thing that captured her. Emptied a clip into it and it died. They can be killed just like you and me."

Reese seemed to contemplate on that. Nan's eyes were drawn to movement outside the building's front window. There were more molt weevils than Nan could count. Nan and Reese had cautiously entered the building through the front entrance, but others outside the doors were less fortunate and were now encased in cocoons. Several creatures were sliming their way up the glass. Seeing their white underside flesh, and the gaping orifices at the apex of where legs met torso, totally disgusted her.

"That's so gross!"

Nan turned to see Mollie pointing at the same creature.

"They can climb? Can they get in here?" Mollie asked.

The man who'd driven the pickup truck came over to them. He was burly and had a long gray beard. *This guy's got a strong biker influence*, Nan thought. "Can they?" Nan repeated Mollie's question.

The bearded man walked up to the glass and tapped on the window. "They have teeth. You can see them there, in that orifice. They chewed through the wooden fence out front, but this building is mostly corrugated steel and, of course, some glass. They don't seem to be able to penetrate either."

"So we're safe?" Mollie asked, matter-of-factly.

The bearded man turned back toward Nan and Mollie. "The roof isn't solid steel like the walls. Wood, paper, tar, some rock... definitely not solid, and I suspect they'll be able to munch their way through it without much trouble."

Nan and Mollie continued to stare at the man.

"My name is Gus. I own this large equipment dealership."

"Hi, Gus, I'm Mollie. This is my mom, Nan, and that guy is Agent Reese."

"Is there anyone else here?" Reese asked. "This place is huge; it's like an aircraft hangar. You can't be the only one around."

"We're actually closed today. We have an open house next week. People come from all over the country to see our newest model Caterpillars."

Mollie made a face.

"Not that kind of caterpillar, Mollie. We sell big trucks and tractors... heavy equipment," Gus said. "I suppose we could shoot at the things from the roof, but that'll only provide us a short-term reprieve. My limited amount of ammo won't last long."

Two more molt weevils joined the others and began sliming their way up the glass.

"It's not just the glass. They're on the outside walls as well," Gus said. "I may have an idea." He rushed out of the front reception room and down a hallway.

Reese followed, with Nan and Mollie running behind him. With the electricity out, the back offices were dark. Nan could faintly see ahead that either Gus or Reese had turned on a flashlight. She reached down and took Mollie's hand. "Stay close to me."

"I wish you'd let me bring Teardrop."

"I wish I had too."

More light streamed in from ahead. As they approached an open doorway, Nan could see that the rear of the building was an immense space. Completely open all the way to the ceiling two hundred feet above, several large, framed skylights allowed in just enough light to provide visibility below. She saw the structure truly was a dealership, just as Gus had said. Large Caterpillar equipment was on display and the employees had gone all-out for their upcoming open house.

Bright yellow tractors of various sizes filled the space. Each was positioned in a staged display-like setting—a backhoe doing roadwork; some kind of crane grabbing trees in a mock forest; a pipe-laying machine perched over a ditch; a purple pipe hanging from thick metal cables. It seemed the equipment got larger and larger, and the mock displays got progressively more elaborate, all the way back to the far end of the building, which was dark.

Gus sidled over to Nan's side. "Impressive, huh?"

"Yes, that's quite an inventory."

"You're looking at over one hundred million dollars' worth. And the ones here are floor models... not inventory." Gus, with Reese close behind, headed to an area that looked to be primarily storage. Five fifteen-foot-long rows of thick, heavy gauge steel shelving reached high above their heads. He came to a stop at a grouping of ten large oil drums sitting on the concrete floor.

"Most of this equipment requires special lubrication. What we have here is specially engineered equipment grease. Stuff's slippery as hell."

Reese knocked on one of the drums with his knuckles. "You're going to throw grease on the things—then light them on fire?"

Gus laughed out loud. "No, but that's not a bad idea. We're going to make it more difficult for them to crawl up the sides of the building. We'll use that crane over there to transport the drums up to the roof."

Mollie looked up at Nan. "I was up there, Mom. It's really high!"

Gus continued: "I'll need your help... even using equipment it will be a fair amount of work."

"I'm not averse to hard work. Just tell me what to do."

It took nearly four hours to maneuver the grease drums onto the roof. Gus had configured a wooden pallet, secured with four cables at each corner, to a crane that extended all the way up to the ceiling, where two trapdoors opened, allowing them outside access to the roof. Both Gus and Reese were drenched in sweat and grime.

Mollie was put in charge of reporting on the status of the molt weevils. Up on the roof, she ran from one side of the building to the other, yelling at the top of her lungs: "They're halfway up over here!" or "They're three-quarters of the way up on this side!"

Nan, arms crossed beneath her breasts, stood on the roof looking south toward Cheyenne Mountain. They were fine for now, but she needed to get to the NORAD and USNORTHCOM Alternate Command Center. She wondered if anyone there was still alive. Looking down below, her breath caught in her chest. "Good God," she murmured to herself. The ground below was nearly covered with molt weevils.

A virtual brown sea of jittering movement. It was obvious the things were reproducing at an astounding rate. Was the whole planet covered with them? Were they the means the Craing was using to take control of Earth? Her eyes moved back toward I-25 and the near-endless line of immobile cars stranded north and south. By every car, there were cocoons haphazardly strewn about—some on the road, others lying atop hoods or car roofs.

There wasn't a live human in sight anywhere. Were they the

only survivors in Colorado Springs? Nan could not remember ever feeling this isolated and alone. She let her hand slide down to her lower belly and wondered if her unborn child would survive... *will any of us?* She hailed the one person who could save them.

"Go for Captain," came the familiar voice in her NanoCom.

Chapter 18

Jason heard the desperation in Nan's voice. He wanted to be there for her and Mollie, to protect them. He contemplated doing just that—perhaps he could find a way. He could phase-shift down to the surface. Get them to a safe location. No, he needed to stay and fight the Craing. The very survival of Earth was at stake.

"Nan, you're one of the most resourceful people I've ever met. Whatever it takes, survive. Keep Mollie safe and make sure both of you survive. Do you hear me?"

"Of course, I hear you. You're right. You do what needs to be done up there or our lives down here won't be worth living anyway."

"Know this... if there comes a time when you need me there —to come get you..."

"That's not going to happen."

"If it does... I'll find a way. I don't know how, but I'll get there."

Nan was quiet for several moments and then said, "Okay."

Jason broke the NanoCom connection and looked up to see his assault team staring at him: thirteen, including himself. All wearing battlesuits. They'd practiced flying maneuvers and Jason was not impressed. *There's no fucking way this is going to work*, he thought.

"Gunny has pre-configured each of your HUDs. We will be phase-shifting multiple times, but not as a group. That would draw attention to us. You'll be alone in open space for quite some time. Don't let that bother you. Once we're in close enough, we will jointly shift onto the dreadnought's bridge and the second phase of our incursion will begin. If you have any questions, any at all, now's the time to speak up." Jason looked over the assault team but focused on the shorter members—the replacement bridgecrew. Hesitantly, one held up a hand.

"You, what's your name again?"

"Rup-Lor, Captain."

"What's your question?"

"Won't the other dreadnoughts see us when we take the place of the other crew?"

"Good question. No. We can only do this once. We'll need to jam the comms signals, including video feeds, for ten seconds. That's how long we'll have once we phase-shift onto their bridge. And that brings up another important point. If there's anything visual that is particular to the crewmembers you are replacing, take it from them... things like medallions, or—"

"Vanguard fleet personnel have hair," Rup-Lor interrupted.

"What do you mean they have hair?" Jason asked.

"On top of their heads, they have a small tuft of black hair."

Bristol hesitated and then spoke, sounding somewhat unsure of himself, "Maybe not these Craing. That ship is not a typical Vanguard ship. It's a modified dreadnought, but nothing like the other Vanguard vessels. Hey, I'm basically pulling this out of my ass here, but it's probably a replacement ship. Perhaps for one that was destroyed. I suspect this crew won't be the same elite Craing as those onboard the other Vanguard ships."

Jason continued to stare at the small Craing. *Why is this information only coming to light now? What else were they missing?* Jason let out a long breath. *There's no way this is going to work.*

"Which one of you will be replacing the Ship Commander?"

"I am," Rup-Lor answered.

"You will have multiple inquiries from the other ships regarding that ten-second comms blackout."

"Yes, Sir. I will have an appropriate response: We were having intermittent communications issues and conducted a quick cycling of our systems."

"That sounds believable. Whatever you do, don't panic. Don't act suspiciously in any way. We only need a few minutes to complete the plan, so keep your cool. Got that?"

Every head nodded.

Jason turned to Orion. "Gunny, you'll be tasked with more to handle than anyone else: tracking the locations of everyone on the team; providing any last-minute changes to our phase-shift coordinates; and then, once we're onboard, working with the replacement tactical officer to target and lock on to the other ships."

"Aye, Cap, I've been working with NaNang. He'll be at tactical and from what he's told me, we'll have no trouble targeting those other ships' big plasma cannons."

"One last thing. We're not particularly close to Earth's higher orbit and these ships. That means we'll be traveling millions of miles—it will take us close to an hour. Some of that will be phase-shifting, while some will be propulsion-based, sub-light travel, in order for our internal systems to recharge. Keep an eye on your HUD destination coordinates. Once we're all within close enough range, Gunny will phase-shift us together onto the bridge at the same time."

Again, the team nodded their heads. Jason looked over to Orion. He was counting on her more than ever before. Behind her amber-colored visor, her eyes locked with his.

"I got this, Cap."

"I know you do, Gunny."

Billy was at her side—also watching her. It was evident he was proud of her. It was then Jason noticed he had a stubby, unlit cigar clasped in the corner of his mouth.

"Seriously, Billy?"

Billy winked but didn't say anything.

Jason was being hailed.

"Go for Captain."

"Are you sure you don't want me coming along?"

"No, Dira. I want you to stay here and be ready for any incoming injured. But keep a SuitPac on your belt, just in case." Jason waited for her to respond. After several seconds he asked, "Are you there?"

"Yes, I'm here. Jason... I have a bad feeling about this. Like I'm not going to see you again. That this will be the last time we'll ever speak to each other. Let me come with you."

Jason let his mind return to their last intimate encounter. The magnificence of her body, the warmth of her lips on his. How her eyes... so close to his own... eyes that seemed to pierce the depth of his very soul. "Hey, I'll be back before you know it. Our time together is far from over." Although he'd said the words, he too felt the same uncertainty. Was this the last time he'd hear her beautifully accented voice? He cut the connection.

"Gunny, let's get everyone out into open space."

IN A FLASH JASON, WAS ALONE IN SPACE. He looked to his left. There it was—no more than the size of a quarter: Earth, like a distant beacon, glimmering blue and white against the blackness of space. He reviewed his HUD readings. The next phase-shift would take place in five minutes. He goosed his spacesuit thrusters to align himself toward Earth, throttled up to its full speed capacity, and cut propulsion.

As Jason jetted through space in silence, he brought up the thumbnail feeds from the others on his team. If everyone had done what they were supposed to, he'd be seeing perspectives similar to his own—namely, Earth should be front and center for one and all. The twelve thumbnail feeds did, in fact, have Earth's position right where it was supposed to be. So far so good. He was being hailed by Lieutenant Commander Perkins on *The Lilly*.

"Go for Captain."

"Captain, we've picked up an interesting interstellar comms from the Craing worlds."

"Can't this wait until I'm back onboard, XO?"

"I'm not sure. Ot-Mul, the Craing we know as the Chief Commander of that fleet of dreadnoughts, is being recalled back to Terplin."

"That's nothing new, XO."

"Apparently, there's an uprising, Captain—resulting from our destroying key government and military infrastructures on the Craing worlds. It started with the students but it's spreading. Millions have taken to the streets; some military and police groups have gone so far as to join the rebellion. What remains of the ruling government, mostly those next in line, like high overlords, see that the masses smell weakness... that this is their chance to strike. As acting Emperor, Ot-Mul is clearly needed back on Terplin, if there's any chance to bring back stability."

In one respect this was incredibly good news. Hell, could this be the proverbial *light at the end of the tunnel*, the end of the war with the Craing?

"What's Ot-Mul saying? What's he doing with this request?" Jason asked.

"It's hard to say. They're attempting to better encrypt their comms transmissions, and to some extent, it's working. From the bits and pieces we have deciphered, Ot-Mul has reluctantly agreed to return to Terplin immediately."

"Not now!" Ot-Mul said aloud, pounding his fist onto his desktop. Alone in his quarters, he clenched his fists in fury. To be this close to victory. To witness for himself the final downfall of the Allied forces—to conquer the planet called Earth and step upon its soil, knowing the last of the Craing enemies had been defeated. But apparently, that was not to be. There were new enemies—enemies among his own kind. Shortsighted imbeciles who would erase all that had been gained. Conquest after conquest for two hundred years—extending to the far reaches of the Universe—was that all for nothing?

Ot-Mul sat back in his chair, forcing himself to calm down. *Clarity.* He could turn this around. Not only would he squelch the uprising back on the home worlds, but he'd also accelerate *The Great Space* initiative. That would start today... right now. He pressed a button on the intercom unit on his desk.

"Yes, my Lord."

"My Second... You will ensure these four things take place. One, you are to prepare my schooner. I will be leaving for the home worlds immediately. Two, you are to continue taking control of this planet. You will eradicate all human existence and subsequently defend her as you would any of the Craing worlds. Third, upon the arrival of Fleet 9, Fleet 173, and Fleet 25, the Allied fleet will be destroyed. No ship will be spared, no survivors taken prisoner."

"And the final directive, my Lord?"

"First, it is time for your advancement. Vik-Ta, I am promoting you to Vice-Commander. Other than myself, no one wields a higher military rank. I trust you are up to the task?"

"I am honored, my Lord. I am up to the task."

"Trust is everything, Vice-Commander Vik-Ta... tell me I can trust you."

"I am your servant, my Lord. You will not regret the faith you have placed in me."

"That is good. The fourth directive, Vice-Commander, is this: You will give the order to implement *The Great Space* initiative."

Chapter 19

oth Reese and Gus had telescoping poles with extra-
large broom mops attached to one end. Reese was the
first to dip his mop into one of the opened grease
drums. He swooshed it around and pulled it out dripping with
the black, viscous, gooey liquid. He hurried to the nearest ledge
and slopped the mop over the edge, letting the grease waterfall
down the building's metal walls.

Mollie stood several feet off Reese's side to observe the
results. "You're going to need to keep slopping more of that stuff
on the walls. It's not reaching down far enough."

Reese gave Mollie a blank stare that said *yeah, I know that
little girl...*

Gus, now with his sopping mop, hurried to the other side of
the roof and slopped more grease down that wall. Back and
forth the two men continued until the first drum was emptied
and two walls were completely covered—all the way down to
the ground.

"It's working! They're falling off the walls," Mollie yelled
excitedly.

Nan screamed and pointed, "Over there!"

Two legs of a molt weevil had crested one of the still ungreased walls, pulling itself over the edge. Gus left his mop standing upright in the grease drum and picked up the double-barreled twelve-gauge shotgun he'd kept close by him on the roof. Too casually for Nan's taste, he walked over to the molt weevil, which was now pulling the rest of its repulsive torso over the edge of the roof. He pointed the rifle and fired. The top portion of the creature disintegrated in a mist of brown sludge. Gus stepped forward and punted the rest of the carcass over the roof's edge.

Mollie ran forward to see it land. "No... Stop, Mollie!" Nan yelled, but her daughter was already at the edge. Mollie's eyes, suddenly the size of saucers, froze and she stood paralyzed as another brown serpent-like leg appeared and quickly wrapped itself around one of her thin ankles.

"Gus! Mollie's leg," Nan yelled.

Startled, Gus fumbled open his shotgun's dual barrels and tried to extricate the two spent shells. His hands were shaking and moving excruciatingly slow. Nan knew she was too far back to reach Mollie in time herself.

Fortunately, Reese was already on the move. His muscular, athletic legs drove him forward. Arms pumping—his stride extended wide, like a track star.

Shooting the thing at this point would not be an option—Mollie would simply be pulled over the edge along with it. From ten feet out Reese dove. With both arms outstretched, he hit the rough gravel, and his momentum carried him forward. The speed in which Mollie's foot was pulled out from under her caused Nan to scream again. Now on her backside, Mollie turned away from the molt weevil and the approaching roof's edge. She was being pulled backward. Her ten-clawed fingers dug into the roof's gravel-covered surface as she was steadily dragged toward the creature's body.

"Help me! Mom!"

Reese was still sliding on his chest like he was body surfing; he brought his fingers within inches of Mollie's own, but his momentum suddenly slowed. He began frantically peddling forward with the tips of his shoes, but the gravel had no traction. Mollie continued to be pulled backward. She now gazed back toward the ugly creature. She kicked at it with her other leg, but the beast caught that too in one of its free tentacles. Terrified, Mollie turned back around, one more time, in search of her mother. Running, Nan knew she was still too far away to do anything to help her.

Swimming awkwardly on the loose gravel, Reese brought one hand down and positioned it on the roof. In a last-ditch effort, he lunged forward. The tips of his fingers found the tips of Mollie's—then her hand was clasped in his. Somewhere along the line, Gus had reloaded. With the muzzle of both barrels placed point-blank between the molt weevil's eyes, he fired.

FOR THE REST OF THE AFTERNOON, NAN ENSURED that Mollie stayed close to her side. Gus and Reese finished coating the other walls with grease. While holding her hand, she let Mollie look over the edge.

"Look at them. We're safe up here and the stupid things can't get to us. Ha-ha-ha!" Mollie said, scowling down at them. She made a mean face and stuck out her tongue.

Covered from head to toe in grease, Reese and Gus joined them at the edge. "This definitely bought us some time, but I'm still tasked with getting you to the mountain," Reese said, looking over at Nan.

"Good luck with that, Agent Reese," Nan replied. "There's an ocean of those things down there."

Mollie looked up at Gus. "You don't have a boat in that big garage down there, do you?"

He chuckled and shook his head, then his features turned serious.

Reese put a hand on the older man's back. "Don't worry about it... A boat wouldn't really do us much good."

"No, a boat wouldn't... but something else might. Come with me, all of you. Let me show you something. Hurry, before the sun goes down."

Reese, Nan, and Mollie followed Gus as he gingerly hurried down the long metal staircase leading to ground level. Once down, they had to catch their breaths; Gus was huffing and puffing more than the others; his greasy Grateful Dead T-shirt had dark underarm sweat stains.

"You okay, brother?" Reese asked, watching Gus struggle for air.

"I'm fine. 'Spose it's time to stop smoking."

"Smoking is a nasty habit, Gus," Mollie chimed in.

"Yes, it is. Most definitely, young lady, I'm gonna quit—I promise you that. Come on... Enough standing around. This way."

Gus headed off toward the large equipment displays. Nan, bringing up the rear, took in what looked like artfully arranged *mini-movie-sets*. Manikins dressed in overalls, bright orange road-crew vests, and hard hats posed in mid-motion behind big steering wheels or standing atop mounds of plowed dirt. Just as Gus had said earlier, the equipment grew in size, and the displays became more and more elaborate the further into the garage they went.

"How far do we have to go?" Mollie asked from the middle of the group.

"All the way to the end of this row," Gus replied.

They were currently passing something called a Highway

Miner, at least that's what the display sign indicated. Massive, it appeared that it was used to make multilane highways. There was something unsettling about machinery this size, Nan thought. Perhaps it was how unsubstantial it made her feel. The group slowed and fanned out in front of something so goliath, so mountainous, they had to crane their necks back to see to its very top.

Gus took a few steps forward and turned toward the others. "Why... you're looking at, ladies and *gentleman*, is the Caterpillar 797F... the biggest damn truck in the world. Nominal payload capacity is a staggering 400 tons. We're talking a machine with a whopping 4000 horsepower!"

Nan continued to stare up at the massive dump truck. A bright shiny yellow, it was as big as a building—easily two, maybe three stories high and fifty feet long. The wheels alone were twice the height of an average man.

"I bet it has a cool stereo. How fast does it go?" Mollie asked.

"About forty-two miles per hour is her top speed."

Mollie nodded, standing there and taking it all in, her hands on her hips. "Um... why are you showing this to us?"

Nan had to smile. She had been about to ask the very same question.

Reese spoke up before Gus had a chance to answer. "This is our ticket to the mountain. This is our boat." Reese walked over to one of the gigantic black rubber wheels and reached up with one arm. It didn't come close to reaching the tire's top. He smiled. "What else would be able to traverse a landscape six feet deep in molt weevils?"

Mollie turned and looked at her mother with a furrowed brow.

"What is it, pumpkin?"

"If those things can climb up the side of a flat building,

they'll be able to climb all over that machine. And I don't think we're all going to fit in that little cab area up there."

Nan, Mollie, and Reese turned to look at Gus.

With a bemused expression, he said, "We still have two more drums of that grease."

Chapter 20

In a matter of minutes, the overhead skylights had gone dark. It was nearly impossible to see even five feet away. Gus and Reese had rushed off toward another area of the building. Nan and Mollie sat together below the bottom rung of a stepladder at the front of the big truck. Nan didn't like the way Gus looked. His color was off. Even with the dirt, grime and grease, his pallor just looked wrong—and what was with that profuse sweating?

Reese suddenly appeared out of the darkness, pushing something and positioning it near the truck. Nan had seen similar electric generators at the scrapyard. This one was brand new and was labeled a Honda EB5000. She figured the 5000 related to the unit's output watts. This certainly should provide serious job site electrical power.

"These should brighten things up a bit," he said good-naturedly. He had five large lights and stands loaded onto a flatbed trolley and several coiled-up extension cords. He went to work setting up the lights around the perimeter of the truck and then ran the extension cords back to the generator.

"Hey, Reese?" Nan said.

"Yeah?"

"Does Gus seem okay to you?"

He stopped and looked back at her from the rear of the truck. "I don't know. Not really. Guy's sweating more than he should. You think he's queued up to have a heart attack or something?"

Nan shrugged, "I'm not a doctor, but yes, I kinda do. He must be pushing seventy. This is a lot of manual work for a guy that age... not to mention he's carrying around a fairly substantial paunch."

From the other side of the building Nan heard an engine kick over. Sounds of machinery moving back and forth from one place to another echoed up to the metal rafters high above. Within several minutes, Gus arrived sitting atop a brand-new CAT TL1055C forklift.

Mollie was on her feet and strutting toward Gus. She gave the internationally known sign to cut the engine: a straight finger making a slicing motion across her throat.

Gus did as he was told and leaned out, looking down at the impetuous nine-year-old. "What is it you need, missy?"

"My name's Mollie, not Missy, and you need to come down here. You're going to have a heart attack any minute."

Nan shook her head. She had to remember Mollie was like a sponge. Anything Nan said or did, Mollie soaked up. And added to that fact, Mollie was just about the bossiest person alive. Gus had left a multipack of water bottles for them earlier. Nan tore into the plastic and extricated one. She joined Mollie at her side and held up the bottle. "She's right, Gus, a ten-minute break. I insist... you're going to get hydrated before you do anything else."

He looked ready to argue the point, but then shrugged it off and climbed down from the forklift. He took the water bottle, unscrewed the cap, and downed the bottle's contents in one long swig. He patted Mollie's head and looked at the job Reese was doing with the lights.

"What do you think?" Reese asked.

"Good job." Gus plugged the remaining cords into the outlet strip on the generator's front panel. He turned the ignition key. The generator kicked over on the first try and the five high-power spotlights came alive. The truck and surrounding area were bathed in bright white light.

At the front of the forklift, Gus had loaded a pallet with the two remaining drums of grease. How he'd maneuvered the things onto the pallet by himself was a mystery to Nan. The guy was some super kind of worker.

A loud screeching sound pulled everyone's attention to the other side of the building.

Mollie moved closer to her mother, while Gus and Reese looked at one another.

"That sounded like the metal siding being yanked away from the building," Reese said.

"That's exactly what it sounded like," Gus said. He retrieved both his flashlight and his twelve gauge from the cab of the forklift and gestured for Reese to follow him.

Nan waited for a moment and then grabbed Mollie's hand and followed after them. There was no way she was going to be left there alone and weaponless with those creatures lurking about. They had to run to catch up to Reese. He looked back over his shoulder when he heard their approach.

"I can't see anything, Mom. Is there just one flashlight in this entire building? What's that about?"

"I don't know. We'll ask Gus for one as soon as we get a chance, okay?"

Nan found herself closely observing every shadowy shape they passed by. She was quickly getting freaked out. So far they'd only seen the telltale straight lines of big road equipment.

Mollie froze and screamed—the sound pierced the darkness and brought everyone down to a crouch. "There's someone standing there. Right there! Can't you see him? I think he's pointing a gun at us!" The last of Mollie's words came out more of a plea for someone to do something. She took Nan's hand and never took her eyes off the dark shape. Gus rushed back and moved the beam of his flashlight across the dark landscape. The beam came to rest on a man's face. The man's unmoving eyes stared back. The smile on his face only added to his creepiness.

Gus laughed out loud, then Reese and Nan started to laugh too. The manikin, positioned with a long metal pipe over one shoulder, was straddling a ditch and waving nonchalantly with his free hand.

"It's just a manikin, Mollie. Good that you're being observant though," Nan said.

Mollie pulled away and stared at the immobile figure. She smiled and let go of Nan's hand. Looking at Gus, she asked, "Why is it you have the only flashlight? How is anyone supposed to see anything?"

Gus didn't have an opportunity to answer—two more loud scraping sounds brought them all back to reality—somewhere close by, one or more molt weevils were trying to break into the building.

"Let's stay together," Gus said as he retraced his steps to the front of the group. Behind him, Reese held his handgun out, his arms extended. The flashlight beam was bouncing off the far wall ahead—they'd reached the section of the building where the noise had originated. They slowed. Then the sound came again—metal was being ripped from structural girders.

Reese tapped Gus's left shoulder and pointed. "It's coming from over there. Down at ground level." Gus brought the flashlight beam to the left but overshot an area where there was movement. He brought it in back again in a slow-moving arc. The beam came to a halt where two corrugated steel panels met. They'd been pried open, pulled outward, at the lowest corner. Nan counted nine separate moving arms. They'd partially squeezed their way through an opening no larger than a dinner plate. Nan brought both hands to her mouth. How many molt weevils had maneuvered their bodies into that one place?

Gus stared for several more moments before turning around. "There's nothing we can do here. The sheer fact there are so many of them has made it damn near impossible for any one of them to squeeze through." He looked at Nan. "That metal siding won't hold for long. We need to get you all moving out of here within the hour."

Nan nodded her head rapidly. "Or sooner. We're okay with sooner."

NAN TOOK UP A GREASE MOP NEXT TO REESE, which freed Gus up to accumulate supplies for their upcoming trip. He scooted around the building with his forklift... stopping long enough to load up anything and everything they would possibly need. With a payload capacity of 400 tons, he wasn't worried about overfilling the damn thing.

Mollie sat up high in the cab of the Caterpillar 797F. There was no safer place for her to be. Nan and Reese covered virtually every inch of the huge dump truck's exterior—tires, sides of the truck, even the undercarriage. What was once a new bright yellow Tonka toy-looking machine was now a dingy-black.

With multiple trips, Gus used the thirty-foot lift range on

the forklift to add multiple pallets of supplies and equipment into the big truck's dumping bed. Reese, now up in the truck's bed, used a hand truck to position the delivered items such as tarps, several diesel generators, two self-contained chemical outhouse units, fuel, sheets of plywood, steel struts, a hydraulic jack, and what remained in the grease drum.

Also, food supplies from three different vending machines and two filled refrigerators, two of Gus's hunting rifles, the twelve-gauge, and multiple boxes of ammunition and buckshot shells, lots of water, rope, and ladders, and large quantities of varied odds and ends. He also included the front lobby's sectional couch, since only two adults could sit in the enclosed cab comfortably. Except for the one still being used, the big spotlights were doused and added to the payload as well.

Nan was now sitting next to Mollie in the cab and watching the two men. Pushed to exhaustion, they finished the last of their pre-launch duties. Nan and Mollie were each given their own foot-long Maglite. Periodically, Nan pointed her beam back toward the area where the molt weevils had breached the walls. The screeching sounds had increased and she and the others knew it was only a matter of time before the creatures would pull a metal panel free and swarm into the building like ants invading a picnic.

Everything that could be done was done. Gus and Reese were moving quickly, despite obvious exhaustion. Reese was the first to head up the metal stairway toward the cab, over two stories above him. Gus waited on the bottom step, catching his breath. Nan watched him, kept her eyes locked on him and wondered if he had the stamina and strength to climb the twenty or more steps before him.

Nan stood, leaned over the steering wheel, and watched Gus, some twenty-five feet below her. The plan was for him to slop more grease on the steps below him as he ascended the metal stairway, leading up to the 797F's cab above.

Everyone stopped. A vibrating rumble shook the building's metal siding. Heads turned this way and that. Nan pointed toward the back corner of the structure. "I think it's coming from over there."

The rumble soon turned to violent shudders and jolts.

Chapter 21

The hour of jetting across open space in a battle-suit gave Jason time to think about their plan to board the dreadnought. He also had time to take in the magnificence of the view—of Earth with her brown and emerald-green continents and the contrasting azure oceans. The moon hovered in the distance like a watchful, unassuming, sibling.

His thoughts were interrupted by a hail from Perkins.

"Captain, a small schooner has left the command ship. Ot-Mul is on his way back to Terplin."

Jason saw a tiny white speck in the distance and used his HUD to magnify it. The schooner was now just another, albeit smaller, bug-shaped ship.

"I'm sure that's not the last we'll be seeing of him."

Jason cut the connection and took in the bright spectacle of Earth before him. The planet filled most of his field of view. What was happening down there? Would the molt weevils eradicate the human race? Over the past hour, he'd added both Nan's and Mollie's life icons to his HUD display. But his priority, his concentration, needed to stay focused on what lay ahead of him less than ten thousand miles away—that minimally modified Craing dreadnought.

Jason answered the incoming hail from Orion. "Go for Captain."

"We've all reached a distance close enough to phase-shift, Cap. I've instructed the others to wait; hold up at their current coordinates."

Jason slowed and brought himself to a stop. "Very good, Gunny." *So this is it*, he thought. The moment had come that could determine the fate of Earth and, most likely, that of the Universe. His confidence in the success of the mission had not increased one iota, but something else had: his willingness *to fight the good fight* regardless of the outcome. He supposed that's what happened after spending an hour in space looking at something so magnificent, so precious, as Earth... his home.

"Cap? You there?"

"I'm here. And you're going to put us all precisely in the right place? Are we poised to jam comms for ten seconds?"

"Everything's ready, Sir. On your *Go*, we move."

Jason took another few seconds looking at Earth, and then at the boxy Craing dreadnought not so far off in the distance. "Go."

Jason saw the dreadnought's big red icon on his HUD flicker once and then disappear completely. In mutual flashes of white light, he and the others were phase-shifted onto the bridge of the Craing warship. Everyone moved with well-practiced efficiency. Multi-guns had previously been set to stun. Jason and Billy fired, and within seconds they'd taken down the three senior officers on the raised platform at the back of the bridge. Jason had hoped these crewmembers would not have the tuft of black hair atop their heads, that they were, indeed, a last-minute replacement crew. To his relief, they were all hairless.

The three Craing assigned to replace them—NaNang, Drig,

and Rup-Lor—rushed forward, retracting their battlesuits back into the small SuitPac devices worn securely on their belts. Medallions, as well as other distinctive pieces of clothing, were stripped off the inert Craing bodies and repositioned appropriately on their three replacements. As Jason and Billy grabbed up the unconscious officers' bodies and moved them out-of-camera view, NaNang, Drig, and Rup-Lor took their seats on the raised platform. Rizzo and Orion worked with the same well-practiced efficiency, stunning key Craing crewmembers at their posts. As expected, there were far more remaining Craing bridge crewmembers than they had replacements for.

As unconscious Craing crew were dragged away from their posts, Gaddy paced up and down the multiple rows of consoles. "No one move! You even twitch, you'll die! Follow the orders given to you and you will live to see tomorrow. Do you understand?" she asked, speaking in Terplin. "Don't move! Don't attempt to contact the rest of the fleet! Keep your heads down... act natural." Gaddy looked over to Jason and shrugged.

Jason, Billy, Orion, Bristol, Rizzo, and Gaddy stepped backward and stood with their backs up against bulkheads at predetermined, out of camera view, positions. Orion quickly darted to her right. One of the unconscious crewmembers had an arm flung outward in full view. She flopped it onto the Craing's chest and jumped back to her hidden position. Jason watched the mission elapse timer on his HUD and saw they were now at twelve seconds and counting. The dreadnought's red icon flickered back on.

Immediately the comms station erupted in tones, which indicated there were incoming hails. The replacement Craing comms officer quickly glanced toward Jason and answered the first hail. Within seconds, Rup-Lor, wearing a gold medallion around his neck and sitting in the Commander's seat, began addressing the Vanguard Fleet Commander. Although he was speaking in Terplin, Jason's NanoCom translated his words to English.

A twangy, high-pitched voice filled the expansive bridge area. On the display screen, an angry-looking Craing officer with a patch of dark hair atop his head peered back.

"Report! Why did all of your ship readings go totally dark? Explain to me exactly what your current status is. Answer me, Commander Cal-Mal."

"Yes, Sir. I assure you, all is well. We have been experiencing multiple communications issues... Sir. It was only by cycling our bridge communications station completely off, and then on, that we've been able to reestablish communications with the rest of the fleet. I apologize for this disruption. Our vessel has had multiple such issues in recent days, Sir."

"I knew accepting a replacement non-Vanguard ship would be a big mistake," the angry Craing Commander spat. "What can be done to rectify this problem?"

Jason could not have wished for a better reaction.

"Just several more minutes to double-check the operation of that one station. We will be dark again for no more than two to three minutes, maximum."

The Craing Commander looked as if he was going to blow a gasket. "Two or three minutes! Do you understand the importance here? All ships are to remain at battle stations on high alert. The command to attack could come at any second. You get this problem fixed immediately or you and your head will be separated by the edge of a warrior's Klaxon sword!"

"Yes, Commander. We'll proceed with all due haste."

Again, with Orion's silent OK back to *The Lilly* to start jamming signals, the dreadnought's icon disappeared from Jason's HUD. Jason relaxed, realizing he'd been holding his breath. Orion rushed over to the tactical station. She was simultaneously communicating with Perkins back on *The Lilly*. Jason felt his heart rate double. He had to consciously slow down his breathing. Any mistake now would surely bring those big Vanguard guns to life. One misstep, a miscalculation, and not only would this ship be atomized in a millisecond, but Earth, too, would quickly come under attack. Orion was crouched next to the Craing sitting at the tactical console. Jason stood behind them both and watched the small display in silence.

One by one the Vanguard dreadnoughts were selected and the precise coordinates of their massive plasma cannons were targeted. A total of four times they went through the same routine of selecting a dreadnought and targeting and locking on to their plasma guns. Jason heard Orion quietly murmuring— she was talking to Perkins. Undoubtedly, *The Lilly* was already locked onto the two dreadnoughts within their line of sight. Now it would be a matter of timing. The attack needed to come at precisely the same moment.

Orion looked back over her shoulder and nodded her head. Jason looked up to see Billy had raised his visor and lit the stubby cigar in his mouth. "What do you say we kick some Craing ass, Cap?"

Three minutes had passed since the dreadnought had gone dark.

"We have an open channel with *The Lilly*, Cap," Orion said, looking up at him.

"Fire!" Jason ordered.

Chapter 22

Jason was not prepared for the jarring recoil kickback the massive plasma cannon produced. As their stolen dreadnought's big gun continued to fire, the dreadnought's bridge relentlessly shuddered. Bristol had found an open post and soon configured the main screen to provide bare-bones logistical information.

Icons for each of the seven Craing dreadnoughts, as well as an icon for Earth, were displayed. Compared to the highly advanced Caldurian technology Jason was used to, this Craing ship's display looked almost comically obsolete. *The Lilly*, with her unique ability to evade most ships' sensors, was not showing up on the screen. It was only her own powerful plasma pulse readings that gave any indication the ship was there at all.

The one area where Craing technology had always shone brightly was in its shielding capabilities. Bristol had been tasked with finding any and all weaknesses to their shield. As he sat at the console, his irritation grew. "Those other Vanguard ships... their shields... are a factor of five more superior to what this piece of shit ship has."

"Cap," Orion piped in, "looks like *The Lilly*'s taken out two of the Vanguard ships' big guns. She's maneuvering to assist with the other four... make that three; we just took out one ourselves."

"Our shields are down to twelve percent," Bristol said.

"He's right, Cap. All three of the remaining Vanguard ships are pounding our shields. We're no match for them."

"Down to three percent!" Bristol said, his voice cracking in desperation.

All eyes were on Jason as he continued to watch the display. "Let's get out of here. Abandon ship!"

Even before Jason selected the proper HUD menu for phase-shifting, Orion had phase-shifted all of them away together—three thousand miles out into open space. From his new vantage point, Jason watched as the three black Vanguard warships focused on the ship they'd just evacuated. Its shields were obviously down—mass explosions began erupting from multiple areas on its hull. Seconds later the dreadnought simply ceased to exist. It had been atomized—one second it was there, the next it was not.

The Lilly moved in behind the assault team with such stealth, Jason had to do a double-take when he saw her advancing behind them. He was being hailed.

"Gunny, get us all onboard."

WITHIN TWO MINUTES JASON ENTERED *The Lilly*'s bridge. The Admiral was seated in the command chair, his familiar baritone barking orders to one of his fleet commanders, whose face was among two others on the overhead display. When the Admiral saw Jason enter the bridge he stood, gestured for Jason to take the seat, and continued on with his multiple conversations.

"Priorities change, Captain Rush. Let me confer with

Captain Reynolds and we'll continue this discussion within the hour." All three feeds disappeared from the overhead display.

"Good to see you back in one piece, Jason."

"Thank you, Admiral."

"The problem is, we still have six dreadnoughts orbiting Earth; three still have their big plasma guns."

Perkins gave up his seat at tactical and let Orion sit down.

Jason was irritated by his father's lack of appreciation. Not only was there one less dreadnought orbiting Earth, but three of the remaining six were a far lesser threat than they'd been minutes earlier. Were they still capable of destroying an entire planet? Jason was unsure.

He looked to the logistical display and realized the Vanguard Fleet Commander may have made a crucial mistake. All six of the huge dreadnoughts now occupied relatively close space, the near side of Earth's upper orbit.

"I think, with the help of what remains of the Allied fleet, we can take out the rest of those dreadnoughts in one well-orchestrated attack," Jason told the Admiral.

"My thoughts exactly, Captain. Although some of my fleet commanders think it far more prudent for them to maintain their present position—hold their current line against the arrival, later today, of Craing fleets 9, 173, and 25."

"As you said, Admiral, priorities change. Right now, the dreadnoughts are vulnerable. If the Craing are defending themselves, there's a good chance they won't be firing on Earth. My suggestion would be to flank them from both sides, cutting off their ability to maneuver, while pounding them from our current position."

The Admiral stared at the logistical display and nodded. "That will be our plan." He brought two fingers to his ear and was back communicating on his NanoCom to his fleet commanders.

"Orion, prepare all tubes for our fusion-tipped phase-shift missiles."

"Aye, Cap." A quick moment later she said, "Tubes loaded and phase-shift timing configured."

Hundreds of small yellow icons moved across space. The remaining four hundred Allied warships, now split into two groups, were almost in position. Jason knew they were taking a monumental risk here. The Vanguard ships could easily still fire down on Earth—perhaps out of desperation, or as a last-ditch show of revenge. Since some of the Vanguard dreadnoughts' big guns were now disabled, they might not be able to completely destroy Earth—atomize her outright, as they'd done to so many other worlds recently—but they certainly could lay the planet to waste, to the point she would be uninhabitable.

Both the Admiral and Orion signaled they were ready.

"Fire all tubes, Gunny," Jason ordered.

Jason heard his father give the command to his fleet commanders to engage the enemy.

The six cube-shaped Vanguard warships were lined up in Earth's high orbit, one after another, like black dice. The three dreadnoughts clustered in the middle still had their big guns and immediately came alive, with dramatic results.

"They know we're here, Captain. They have a lock on us," Orion said. Even before she'd finished her sentence, *The Lilly* was taking fire. The Admiral was thrown to the deck, while the others reached for something solid to grab onto.

"All three of their big guns are concentrating fire on *The Lilly*, Cap."

"Shields?"

"Dropping fast; down to fifty percent, Cap."

The overhead display showed a magnified view of the six, clustered-together, dreadnoughts. The first rounds of *The Lilly*'s fusion-tipped missiles were closing in on their targets. Within seconds they reached the dreadnoughts' outer shields. One by one the missiles flashed and disappeared, only to flash into view again—having phase-shifted onto their far side. Explosions—hundreds of them—erupted from the six dreadnoughts' outer-facing hulls.

Allied warships fired their plasma cannons toward the now penned-in dreadnoughts from both flanks. The combined fire-power was taking its toll. Explosions, albeit short-lived in the vacuum of space, were coming with more frequency.

"Shields down to ten percent, Cap."

"Cease fire, Gunny. Helm, phase-shift us ten thousand miles out to our starboard."

"Aye, Captain," McBride acknowledged.

In a flash, *The Lilly* changed position. Unless the Craing had a direct visual sighting on her, they were undetectable to the enemy. Two dreadnoughts, one right after the other, blew apart. They'd been closest to the Allied ships.

"That'll make our boys cheer," the Admiral said with a grin.

"And girls too," Orion added.

"And girls... I stand corrected, Gunny."

The celebration was short-lived. With *The Lilly* no longer the center of their attention, the three big Vanguard plasma cannons were concentrating on individual Allied cruisers—both heavy and light vessels. With astonishing speed, more and more Allied ships disappeared. Jason tried, unsuccessfully, to keep the increasing Allied death rate from his thoughts.

"Shields are back up to sixty percent, Cap," Orion said.

"Resume firing fusion-tipped phase-shift missiles, Gunny. Take out the center three ships first. Deploy rail and plasma cannons. Fire everything we've got until there's nothing left of them."

Jason watched the display, his eyes going back and forth between the logistical and live-view segments. In a rapid flurry of explosions, five dreadnoughts soon became four, then three, and then—with two final colossal explosions—zero.

The bridge erupted in cheers and hollers—the loudest emanating from the Admiral. Pumping his fist in the air, he turned toward Jason: "That's how you do it. That's how you win!"

Jason smiled and accepted the ensuing hug from his father. But Jason's eyes never left the logistical display segment, and the ship count readout at the bottom of the screen. One hundred and five ships remained. Nearly three hundred warships lost in a matter of minutes—thousands of men and women now dead.

The Admiral stood back, and his eyes too fell on the logistical segment's remaining ship count numbers. "Oh my God."

Chapter 23

Nan screamed through the windshield, "Get up here, Gus!"

There were several loud screeching sounds, followed by the sound of metal siding crashing to the concrete floor.

Mollie, who was standing directly to her left, opened the cab door and peered down. "Hurry up, Gus! They're coming. Move faster!"

Nan could hear footsteps above her. A flat ten-foot overhang attached to the truck bed covered the entire cab, as well as the metal deck leading to it. Nan heard Reese up there pumping the twelve-gauge.

What she could see of the concrete floor below quickly changed to a tumultuous, writhing mass of hundreds, maybe thousands, of molt weevils. Serpent-like arms, constantly probing, wrapping, and slithering, created a choppy ocean effect. The lone standing spotlight went down but stayed lit. Its wide swath of light moved and played against the high ceiling above and caused dark shadows to rhythmically dance back and forth.

Gus picked up his pace. He dipped his mop into a five-gallon drum of grease at his feet, quickly swooshed it around, and slopped more of the viscous contents onto steps below him as he ascended upwards. Nan noticed he had neglected to coat the metal banisters. A slithering tentacle reached from below and wrapped itself around the bottom railing. Out of the mass of moving bodies, a single torso rose several feet into the air—its other arms probing for any non-slippery surface to grasp on to.

Both Nan and Mollie reflexively ducked as a thunderous blast came from overhead. Reese had fired down from the over-hang, taking off the molt weevil's arm and driving the creature back into the writhing mass. Gus looked up at Reese and gave him a quick wave. He looked back the way he'd climbed and saw his mistake.

The grease was ridiculously slippery; there wasn't a way for him to go back down with his mop to grease up the railings. Placing the mop higher on the steps, Gus hefted up the bucket, getting a good hold on its edges, and, in one fluid motion, swung the bucket outward. Half its contents flew forward into the air in a wide arc. The grease splattered down, covering the stairs and both railings. Satisfied, Gus climbed back up, retrieved his mop, and finished coating the rest of the stairs below him as he rose.

Gus reached the metal deck and appraised his handiwork. The grease was keeping the molt weevils at bay. He turned and looked at Nan still watching him from the cab. "What do you say I get this thing started and we head on out of here?"

"I think that's a good idea," she answered back.

Mollie and Nan cleared out of the tight, two-man cab to let Gus inside. He positioned himself behind the wheel breathing rather heavily, and Nan thought she heard him wheezing. She sat down in the passenger seat while Mollie stood in the open doorway.

"Are you okay, Gus?"

"Stop worrying about me. I'm fine." Gus reached for the radio, turned it on, and spoke into the mic. His deep voice was amplified over the truck's PA outside: "Reese... find something to hold on to. And get yourself in the bed. This is going to be a rough ride." He replaced the mic and brought his hand over to the center panel and the three-position ignition dial.

He looked over at Nan and Mollie. "Here's hoping the battery isn't dead." With that, Gus turned the knob.

The big V-24 quad-turbo diesel engine roared to life. Even inside the cab, the noise was near-deafening. Mollie's eyes went wide as she covered her ears. Gus gestured for her to come all the way inside the cab. She sat on her mother's knee and pulled the door shut behind her. That helped somewhat.

Next, Gus turned on the four big headlights. The molt weevils below had moved away from the truck, obviously sensitive to either the noise or vibration, from the big 797F's engine.

Nan was surprised at how simple the controls were. Not all that different from any other truck. The cab was also fairly comfy, with plush bucket seats and what looked like a high-end, in-dash stereo system. Gus put the truck in gear, let off on the brake, and coaxed the behemoth vehicle forward. He was saying something but his voice was hard to hear over the engine noise, "... and make sure that the truck is always moving when you turn the steering wheel."

Nan nodded, not real sure why he was telling her this. She had no intention of driving the thing. The prospect alone scared the hell out of her. As the truck picked up speed, molt weevils tried to scurry out of the way. Those that were too slow, or didn't understand what was happening, found themselves flattened beneath wheels that supported one hundred and fifty thousand pounds of American-built engineering.

Mollie saw the wall approaching up ahead and looked over

at Gus. "There's no door there. You know that, don't you? Stop, Gus, you're going the wrong way!"

Gus glanced at Mollie and then at Nan; both looked nervous. Gus changed the seven-level transmission selector from second to third and the big truck lurched forward, continuing to gain speed. Several seconds later he shifted into fourth gear, bringing the truck's speed to fifteen miles per hour. "I'd hold on to something," Gus yelled.

The 797F plowed through the south wall of the building without slowing in the slightest. Metal girders snapped like twigs and metal siding sheets tore out of the way as easily as if they were slices of cheese.

The building-sized dump truck continued forward into the late evening darkness. Gus brought the truck's gear back down into third, reducing their speed to less than ten miles an hour. They began progressing up a slow rise. Headlight beams illuminated a field of tall, wheat-colored chaparral grass. There were fewer molt weevils here, although every once in a while, some skittered out of the way to avoid being flattened. The terrain worsened the further they moved away from the Caterpillar dealership. Gus was forced to gear down to second, reducing their speed to five miles an hour, then drove steady around that slower rate. Nan watched the speedometer, realizing that getting to Cheyenne Mountain would take several hours, at a minimum.

"You know where we're going, Gus?" Nan asked.

"Anyone who lives around these parts knows the way to the Cheyenne Mountain entrance."

Nan gestured for Mollie to get off her knee and the two of them left the cab and stood upon the metal grate decking that ran around the front of the truck. "Don't let go of the railing, Mollie." Mollie looked up at her mother with an expression that said... *I already knew that.*

A rope-like ladder, actually made of small metal chain links, fell from the overhang above. Reese peered over the edge, nodding to Nan, and said, "Can you take this?" He passed her the twelve-gauge, tossed down a box of shells, and then climbed down the ladder. Nan and Mollie sat on the deck, their feet hanging free over the edge. Reese stepped behind them and checked in with Gus. Nan heard Reese ask him how he was holding up and to let him know when he wanted to be relieved. A moment later, Reese was sitting next to Nan on the deck.

Nan looked over at him. "You got things organized there okay?" she asked, gesturing toward the truck bed behind them.

"It's a big space... even with all the crap we've brought along... lots of room left." He continued to look forward as the truck slowly traversed the slight rise. "You know, this reminds me of my Navy days. I'd stand at the prow of the *Arlington*, a destroyer, at night and look out at the dark sea, the stars... sometimes a whale or dolphins would crest the surface."

"So, you're a Navy man?"

"Yep. Petty Officer—"

Mollie interrupted him. "My dad's a Navy man, too... now he's a spaceman."

Both Nan and Reese laughed. "Your dad's famous, Mollie. Most people know who Captain Reynolds is... just as they know your mom is the secretary of inter-stellar relations, answering directly to the President."

Mollie beamed at that and simply nodded.

"So you work here in Colorado... out of the Denver office?"

"Yes. Both Agent Clark and I." Reese's expression changed with the realization that she was no longer alive.

Nan changed the subject. "What were your orders? I mean, pertaining to my daughter and me?"

"Simple... get you both to Cheyenne Mountain at any cost, including my own life."

145

"We appreciate it, Agent Reese. Do you have a first name or does everybody just call you Reese?"

She watched the agent squirm at the question. Seeing this rare bit of vulnerability made her like him that much more.

"Um, I actually prefer Reese, ma'am."

Mollie giggled. "What's so hard about just telling us your name?"

Nan watched Reese's reluctance and wondered what the big deal was. In the darkness, she could barely make out his face. She realized he was handsome—muscular build, smooth mocha skin—and he had a young *Denzel-Washington-thing* going on.

"I'm sorry about your partner," Nan said, letting him off the hook about his name.

"Thank you, ma'am."

"I'm Nan; you can knock off that ma'am stuff."

The truck cleared the field and was leveling out onto a paved, two-lane road. The truck took up both lanes, as well as several feet on each side of the road. Their speed increased and leveled off for a while.

Nan stared at the road ahead and then leaned forward. "What is that?" Something was up ahead—something long and *greenish*. As they drew closer, Nan realized it wasn't one thing—but many. Like wrapped-up mummies, illuminated in the wash of the headlights, there were increasing numbers of cocooned bodies. Each lay haphazardly at odd angles, atop the blacktop. She saw more and more of them off into the visible distance.

Gus brought the truck to a stop and continued to idle there. The cab door opened and he peered out. He looked perplexed and said, "What should I do? Should I just run over them?"

Chapter 24

The *Minian's* bridge, for the most part, was looking good. Consoles were reassembled and closed up. In addition, tools and test equipment were returned to their proper locations. A good amount of progress.

Ricket knew he was well suited for solitude. Two hundred years as a cyborgenic being probably had a lot to do with that. He was comfortable with his thoughts; he liked his own company. He enjoyed problem-solving—that was his creative outlet.

Granger, on the other hand, was not built for solitude. Ricket had watched him over the last few days and quietly took note of his mounting problems being onboard this massive mile-long vessel—a vessel with just two other people to converse with. The once confident, gregarious Caldurian had become introverted and mopey. Sergeant Toby Jackson, Granger's overqualified Delta Forces security guard slash babysitter, also seemed to be struggling with the solitude aspect—but nowhere near to the extent Granger was.

Ricket had spent nearly all of his waking hours either in his lab, here on the bridge, or making repairs to the various other missing or inoperable systems around *The Minian*. As Ricket's familiarity with Caldurian technology increased, his dependency on Granger's assistance declined. In retrospect, that had been a mistake. An uninvolved Granger was a dangerous Granger.

Now, as Ricket sat facing the tall Caldurian who was pointing a pulse pistol towards his heart, Ricket assessed the situation. Where was Sergeant Jackson? Had Granger killed him? What did Granger hope to accomplish? The truth was, he could no longer return to his own kind, the progressive Caldurians that preferred to roam the Multiverse. They certainly would not welcome him back after he'd absconded with *The Minian*... and the other Caldurians, the Originals... they'd left him high and dry at the first sign of violence back in Craing space at the Ion Station. Where would he go?

"What is it you want, Granger?" Ricket asked.

"I want control of this ship," he said, gesturing with his free hand to the ship around him.

"Ship repairs have steadily progressed. We are nearly done... ready to power on the ship's propulsion system, get the drives back online," Ricket said.

"And you'll continue with that. The difference now is that we won't be returning to Earth."

"Without the help of *The Minian*, Earth, and the Alliance... we will be lost," Ricket said.

"That is unfortunate. But my situation dictates I leave this sector with all due haste. I've had a lot of time to think about things. For instance, what happens once this ship is repaired? Am I to be an indefinite prisoner on this or another ship; or perhaps back on Earth?"

"That depends. Where is Sergeant Jackson?"

"He's fine. I promise."

Ricket waited for more specifics.

"Fine. I tagged him with a stun pulse. He's locked in the ship's brig."

Ricket tried to remember where the brig was on *The Minian*. "I'm not unsympathetic to your situation. But I cannot allow—"

Granger cut him off. "I'm quite familiar with the workings of this vessel, Ricket. I've changed the command protocols. At this point, the AI will respond to my commands and my commands only. I'm sorry, Ricket. I like you and I have no intention of hurting you as long as you follow my orders... which include completing the repairs on this ship."

Ricket almost felt bad for the Caldurian. But Granger wasn't the first person to underestimate him.

"Granger, in actuality, you have not reassigned command protocols for *The Minian*. You were not interfacing with *The Minian*'s AI, you were interacting with my advanced nano-device interface. As long as I'm tied in, as I am, there is no user or command-level exchange that I am not aware of. To make my point, you used a passcode registration of..." Ricket proceeded to spool off twenty-seven alphanumeric characters of the Caldurian alphabet.

Granger stared back at Ricket for several seconds. Before he could say anything further, two security drones hovered into position, one behind and to the left of Ricket and one directly behind Granger. Both drones were in high-alert mode with their primary weapons dispatched.

Granger didn't move for several beats before slowly releasing his grip on his gun and tossing it onto Ricket's lap. "You win."

"It seems to me, Granger, you spend an inordinate amount of time with subterfuge... trying to outsmart others. I think you could call it being a con man. Concepts such as friendship and loyalty play no part in your life. It is unfortunate and I suspect the reason you keep finding yourself in this same predicament."

"So you're telling me we were friends?"

"No. I don't trust you... I never have. Friendship is earned. Friendship comes with a price, one that you would need to figure out for yourself."

Granger snickered at that and shrugged. But Ricket saw that his words had penetrated Granger's cynicism—how much, he wasn't sure. "Please go and release Sergeant Jackson from his cell."

"You have command-level interface capabilities with the AI. You can easily do that yourself."

"Yes, quite easily indeed. But this way you have the opportunity to apologize to Jackson," Ricket said with a smile.

Granger snickered again and stood and saw that the two drones were gone. Ricket tossed Granger his pulse weapon. "In ten,to bring the drives back online. I could use your help with that."

Granger smiled. "I doubt you need anyone's help, but sure. I'll go ahead and let the soldier out of his cage."

Ricket watched him leave and let out a breath. Unaccustomed to this kind of deception, Ricket had been bluffing. He had memorized Granger's command passcode, seeing it deep within the trillions of lines of code of the AI's core. Ricket used that same code now to log in and revert the command protocols back to himself. He also reconfigured the AI to alert him to any other potential breaches of this nature in the future.

RICKET HAD PUT IN A REQUEST TO THE *Determined*'s commanding officer, Lieutenant Commander Douglas, to move additional personnel over to *The Minian*. The solitude situation was an easy fix, one he should have thought of previously.

Within an hour, twenty-five crewmembers transferred over to *The Minian*; although this was not a substantial number of people, it had an immediate impact on the overall ship-wide atmosphere. Now there would be sufficient crew to man key departments including tactical, engineering, bridge/navigation, medical, as well as command and operations.

But having this new crew wouldn't do anyone any good if *The Minian*'s drives couldn't be brought back online. Ricket had done all that he could, including manufacturing thousands of new parts via the phase-synthesizer. In effect, he'd had to re-engineer much of the drive technology and develop the necessary parts on the fly. In concept, it all should work, but the truth was, Ricket wasn't one hundred percent sure it would. All this was accomplished while at the same time, he stayed current on what was happening back on Earth. Ricket had not slept—had not eaten, had done only those things that would get *The Minian* back into the fight with the Craing.

From his last conversation with Captain Reynolds, miraculously they'd destroyed the Vanguard fleet of dreadnoughts. An impossible task in its own right. But the approaching three fleets, Fleet 9, Fleet 173, and Fleet 25—comprised of no less than five thousand warships—would be impossible to defend against without *The Minian*'s presence there.

Ricket stood alongside Granger and one of the new engineering crewmembers, Seaman Steinway, in engineering. He was feeling dizzy and nauseous. Ricket was unaccustomed to illness. Cyborgs didn't get sick. Even now, with his millions of internal nanites working overtime, his body was rebelling. But he'd continue to push forward or die trying.

Ricket and Steinway manhandled the thick cable into place, having connected the last of three optical power cables on the primary substrate. Ricket measured the energy levels on each with a portable test device and nodded.

"That was the last of them," he said. Ricket turned to Granger and gestured toward the primary engineering console. "I'd like you to have the honor of initiating the power-up routine."

Granger looked surprised. "Thank you, Ricket. I would like that." He stepped over to the console with its now operational holo-display interface. He keyed in the start command which activated the system to initialize. Both massive drives, only the ends of which protruded into engineering looking like the noses of two Goodyear blimps, now buzzed to life.

Ricket felt exhilarated and then fell to the deck, unconscious.

Chapter 25

Jason entered the Captain's ready room to find the Admiral finishing up a conversation with the President of the United States and several others—each with their own video feed window up on the integrated wall screen.

Jason walked further into his cabin and found Boomer immersed in a game. When he heard his father finish his conference call he reentered the ready room.

"What's new?" Jason asked.

The Admiral stood and stretched. "Two hours of video-feed briefings with officials from Washington, as well as with several leaders from the few remaining Allied worlds."

"I saw you speaking to the President," Jason said.

The Admiral looked shaken. "Yes, for a few minutes there at the end. Things aren't good. His security detail has had to move him and his family three separate times. Seems the molt weevils have managed to breach the White House's underground bunker, as well as two other supposedly secure locations. The Capitol building now contains hundreds of cocoons... many were U.S. senators and congressmen." The Admiral made a beeline to the liquor cabinet where he poured them both a drink. "How are Nan and Mollie? Have they made it to safety?"

Jason had just ended a NanoCom conversation with Nan—she'd assured him that she and Mollie were fine, still on their way to Cheyenne Mountain and that they'd probably make it there some time that night. But Jason didn't buy her act... her pretend confidence that everything was fine and that he needed to stay in space and protect the planet at all costs.

Jason took the tumbler and shook his head. "Still en route. Hoping to get to the mountain later tonight. Seems the molt weevils are multiplying at an astounding rate. It won't be long before they literally cover every inch of—"

"It's like that throughout North America. Hell, the entire Western Hemisphere, Jason. I know you're worried about them. You're probably tempted to rescue them."

Jason didn't answer, but his expression answered the question... *of course, he was tempted.*

"Don't do it, Jason. For one thing, where would you bring them? Here in space? You know what's coming. I don't need to tell you what our odds of survival are against those approaching five thousand Craing warships, do I?"

"What else did the President say?" Jason asked, changing the subject.

"Earth has never been in greater jeopardy—reports of the infestation down on the surface paint a truly desperate picture. While we're up here battling the Craing in space, the general populace below is being eradicated at an alarming rate. On the flip side, we have reports that the Craing Empire itself is perilously close to crumbling. Which explains Ot-Mul's quick departure. Jason, your bombardment of the Craing worlds' key military and government installations accomplished a tremendous amount. Probably more than you anticipated. Things are finally changing there."

"I only hope Earth survives long enough to see that empire fall," Jason said.

"The problem with desperate situations is that they often require desperate decision-making. I've been in contact with our Mau friends... homeless now, they conveyed more discouraging news regarding Craing deployments. Hundreds of Craing fleets are moving into that sector's star systems, indicating *The Great Space* operation has fully begun. The Mau are seeing the systematic obliteration of planets. It seems the Vanguard dreadnoughts we destroyed were actually a prototype methodology, one that has been uniformly replicated. Together, seven retrofitted dreadnoughts' combined strength can atomize a planet in minutes."

"So, while anarchy spreads among the populace at home, Ot-Mul continues his predecessor's insane plan to continue *The Great Space* wipeout," Jason said, draining his drink and slamming his glass down on the table. "Suddenly, winning this war has become more about taking out Ot-Mul than it is defeating the Craing's military machine."

"I'd have to agree with that." The Admiral swirled what remained of his whisky at the bottom of his glass. "*The Minian* will be arriving here in Earth space within the hour. Ricket has done the impossible—brought that magnificent ship back to nearly full strength. With what's left of our fleet, along with *The Minian*, I think we can hold off those three approaching Craing fleets."

"What are you saying, Dad?"

"What's the best defense?"

"A great offense. I know where you're going with this. You want me to go after Ot-Mul. Read my lips: it's IMPOSSIBLE. I've been to Craing space recently; I've seen the countless warships moored there for as far as the eye can see. And that's not even talking about getting onto the planet itself!"

Mark Wayne McGinnis

"What's at stake is humanity itself. Come up with a damn plan, figure it out... you've done it before. Take *The Lilly*, and that same convoy, back to the Craing worlds. Find Ot-Mul and his supporters and take them out. At all costs, son... take them out."

Jason realized Boomer was standing in the doorway. "Hey, sweetie, what are you up to?"

"We're going back to the Craing worlds?"

"No. You'll be staying here with Grandpa, kiddo."

With a furrowed brow, Boomer sat down next to the Admiral.

"I'm sorry, but you'll be safer—"

She cut her father off. "I know that, Dad. I want to talk about something else."

Surprised, Jason and the Admiral glanced at each other. "What?"

"I've been talking to Mollie."

"What do you mean, you've been talking to her?"

"Well... NanoTexting with her."

"That's good, Boomer. It's time you two became closer," Jason told her.

"Anyway, I wanted to ask permission to send her Teardrop."

Jason sat up straighter in his seat. *Why hadn't he thought of that?* "That would be an amazingly kind thing to do. They need the help. Yes... Teardrop would help keep them safe."

"It wasn't my idea, it was Mollie's. She told me she figured out how to NanoText with the other Teardrop... the one they had to leave back in Washington."

Jason recalled the recent past realms of time situation on Earth, which culminated in there being not only two Mollies but two Teardrop drones, as well.

Boomer continued, "Mollie contacted her own Teardrop

and it's now on its way to Colorado Springs. I want to send her my Teardrop, too.

"Will I stay with you, Grandpa?"

The Admiral looked to Jason and saw him nod. "Yes, Boomer, we'll be staying on *The Minian* when it arrives, until your dad returns."

"Good, there's still lots and lots I haven't explored there!"

Both Jason and the Admiral smiled but looked worried just the same.

SEATED IN THE COMMAND CHAIR, JASON WATCHED as six gleaming-white heavy and light-cruisers approached and came to a stop. It was the same U.S. convoy that had accompanied *The Lilly* on their previous mission to the Craing worlds. Now there was an additional heavy cruiser—one still painted the typical, drab, grayish-tan color. It slowly moved in to join the convoy of ships.

"*The Revenge* has joined the convoy, Captain," Perkins said.

Jason had recently given his brother, Brian, the ship's command. The ship's previous owner, Captain Stalls, was still imprisoned within *The Lilly*'s brig. Jason wondered if it had been Brian who'd renamed the ship.

Two more vessels, *The Determined,* and *The Minian,* arrived; the latter's size dramatically dwarfed all the other ships.

"I have returned, Captain."

Startled, Jason saw Ricket standing to his right. His features had changed—from those of Nelmon Lim back to Ricket's own. He was wearing a new battlesuit with the helmet retracted.

"Welcome back, Ricket. We've missed you," Jason said. He watched Ricket take in that last bit of information without any reaction. He may have left his cyborg body behind months previously but it would probably be quite some time before his interpersonal social skills evolved—if ever. Truth was, Jason wouldn't change a thing about his brilliant Craing friend and was glad to see he was himself again.

"Captain, *The Minian*, as you undoubtedly have noticed, has been repaired to a level where she can traverse space under her own propulsion systems. Also, navigation, weapons, and shields are operating within satisfactory parameters."

"Excellent, Ricket. Any problems? How was Granger?"

"No significant problems, Captain. Granger... is a person without any loyalties... allegiances. I am not well-suited dealing in such matters; perhaps you can speak with him."

"Should I be worried? Can he be trusted?"

"He has shown himself to be untrustworthy. I do believe there is hope for him, though, in that regard. But again, this is not my area of expertise."

"Understood. On another subject, *The Minian* will stay here in defense of Earth under the Admiral's command. *The Lilly*, along with the convoy, will embark on another mission shortly. I want both you and Gaddy along with us."

Jason noticed Ricket's demeanor change ever so slightly at the mention of Gaddy's name. "Yes, Captain, I will return to *The Minian* to retrieve my things."

Ricket left the bridge as Orion entered. Once seated, she added a new logistical segment to the overhead display. Varying-sized icons represented Earth, their small convoy of ships, including *The Lilly* and *The Minian*, as well as the three approaching Craing fleets.

"How much time do we have, Gunny?"

"At their current speed... two days," Orion answered.

"It's no secret that the battle of all battles is coming, Gunny. They'll need the very best on tactical. I'll do my best to be back here before those fleets arrive, but there's no guarantee. Take this bit of down-time getting to know *The Minian*'s defenses...

like *The Lilly*, she's an incredible ship. She'll need to be. And you'll need to be just as amazing."

"I'll do my best, Cap."

"That's all I can ask of you. Listen, we're heading out within the hour. You may want to say your goodbyes to Billy..."

Orion held his stare for several long seconds. Jason had never suggested such a thing before, saying goodbye, anytime previously. Perhaps only then did she fully understand that he didn't expect them to return. That this, most likely, would be a one-way trip—*The Lilly*'s last voyage.

Chapter 26

"**G**o around them," Nan said.

"Just so you know, that will slow us down considerably. It's not like they'll feel it," Gus replied.

Nan stared at the cocooned bodies lying on the road. "They've already endured a terrible fate. We're not going to disrespect them in death as well."

Gus disappeared back into the cab. The big truck accelerated forward several feet, turned off the pavement, and slowly continued onto the grassy field.

Reese made a sympathetic face. "You know... bodies aren't only lying on the street. They're all over the place, including this field."

Mollie looked disgusted.

"I'm well aware of that," said Nan. "But there's a difference between consciously knowing you're rolling over something and inadvertently rolling over something."

"Or someone," Mollie added.

Nan purposely averted her eyes from what the headlight

beams might illuminate near the ground. The terrain was becoming more uneven and the slope of the field more precarious. Again, the truck came to a stop and Gus stuck his head out the door of the cab.

Nan looked over her shoulder at him, waiting for Gus to resume his prior argument. She raised her eyebrows. He pointed off to the right, near the side of the road.

"They're here!" Mollie screamed.

Reese jumped to his feet and raised the shotgun.

Nan stood as well and tried to see what Gus and Mollie were talking about. She recognized their unique, hovering, teardrop silhouettes, and let out a breath. "I don't understand how—"

"I NanoTexted them. Actually, I NanoTexted my own Teardrop... the one we left behind in D.C., and then I Nano-Texted Boomer, up in space. She sent us her Teardrop."

Mollie moved closer to the two drones, walking to the far-right end of the metal deck. "Come closer, both of you."

Nan watched as they silently approached. To most people, they would look identical, but Nan and Mollie could see the subtle differences in the duo—the most significant being Boomer's drone, although repaired, showed battle wear from fighting the pirate, Captain Stalls, when she was taken from *The Cutlass.*

Mollie stood with her hands on her hips. "We can't call you both the same name. So, from now on, you, Boomer's drone... we're going to call you Dewdrop." Mollie turned toward Nan. "What should I tell them to do?"

Gus's voice boomed from the cab, "Tell them to protect us from the molt weevils, for God's sake, little girl!"

"Protect us from those molt weevil creatures," she instructed the drones.

"Why don't we have them move the cocoons out of our way on the street?" Reese added.

Mollie turned back to the drones and told them, "Also, clear a path up on the street so we don't run over the cocoon things."

In the darkness, Nan noticed both drones had deployed their plasma cannons from the compartments at the center of their torsos. Without warning they each began spinning and firing at unseen molt weevil targets. Dewdrop moved to the back of the truck, while Teardrop moved to the paved street and started using its articulating arms to clear the cocooned bodies far enough off the roadway for the truck to pass through.

Gus powered the truck back onto the now-open road. Teardrop moved farther up the road to clear away more cocoons, while Dewdrop acted as sentry and shot at any approaching molt weevils. The engine noise grew louder as the truck picked up speed.

The Caterpillar dealership they'd left behind was in a relatively remote industrial section of town. Now, they were approaching an expansive neighborhood off to the right. Not only were there far more cocoons lying scattered on the streets but there were also significantly more attacking molt weevils.

Nan watched as the two drones continued to spin and fire pretty much non-stop. She wondered how long they could continue—would they need to rest—to recharge?

Mollie cupped her two hands over her nose and mouth as the smell of burnt molt weevil flesh filled the air. Between the fumes and the growing number of dead carcasses, Nan was fighting back nausea.

As the streets narrowed, more and more cars parked by the curb, and Gus turned west on Lake Avenue, which was better—more of a thoroughfare. As their speed increased, Nan was sure they were pushing the upper range for the 797F. Now there were fewer attacks—giving the two drones a much-needed reprieve.

The truck started to slow down again. Nan, standing on her tiptoes, saw that the road ahead was split by a grass island divider. The track, the distance between wheels on the same axle, was clearly wide enough to span the divided roadway. "Gus, you do see those trees... don't you?" Nan yelled.

He replied using the PA, "Of course I see the trees. I suggest everyone hold on to something."

Nan pulled Mollie in tight and clenched her jaw just prior to the front end of the 797F careening into the first tree's thick trunk. It toppled over as if it were made of rubber. Every three or four seconds, another tree went down. There were some instances when the wide tires rolled over a wrapped cocoon. At this point, Nan was rethinking her stance on avoiding them: *Why bother?*

Up ahead was the entrance to the Broadmoor Hotel. Dual rows of perfectly manicured pines lined the circular drive; a posh Mediterranean-style building standing several stories high sat perpendicular to Lake Avenue. The truck turned south, crossing over the island, and headed down a somewhat narrower street. Again, abandoned cars were parked ahead on the curbs.

Nan looked over to Reese. "What's Gus doing? Doesn't he see there's no room for the truck to go in this direction?"

Before he could answer, Gus jerked the wheel toward the west again and drove across the hotel's parking lot. They picked up speed and headed toward a row of bungalow-style buildings. Gus laid on the horn. It was now obvious to Nan what Gus intended to do, and she only hoped the bungalows weren't currently occupied. But Gus surprised her by bringing the truck to a stop.

Back on the PA again, Gus's voice echoed into the street,

"Everyone climb up and get back into the bed. Get under cover."

Mollie wasted no time climbing up the ten-foot-high rope ladder. Once she'd disappeared over the edge, Nan followed. She looked back and saw Reese had joined Gus in the cab. Crouching low, she traversed the long steel overhang and found another rope ladder leading into the bed. As she turned and started down the ladder, the truck lurched and Nan held tight onto the top edge of the truck bed. She looked up just in time to see the front end of the 797F plow into a two-story-high bungalow.

The sound of timber, drywall, and concrete smashing beneath six twelve-foot-tall tires made her cringe. She figured Gus was keeping the accelerator down to the metal because the big dump truck's progress didn't slow. In less than five seconds they'd cleared the debris and were cruising along on the Broadmoor's first-hole golf course fairway, heading southeast. Nan climbed down the rest of the way into the huge truck bed and saw all the stuff Gus and Reese had loaded in there. Mollie waved from the middle of the sectional couch.

Nan regretted not bringing her flashlight with her but didn't think she'd have been able to climb the ladder and hold on to it at the same time. She navigated around pallets of equipment and made it over to the couch, sitting down next to Mollie. The Broadmoor's lush thick grass beneath the truck's tires made for a comfortable ride. Nan scooted in close to Mollie and put her arm around her. For the first time in hours, perhaps days, Nan let herself relax. She kissed Mollie's forehead and looked up to the nighttime sky.

"Look, Mom, the Milky Way."

Pitch-black against the star-filled heavens, silhouettes of tall oak trees paralleled both sides of the fairway. Nan remembered

Gus saying the truck was three stories high... so how high were these trees? Four stories?

The truck moved closer to the right side of the fairway—next to the big oak trees. Suddenly paralyzed with fright, Nan couldn't scream—she couldn't move. She could only watch as the all-too-familiar shapes of three molt weevils leapt from outstretched tree branches into the truck bed.

Chapter 27

Mollie saw them too and, unlike her mother, she had no problem screaming. Unfortunately, Reese and Gus weren't able to hear her within the truck's highly insulated cab—a cab designed specifically to block out much of the thunderous engine noise.

The other problem was neither drone was close by. Teardrop was one hundred and five yards ahead of the truck, repositioning stray cocoons off the path of the oncoming vehicle. Dewdrop was seventy-five yards away, on the other side of the fairway. It had detected more of the molt weevils' alien signature high up in the treeline and had moved over there to eradicate five of them.

Nan had seen these things move and knew she and Mollie were in grave danger. Now, seeing one of the creatures approach them, her paralysis vanished. She and Mollie leapt over the back of the couch and slowly backed away. A noise behind them, and then another noise off to their right, let them know where the other two creatures were. They were surrounded. Mollie continued to scream, and Nan wondered what was taking the two drones so long—

She didn't have time to finish that last thought. Two of the molt weevils flew onto them with amazing speed. Nan felt Mollie yanked from her arms as she was lifted into the air by multiple powerful appendages. Something was sprayed into her face and now a different kind of paralysis held her rigid. She couldn't yell out or even blink her eyes. She could only observe as if she were a bystander viewing a horrific car accident, too removed to do anything to help. Nan felt her body begin to spin.

Around and around, the world was a spinning blur around her. Had she just seen Mollie being cocooned too, mere feet away? Slimy mucous oozed from protrusions on the molt weevil's neck, while its serpent-like arms spread the substance over her body. *This is what Clark experienced... this is how Clark died.* Nan could see enough of her own body to know that the process was near completion. Finally, the top of her head and then her eyes were covered as well. Nan knew she appeared no different from the thousands of other mummies they'd seen lying everywhere. At least the spinning had stopped. *This is when I die.* She waited.

Nan heard muffled sounds nearby—as if she was underwater, several feet beneath the surface of a pool. Was that plasma fire she heard? *Why am I hearing anything? I should be dead!*

She felt movement. Her cocoon was being lifted. *God, not again.* She heard ripping, tearing sounds. Yelling. Someone was yelling for her to hold on. *Hold on to what?* Fingers frantically ripped and pried at the dried material on her face. First one eye was uncovered and then the other. Nan saw Reese above her, his face taut with fear. He pulled the cocoon away from her mouth.

"Nan! Wake up... Come on back to us, Nan!"

"I'm here. Just stop yelling," she said, her speech still slurred from whatever it was the creature had sprayed into her face.

He peered down into her eyes, looking concerned. "You're okay? Are you hurt?"

"I don't know. You need to help Mollie. Get Mollie out of that thing."

"She's almost freed. Gus is helping her."

"Is she... is she alive?" Nan asked, the words catching in her throat.

"Yeah, she seems to be fine. You both are."

"Thank God. Now get me out of this thing."

It took ten minutes for Reese to completely extricate her from the cocoon. Nan rubbed her face in her palms. It felt as if she'd lost more than a few layers of epidermis, but that was about the extent of her injuries. She and Mollie returned to the couch, sitting close, their arms around each other.

"I've never been so scared in my entire life, Mom."

"Me neither, pumpkin. Me neither."

"I thought for sure you two were goners," said Gus. "If it wasn't for us seeing the rapid return of the two robots—"

"Drones," Mollie corrected.

"Drones, whatever, I wouldn't have known there was a problem. Hell, who would have thought those things would be hiding in the trees?" Gus asked, looking guilty.

"It's not your fault, Gus. We're both fine now." Nan turned to Teardrop and Dewdrop. "Thank you both. You saved our lives."

Teardrop answered, "You're welcome, Nan Reynolds."

"What did I tell you about saying people's last names? That sounds stupid," Mollie reprimanded.

Teardrop didn't reply.

Nan sat up and then stood. She hurried to the front of the bed and climbed halfway up the ladder. In the distance, she saw several cocoons on a nearby putting green. "Teardrop. Can you go over to those cocoons... scan to see if someone's still alive?"

"I do not need to go over there to provide that information."

Exasperated, Gus looked at the two drones. "Well, are they f-ing alive or not?"

"Yes. Both humanoids are alive and healthy within their cocoons."

"Go get them. Bring them back here. Hurry!" Nan urged.

Reese and Gus moved the couches out of the way to provide more room. The first of the two cocoons was dropped off and Reese quickly got started ripping at the cocoon material. Minutes later, Dewdrop carefully lowered the second body, which was half the size of the first. Gus and Nan went to work, ripping at the cocoon.

Nan had little doubt that the second cocoon was a child. She glanced over at Mollie and wondered if she should send her away. In all probability, too much time had elapsed. It might be a gruesome sight. They removed much of the dried mucous from the small face and could see the eyes. They blinked.

"Oh my God, he's alive. This little boy's alive," Nan said, wiping tears from her cheeks with the backs of her hands.

Mollie scooted in close and began to help. "Do you think all the cocooned people are alive, Mom?"

"I hope so, sweetie."

"Good thing you didn't let Gus run over them all."

Gus and Nan exchanged glances. "Your mother's a very smart woman, young lady."

"I already knew that," Mollie said, without looking up from her work.

"I need to find Clark," Reese said. The woman he was extricating tried to sit up. Agitated, she asked, "Where's my son? Where's Calvin?"

"Mom?"

She crawled over to the half-extricated child and began to kiss his face. Excited, she screamed his name: "Calvin! Are you alright?"

"I think so. Can you just get me out of this stuff?"

Nan noted the boy was roughly Mollie's age. She liked that he wasn't a whiner. Cute kid. Mollie crouched down next to them. "My name's Mollie. We rescued you. Probably saved your lives."

The mother, blonde, late-twenties, was dressed in a maid's uniform. She looked at Mollie and pulled her into a hug. "Thank you, Mollie." She looked at Nan and Reese and repeated the words, thanking them.

"I need to get back to Clark," Reese said, looking east toward I-25.

"Reese, there are thousands of cocoons out there. How would you even find her? You really sure you want to backtrack through all those molt weevils again? Is this what she'd want, or would she want you to complete your mission?"

"She'd do it for me," he said.

"You know her better than we do... But I doubt that. I need to think about my daughter, Reese. I almost lost her. If you're sure about going back for Clark, I'm sorry, but you'll be doing it on your own."

Reese seemed to weigh that in his head. "No, you're right. I have a job to do here."

"Why do they do this to people? Make them into cocoons?" Mollie asked no one in particular.

It was the young boy, Calvin, who answered. "You seriously haven't figured that out?"

"Figured what out?" Mollie sneered back.

"Dinner, lunch, maybe a late-night snack? It's obvious, they're wrapping everyone up for their food supplies."

Mollie made a face. "That's totally disgusting."

Calvin seemed to take pleasure in her reaction. "A lot of insects do the same thing. I guess we now know what it feels like."

Gus rooted around in one of the pallets of equipment and came up with several battery-powered lanterns. He had Reese help him jury rig several tarps over their heads, using tall aluminum poles and rope.

Out of breath, he stopped in front of Nan. "What next?"

"We keep going."

"And the cocoons?"

Nan looked at the others. She bit her lower lip and took in a breath. "We keep going. Any cocoons directly in our path we bring up here and extricate the victims."

Gus seemed to like that idea and headed toward the rope ladder.

"You two need to stay close. We don't want a repeat of what just happened," Nan told the two drones.

"Yeah, you're an embarrassment," Mollie added.

Calvin fully noticed Teardrop and Dewdrop for the first time. Mouth open, he looked at the two and then at Mollie. "Are those real? How do they hover like that?"

"Of course, they're real," Mollie said. "They're both in trouble right now or I'd introduce you to them."

Chapter 28

Admiral Reynolds told everyone to take a seat and to settle down. "Listen up... thanks to Gaddy's home planet connections, some of which were her fellow student dissidents back on Halimar, we've received invaluable information." The Admiral gestured toward the display. "As you can see for yourselves, the Craing populace has taken to the streets... they can smell freedom in the wind and we're guessing full-out revolution is near at hand."

All eyes were on the display. Every seat was taken around the ready room table, leaving *standing room only* for as many others. Jason and the Admiral wanted to get the officers and key personnel together one last time before *The Lilly* embarked for Craing space.

The video feed showed thousands upon thousands of Craing people assembling, marching, and, in some locations, skirmishing directly with military police. Hand-made protest banners and signs waved back and forth in the air.

Gaddy raised her hand.

"Go ahead, Gaddy," the Admiral said.

"We only have these few video clips from cities on Halimar, but this is also happening on the other Craing worlds. It's just a matter of time before we'll be seeing full-out revolution."

Sitting directly across the table from her, Jason watched Gaddy and saw the pride on her face. He asked, "So the next question is, what's happening with the empirical government? Where's the seat of power located now that the Emperor's Palace has been obliterated? We find that location, we'll find where the remaining high priest overlords are hiding... and perhaps, if we're lucky, where the new acting Emperor—Ot-Mul—is hiding too."

Billy, sitting next to Orion, spoke up: "What's the plan once we enter Craing space, Cap?"

"More information is coming in from Halimar all the time. With the help of Gaddy's friends, we think we're closing in on several possible locations," Jason told him.

"Would it be possible to directly assist the revolutionaries?" Gaddy asked.

"Possibly," the Admiral replied, "if it doesn't interfere with our mission. Our biggest problem is one we've encountered before. According to the nearby Allarians in the Orange Corridor, although many thousands of Craing warships have left Craing space—undoubtedly to implement *The Great Space* directive—there are still too many warships present for us to approach any of the seven worlds."

"Well... we no longer have *Her Majesty*. Going in cloaked certainly isn't an option anymore," Brian said, leaning against the back bulkhead.

"There is another option," Ricket said.

Everyone turned to look at him.

"Don't be shy, Ricket. What's the option?" Jason coaxed.

"HAB 12."

Groans emanated from around the room.

Gaddy shook her head. "Oh no... I don't ever want to go back to that place again."

Jason remembered the condition Gaddy had been in after her long trek across that hostile landscape. Hell, he'd lost too many men during *his* weeklong mission within HAB 12.

Ricket said, "Things are different now. The new battlesuits are far more advanced. They're much stronger, and with their integrated propulsion system the trip through would take no more than a day... maybe two."

"Even so, I wouldn't want our team stranded when we come out on Halimar... I'd want *The Lilly* nearby," Jason said, contemplating. "I suppose she can remain in Allarian space." Jason continued, "There's seven planets and we still don't know which one Ot-Mul is hiding out on. We'll come out on Halimar... but without transportation... a ship, I still don't see how this plan helps us." Jason looked over to Ricket and shrugged.

Bristol, quiet until now, had grown more and more agitated in the last few minutes. "Look... we now have incredible manufacturing capabilities with *The Minian*'s phase-synthesizer, right? So, what's the problem? Even if we have physical limitations on how we enter and leave HAB 12's portals and can't directly phase-shift into the habitat... big deal. Why can't we just develop a new ship or shuttle that has a smaller, less than ten-foot circumference? It can be a barebones, basic design. It just needs to get us from point A to point B... right?"

All eyes turned back to Ricket. "He's right. There may even be a small vessel design already loaded into *The Minian*'s manufacturing database."

Jason contemplated the idea. "There are still some potential problems we need to think about. Will a shuttle small enough to fit through the port be big enough to bring a useful-sized team and several days' worth of provisions? And let's not forget about the dangers within the habitat itself. The ship would have to be somewhat battle-ready. We'd need to come up with a plan for what we're going to do once we get to Halimar. There's a lot to think about here, people... so let's not get too ahead of ourselves." Jason looked at the faces around the table. Their expressions said the same thing he was now thinking, they'd have to make it work. "How long will it take for you to determine—"

Ricket held up a hand, "I'm remotely accessing the database now, Captain. One moment, please."

The room stayed quiet while Ricket continued to stare blankly up at the ceiling. He nodded to himself and then brought his attention back to Jason. "I've found three vessel designs that could serve our purpose. Each one fits the proper circumference footprints, while still providing advanced Caldurian technology." Ricket looked over to Bristol. "Excellent suggestion, Bristol."

Bristol looked surprised by Ricket's kind acknowledgment but didn't say anything.

"The new ship needs to accommodate a ten-person team and have acceptable weapons and phase-shift capabilities," Jason added.

"In that case, there is only one design fitting that criterion, Captain. I will need to make several design modifications prior to the phase-synthesizer going to work manufacturing the vessel."

"How long before we have a ship?" the Admiral asked.

"Four hours, Admiral," Ricket answered.

Admiral Reynolds nodded, then cleared his throat. "The other aspect of this meeting is to bring everyone current on what's happening on Earth." He looked over to Jason with raised eyebrows.

"I've been in contact with Nan, who's currently en route to Cheyenne Mountain, in Colorado. The surface of the planet is completely infested with molt weevils. Millions if not billions of people have already been cocooned. But it's possible many of those people are still alive... put in some form of suspended animation. We suspect to be used as food stores later on."

"That's horrible!" Dira said, sitting at Jason's right. "I mean... good, they may still be alive, but horrible they're being preserved, only to be eaten later."

"Can't we do anything to help them down there?" Chief Horris asked.

"We've asked ourselves that same question numerous times, Chief," the Admiral responded. "Certainly, if we didn't have five thousand Craing warships closing in on us we'd be back on Earth eradicating those things. But we've decided our best first course of action is keeping the Craing at bay... defending Earth from here in space."

"Won't we need *The Lilly* here, alongside *The Minian*, for that fight?" Perkins asked.

Jason and his father exchanged glances. "We've gone back and forth with this more times than you can imagine, XO. If necessary, *The Lilly* can call up an interchange wormhole and return back here fairly quickly."

Jason collected his thoughts as he looked at the faces around the room. "I'm sure it's not lost on any of you that right now we have a unique opportunity to bring down the Craing Empire. For over a year it's been a hopeless, daunting endeavor. I have to be honest, when I saw those tens of thousands of Craing warships awaiting deployment just days ago, from right there in Craing space.

I'd nearly given up hope. Figured it would only be a matter of time before Earth, too, succumbed to the Craing's might. But things have changed over the last few days. We've destroyed a Vanguard fleet of dreadnoughts thought to be indestructible. Subsequently, the acting Craing Emperor has fled back to the

Craing worlds... and we've seen the amazing video feeds for ourselves: the Craing populace demanding real change. No longer will they sit idly by while their government continues to slaughter other worlds across the Universe. Right now, we need to stop Ot-Mul's *Great Space* initiative. Yes, we have to defend Earth. But defending the worlds within this sector of space is no less important. So we'll need to at least try to do both simultaneously."

The Admiral stood up. "That's it, everyone. We all have jobs to do... let's get cracking."

Everyone stood and the room started to empty out.

"Cap, who do you want me to pull together for our team?" Billy asked.

"Yeah, I was going to talk to you about that: you and several SEALs. Make sure we have Rizzo, Ricket, Gaddy, and myself. Oh... and Jackson too, our Delta Forces guy. Check with Ricket and ensure there's adequate room for all of us on this new streamlined ship he's conjuring up."

"Not Traveler?"

"Not until I talk to him. He and his kind have paid a heavy price over the past year. I'll let you know."

"I'm coming too," Dira interjected.

Jason felt her shoulder press into his own when she tried to maneuver out of the way as more crewmembers moved to leave the ready room. Their eyes met and Jason felt a near-overwhelming desire to protect her—keep her from the near-certain harm that HAB 12 will inflict. He admonished himself—this is why onboard relationships were such a bad idea. "Okay... Dira too. Work it out and get me a finalized list as soon as possible. We leave within the hour."

Chapter 29

They moved the 797F out to the middle of the fairway, well away from any overhanging trees. Nan didn't like how Gus was looking and insisted they set up camp for the night. Gus and Cindy were not feeling well, so they stretched out on the couch... while Reese, Nan, Mollie, and Calvin got busy organizing the stacks of equipment and supplies in the truck bed.

Nan had never camped a day in her life. It wasn't something she'd even remotely wanted to do. Setting up the new Colman two-burner propane stove was becoming a problem. She swore under her breath as she dug through the box for instructions.

"Just give it to me."

"You're supposed to be sleeping!"

"With you making all that racket?" Gus grabbed the box away from her and had the stove assembled, along with its small propane bottle, and secured within minutes. He tested both burners, making sure Nan watched as he partially turned the knobs, electronically igniting one burner and then the other. But Nan's eyes were on Gus—he was still wheezing, his breathing even more labored than earlier.

"I could have figured it out on my own," Nan said.

"Uh-huh. Where's Reese?" Gus asked.

"Adding more grease. Seems plowing through buildings and driving through tall shrubs wiped much of it off the truck."

"He's down below? Like on the ground?" Gus asked, looking concerned.

"The drones are keeping the molt weevils away. It seemed safe enough," Nan said, but sounded somewhat less sure now.

"What's venison?" Mollie asked, approaching from the other side of the truck bed. She and Calvin each held several big baggies, with packages inside them wrapped in brown paper. Mollie held one up to show Nan the handwritten letters across one of the bags.

"You're definitely not from around here," Gus said. He took one of the bags from Calvin and held it up. "This is God's gift to mankind. This will add a little sunshine to a bleak day."

Nan rolled her eyes. "It's just frozen deer meat, kids."

Mollie made an overdramatic expression of disbelief. "You mean like deer as in Bambi?"

Nan wasn't sure if she was putting on a show for her new friend, Calvin, or just being her typical self.

"You shot it yourself?" she asked Gus with a furrowed brow.

The question seemed to make Gus all the more pleased with himself. "A moving target from over one hundred yards out... yes, damn right I shot it myself!"

Nan handed Mollie a large metal pot. "Why don't you two fill this up with water from the portable reservoir." She watched the kids run off and stood up. "I'll see what else you have hiding in that refrigerator that will go with the Bambi meat. If you're not going back to sleep, maybe you can fire up one of those generators and get us some light. And get the refrigerators powered back up, too. By the feel of that half-frozen meat, things could start spoiling."

Gus gave a half-hearted salute. "I'm on it, boss." He too got to his feet and said, "I think you'll find some frozen vegetables, and maybe some frozen biscuits in there too. Probably buried back behind the bear meat."

Nan checked on Cindy, who hadn't felt well since being extracted from her cocoon. She was curled into a ball. Trying not to disturb her, Nan spread a blanket over her. The night was warm, but Cindy looked as if she was cold. Nan placed the back of a hand on her forehead. *She's got a raging fever!* Nan tucked the blanket in around her and wondered if it was the result of being cocooned. *Was it only a matter of time before she—and Mollie—got sick, too?* No—their internal nanites would protect them. She'd have to keep a close eye on Calvin, though.

THEIR LATE-NIGHT DINNER TURNED OUT surprisingly well. They'd defrosted the bags of meat, veggies, and biscuits in the pot of boiling water and then Gus took over, using two frying pans. Gus had one of the generators going, now droning away at the back of the truck bed. Three electric lanterns provided enough light to see what was what. With the exception of Cindy, they were seated in a circle, plates propped on their laps.

Mollie was hesitant to try the venison, but when she saw Calvin enjoying his portion, she went ahead and tried a small bite.

Reese watched her expression and asked, "Well... what do you think?"

Mollie continued to chew but looked ready to spit it out any second. She swallowed and shrugged. "It's okay, I guess."

Nan took a bite and thought the same thing. It was just okay. Not terrible—but gamey. Distant sounds of plasma fire became so common Nan had stopped hearing them. But when a shadow moved in front of one of the lanterns, she nearly jumped out of her skin. A hand touched her shoulder as Cindy sat down between her and Calvin.

Nan put a hand over her own heart. "You gave me a start there, Cindy. It's good to see you up and around. You feeling better?"

Cindy saw everyone looking at her. "Um... I think so. I'm hungry... that must mean something."

Gus was already up and fixing her a plate. "Maybe I'll start with just veggies and a roll. Don't want to push things," Cindy told him.

Gus looked a bit disappointed. He removed the meat from her plate before handing it to her.

Teardrop appeared from the top of the truck bed and lowered down near the group.

"What is it, Teardrop?" Nan asked.

"There are additional cocoons, Nan Reynolds."

Nan put up a hand to keep Mollie from saying anything. "Cocoons?... Where?"

"As directed, we have repositioned cocoons that potentially lie within the vehicle's forward trajectory."

Nan stood and crossed over to the front of the truck bed. By the time she'd climbed halfway up the rope ladder, she saw what Teardrop was referring to: eight cocoons, in two rows of four, were lined up below, near the front left tire.

Nan climbed the rest of the way up and crouched low on the overhang. As her eyes adjusted to the darkness, she saw hundreds of molt weevil carcasses spread across the fairway. Not only had she gotten used to the sound of plasma fire, she'd gotten used to the smell of burnt flesh. Her stomach churned and she had just enough time to make it to the overhang edge before throwing up.

Reese crouched down beside her and put a hand on her back. "Careful, that's a long drop."

Nan sat back and accepted a handkerchief from the DOD special agent. She took it and wiped the corners of her mouth. "What should we do?" she asked him, gesturing toward the cocoons below.

"Probably should do what we said we would. Free them. But this will have to be the end of doing so for now. There could be hundreds more ahead in our path."

"I don't know... seeing Cindy's reaction. Her being sick made me realize the molt weevils may have done something additional. Infected all of them with something. We need to think about how this could affect others down the road... all of mankind."

"There's no way to know, at this point. But you and Mollie seem fine."

"We're not typical. We've both been imbued with protective nanites."

Reese raised his eyebrows skeptically.

"It's a long story but take it from me, both Mollie and I have alien technology coursing through our veins, and there's virtually no chance either of us will get sick... ever."

"You're serious. Where do I sign up for a bit of that?"

Nan didn't answer, only continued to stare down at the cocoons. "Let's keep an eye on Cindy overnight. If she's still fine by morning when we head out again, we can free those eight."

"Works for me," he said.

Nan wondered at what point Reese had stopped being in charge and she had taken over. She wondered if that was what she wanted. What would be best for the group? But after what she'd been through the last year—captured by the Craing twice... confronting aliens and pirates, she had far more experience fighting aliens than either Reese or Gus, so yeah, she needed to be in charge.

Nan handed Reese back his handkerchief. "Let's all try to get some sleep. I have a feeling tomorrow's going to be an eventful day."

Chapter 30

"Well... I told you we had a problem, Cap."

Jason and Billy stood side by side in the Zoo corridor looking through the portal window of HAB 12.

"After all this time, no one's taken the initiative to move that damn thing?"

"Like whom, specifically, would that be? Someone who isn't particularly bothered by Serapin Terplins, I suppose."

"Have I mentioned you're a smart ass?"

"On more than one occasion," Billy replied.

Jason shook his head and huffed.

"You can tell Gaddy to move it... she was the one who parked it there."

"You're not being helpful," Jason said, looking back and forth down the corridor. "Jack!"

Almost immediately Jack appeared from a hatch, wearing the same green groundskeeper's shirt he always wore. "Yes, Captain. What is it you want?"

"What I want is for you to open this portal window."

"No can do, Sir."

"What do you mean no?"

"If you remember, security level on certain high-risk habitats makes accessing them nearly impossible. I believe Ricket got you in there last time."

"That's right, I remember. Oh, and Jack, my apologies in advance. Over the next few hours, the Zoo will become a little disrupted."

Jack didn't look pleased by that revelation. He grunted something and returned to the hatch he'd appeared from.

With two fingers up to his ear, Jason hailed Ricket.

"Go for Ricket. How can I help you, Captain?"

"We need to access HAB 12's portal. Gaddy's old utility ship is still blocking the window."

"That is a problem, Captain. Surely the vehicle's batteries are now depleted."

"Can you get down here... find a way to jump-start the thing?"

Ricket paused before responding, "Jump... start, Captain?"

Jason was quickly getting annoyed with the delay. Hell, they hadn't even stepped outside yet and already there were problems. "Just Google it, Ricket."

Ricket soon arrived with what looked like jumper cables and a twelve-volt car battery. But at closer inspection, it was something far more sophisticated.

"Captain, once I open the portal, you'll need to move quickly. There's enough of a gap between the vehicle and the window for any number of things to squeeze by and enter the Zoo."

"That's why I have this highly trained Navy SEAL standing by with a multi-gun," Jason responded, nodding toward Billy.

Ricket stepped to the portal access panel, then glanced over to Jason.

Jason triggered the SuitPac attached to his belt and waited

for it to expand around his body. Ricket did the same with his own SuitPac device.

"I'm ready, Ricket. Open it up."

Ricket began tapping in the long string of Caldurian alphanumeric digits from memory. Two minutes later came: *beep beep beep.* The three consecutive tones meant the code was correct and accepted. Ricket nodded toward Jason. "The portal is open, Captain. You have sixty seconds before it closes again."

Jason didn't waste a second. He stepped through the now-open portal window and climbed into the old utility vehicle. "Billy, don't let anything get by you."

Billy triggered his SuitPac. "Nothing's getting by me."

Jason extended a hand down to Ricket and pulled him up into the vehicle. Ricket looked around and then pointed toward an access panel in the back cargo area.

"Without any auxiliary power, this panel isn't retractable," Ricket said.

Jason placed several fingertips within a small rectangular flange where the panel and the bulkhead converged, and he yanked. Two more tries and the cover tore from its mounting hardware. "That better?"

Ricket went right to work attaching his cables to the small ship's propulsion system. A tiny holo-display came alive, and indicators showed that something was happening. Ricket adjusted two of the settings and was about to adjust a third when the utility ship violently shook. Ricket looked up at Jason.

"That wasn't me. Apparently, we have a visitor outside."

"Try to finish up while I take a look." Within five steps Jason was crouching down and looking out the cockpit window. The midday sun was bright and intense and there was nothing visible moving around outside. But the red life icons showing on his HUD told a different story. "This doesn't make sense," he said, trying to correlate the red icons to what he was visually not seeing outside. "There's obviously a lot going on underground because I don't see anything." One icon, if you could even call it an icon, seemed to be bigger than the ship they were standing in. Perhaps it was a swarm of bees, or something not visible to the naked eye. The ship shook again, and Jason lost his balance. He repositioned himself to sit in the cockpit's pilot seat and looked out the forward window again. Now he was able to crane his neck and see almost directly over the top of the utility ship. "Holy shit... tell me you've finished back there, Ricket."

"It would be best to wait several min—"

Jason didn't wait. He already knew how to fly the thing from watching Gaddy, so he slapped at the ignition ON tab below the dashboard. The cargo ship's drive churned and stuttered and then caught. "Hold on, Ricket!"

Jason knew the little ship was on its last legs and he wondered if it had enough juice left to move the twenty feet necessary to unblock the portal window. But as the ship swung violently upward, that was no longer his primary concern. When he'd taken that last look up, he'd seen a creature he wasn't totally familiar with. It was definitely a derivative of the Serapin Terplin. No doubt about that. Only this one was four or five times its size and had wings—ginormous wings, which were flapping to the point visibility was nearly impossible from all the dust being kicked up. The ship was quickly moving up and away from the ground.

"Ricket!" Jason yelled toward the cargo area. "Are you okay?" He managed to get to his feet and moved astern. Ricket, the helmet section of his battlesuit retracted, was lying facedown on the deck. Jason leapt right on top of him and immediately phase-shifted them off the ship.

From a rocky outcropping fifty yards out, Jason watched as Gaddy's cargo ship fell free from the flying Serapin's claws and dropped several hundred feet to the desert floor.

"Cap, I'd give you a hand, but the portal just closed," Billy said.

"You saw it, right? That wasn't my imagination?"

"Oh, I saw it all right. That's one mother—"

"Hold that thought. I need to check on Ricket." Jason rolled to his right, off Ricket, who slowly opened his eyes. They locked on to something he couldn't seem to comprehend.

With a quick glance up, Jason saw it, too. The Serapin was diving down directly at them. "Ricket... hurry and put up your damn helmet!" Jason barked. He brought his arms up and fired from his battlesuit's two integrated plasma guns.

Jason felt the recoil in his arms and shoulders as he continued his concentrated barrage of plasma fire into the beast's head and torso. And then Ricket was firing too. But the Serapin was still coming fast, its jaws wide—foot-long teeth snapping—long strings of saliva trailing off behind its head.

Jason had spotted the rocky cliff outcropping far off in the distance. He knew these suits could phase-shift them substantially further than their old belt configurations could, but in the split second he needed to make the decision he wasn't completely sure it would take them far enough away. Both Ricket and Jason phase-shifted as the Serapin's claws grasped at the empty air where they had been.

Still on his back, Jason got to his feet. His HUD showed Ricket's life icon position to be several miles away. Jason answered the incoming hail.

"Go for Captain."

"The flying Serapin has left the area, Captain. I will phase-shift back to the portal access panel."

"I'll be right there."

At five hundred feet above the desert floor, the view from the outcropping was beautiful. Jason turned and took in the little oasis where, a year earlier, he and his team had camped.

His eyes lingered on the waterfall and the small pond where he'd first held Dira close—kissed her, and knew he'd already fallen hopelessly in love with her. The smile left his face as he remembered that she no longer wanted to be stationed on *The Lilly*. It was just a matter of time before Dira went home to Jhardon.

By the time Jason phase-shifted back to the portal, Ricket was already entering the access code. Two large red icons appeared on his HUD. Jason turned and watched them approach from several miles out. He pumped up the optical zoom level and saw two flying Serapins approaching. *The wingspan on those things is incredible*, he thought to himself.

Beep beep beep. Both Ricket and Jason hurried to the portal window and left HAB 12 behind them.

Chapter 31

As Jason and Ricket stepped back into the Zoo corridor, Billy was already staging the equipment and men for their mission. Some of his team had initiated their SuitPacs and were wearing their new battlesuits. Others, such as Dira, were still dressed in their spacer's jumpsuits. She was busy with her medical pack and didn't look up as he moved by her.

"Captain, I need to finalize the manufacturing of *The Streamline* back on *The Minian*," Ricket said.

"That's what you're calling the little ship, huh?"

"Not me... Boomer offered up the suggestion."

Jason smiled at that. "I like it. *The Streamline*. You still good for our timetable?"

"Yes, Captain. Fifteen minutes is all I'll need."

Jason turned and looked to the opposite end of the corridor. *It doesn't hurt to ask.*

Inside HAB 17, Jason phase-shifted to the outskirts of the rhino encampment. The last time he'd been there, Traveler and the remaining rhino-warriors had been in the process of torching their dome dwellings—never expecting to return. With their home planet destroyed by the Craing, Traveler would spend the rest of his life battling those who'd eradicated his entire species. But as fate would have it, over a hundred rhino-warriors had been rescued from a Craing dreadnought.

New dome structures, far more than were previously there, encircled the circular open space. A roaring bonfire snapped and crackled while several rhinos Jason didn't know tended the fire. *Those are females!* Jason did a double-take. He wasn't aware any of those rescued were female—but it made sense some would be.

Others, including Few Words, appeared from one of the larger domes. Jason met him halfway.

"It is good to see you, Few Words."

"And for me... you too, Captain Reynolds."

"I did not realize there were females among those rescued," Jason said, gesturing toward the three rhinos tending the fire.

"Forty-three," he answered, with pride in his voice.

All of a sudden, Jason regretted coming here—invading what was clearly the start of a new life—a new beginning.

"This is Breeds Often, my mate."

Smaller than Few Words by several inches, she was wider in the hips. She'd been standing behind Few Words but now moved to his side.

"It is nice to meet you." Jason smiled at her. "I hope you are happy here... can make this place your home."

"I am... we all are... grateful to you. You have been added to our morning and evening songs and prayers," said Breeds Often.

Jason, suddenly touched by her words, didn't know what to say. Few Words noticed him looking about.

"He is not here, Captain. Traveler does not live among us as he did before."

"Is he all right? What—"

"He is out there." Few Words pointed to the open plains.

Jason squinted toward the distant horizon but didn't see anything.

"No, not there. Over there," Few Words said, moving Jason's shoulders slightly and pointing again. He heard Breeds Often make a loud, awful sound, which could have been a laugh— Jason wasn't really sure.

Then Jason saw the distant dome and smoke rising from a small fire.

"He will enjoy seeing you again, my friend."

With that, Few Words and Breeds Often moved off. Jason phase-shifted closer to the distant dome.

Traveler was waiting for him. Dressed in battle gear— leather breastplate and heavy hammer hanging from a leather thong at his belt, he said, "Welcome, Captain Reynolds."

"Thank you, Traveler." Jason looked around the small encampment of one large dome and several smaller domes off to the side. From a scraggly tree, several skinned animals hung from ropes secured around their hind legs. "Were you on your way to go hunting?"

Traveler turned his head, looking confused. "I just went hunting. Can you not see the carcasses mere feet in front of you?"

"You're dressed for battle. I didn't know..."

"I'm coming with you. Isn't that why you are here?"

Jason's feelings of guilt returned. "I want to apologize. What I should have done is left you and your people alone. You all have lost so much. Everything. But perhaps this is a new beginning... a chance to rebuild."

"Our two rhino worlds are no more. Gone forever. We deeply mourn the loss. But the only reason the few who remain *are* here is because of you. Indeed, we are happy. This is our home now."

"Well, again, I apologize for disrupting... all this. Be happy, my friend." Jason turned to leave.

"Am I no longer needed? Perhaps Traveler's grown too old and fat to fight alongside his friends in battle?"

Jason looked back at the indignant-looking rhino-warrior. "You've already given us far more than anyone could ask for. I've come to tell you to build your life here. Be happy."

"Do you know the reason I live away from the others?"

"I suppose you like your solitude. You're an independent soul."

Traveler tilted his head back and forth: "Few Words's new mate... the one called Breeds Often... she continually laughs— it's a cackling sound, really... sometimes lasts long into the night. How Few Words tolerates it, I have no idea. I simply needed to move to a quieter place."

Jason laughed out loud. "I think I heard the sound you're referring to."

Traveler continued, "I am a hunter and a warrior, Captain. I live for battle. Yes, I am happy my tribe is growing again and perhaps will thrive in Habitat 17. But I am a warrior who lives to fight... to fight the Craing. To avenge what they've done to my people. I wish to come with you on this new mission into HAB 12. I wish to strike down the one called Ot-Mul... the one who ordered the destruction of my home world."

"So you've already heard about the mission?"

"Yes. I contact Billy often so I can be ready."

By the time Jason and Traveler were back in *The Lilly's* Zoo, Ricket had phase-shifted the new ship into the corridor. Like all Caldurian ships, its design was aerodynamic—ultra-sleek looking. It was immaculately clean, like a new car on display in a showroom; the vessel's deep blue, highly reflective hull sparkled. Jason stood back and appraised the ship. It was ten feet wide, ten feet in height, and easily forty feet long: narrower than the shuttles on either *The Lilly* or *The Minian*, but much longer. Four-foot-tall observation panels, like smoked glass, surrounded the entirety of the vessel. Even the pointed nose of the ship was made from the same dark-tinted material. She was a forty-foot-long blue bullet.

"Do you like it? I named it *The Streamline*."

Jason looked down and saw Boomer in a stance nearly identical to his own, her arms crossed, and head cocked slightly to one side. "It's the perfect name," he told her.

"How long will you be gone?"

"I don't know for sure. With this ship, we'll zip through HAB 12 in a matter of minutes. Finding the Craing leader could take a while. I'll stay in touch with you as much as I can." Jason continued to look down at his nine-year-old daughter. In some respects, she was so different from Mollie, but in other ways, so similar. Dressed in her dark-gray jumpsuit, her hair pulled back tight, she also wore three small throwing knives on her belt. He wondered where she'd gotten them since she'd used her others to fend off a tiger in HAB 4. "Look, I've talked to Brian and Betty, and you'll be spending part of the time with them. Betty will be monitoring your home school studies."

"Okay, Dad. I like Betty."

"Can you try to stay out of trouble while I'm gone?"

Boomer smiled up at her father, with a face frighteningly mischievous.

"I'm serious, kiddo... there's far too much happening right now for you to be getting into trouble. Do I make myself clear?"

"Yes, I'll be good, I promise, but I wish I could go with you."

"I suspect someday you'll be going on your own adventures, little one."

She hugged him and ran off. He heard her say, "I can't wait!"

With all the commotion, Jason was finally able to catch Ricket's eye from the other end of *The Streamline*. They headed toward each other and met at the mid-point of the ship.

"What do you think of her, Captain?" Ricket asked, sounding proud of his handiwork.

"I think it's an incredible-looking ship. I don't mean to sound ungrateful, but do you have any thoughts on how we're going to get her to the port window of HAB 12? A forty-foot-long ship onto a hallway that's not nearly that wide... even at an angle, she won't make the turn."

Ricket was unfazed, which disappointed Jason. Part of him wanted to catch Ricket's typically infallible intelligence in a goof-up. The small Craing man gestured for Jason to follow him. Instead of heading toward HAB 12, he went to the opposite bank of habitats directly across from HAB 12, toward HAB 76. Ricket entered a simple access code and the portal window disappeared. "I've calculated the angle and the required turning radius. HAB 76 will provide more than enough room to make the turn." Ricket smiled. He'd obviously anticipated Jason's desire to trip him up.

"What's in HAB 76? We're not leaving the Zoo open to another kind of diabolical creature, are we?"

"Scans show that this biosphere is comprised solely of plants, trees, and benign, non-poisonous, insects... it's basically a botanical environment, with similar atmospheric levels of oxygen and nitrogen as found on Earth... and on *The Lilly*, for that matter."

"Can we just leave it open like this?"

"I've got it timed to close an hour from now."

Jason hadn't noticed the near-seamless hatch at the middle of *The Streamline*. Like the hatchways on *The Lilly* and *The Minian*, the opening didn't so much open up, in a typical mechanical manner, as it changed its molecular structure. One second the hatch panel was closed—the next, it was gone, and Dira was walking through the opening toward him.

Ricket hurried off to do whatever he needed to do, leaving the two standing in front of each other.

"Did you know this ship has a small medical cubicle?"

"No... haven't been inside her yet."

"Well, come on; let me show you." She turned and moved back inside and made a quick left turn. Jason followed. Immediately he was taken aback at the ship's heightened level of technology. Plush, high-back seats lined the port side of the ship, with an aisle running along the center. Various compartments and storage lockers were off to the right. The interior was bright and expansive due to the surrounding four-foot-tall observation glass panels.

Jason took two quick strides to catch up. His eyes traveled her long slim body and lingered on what he had determined—over many months—was the most perfect derriere he'd ever had the pleasure to witness. With a quick glance over her shoulder, Dira caught him leering and didn't look particularly pleased. *Smooth move, Jason.*

"This is really a miraculous little ship, Captain," Dira said.

So now I'm Captain? Jason watched as she quickened her stride away from him and made another abrupt turn—this time to the right. Jason slowed and saw a small, illuminated MEDICAL sign before him. Two outstretched hands grabbed him and pulled him into the semi-enclosed cubicle. Dira put her hand at the back of his head, while her other hand clutched tightly on his spacer's jumpsuit. She brought his face in close. Their lips met and he felt the tip of her tongue flitter and tease.

Oh God, he wanted her. They kissed, their breaths quickened, and their passion grew. His hands moved over her gentle curves—he'd only just begun to explore the mysteries of her body. Jason's eyes locked on hers—those amazing violet-amber eyes. Dira's long lashes touched his cheeks. He melted into her and her into him and his arms encircled her—pulled her in closer. Voices... several people were approaching. Dira laughed and pushed him away—hard. He lost his balance and fell backward onto a padded gurney. When he looked up Dira was gone, and Billy was looking down at him.

"Not feeling well, Cap?"

Chapter 32

Several last-minute crew additions were made to the roster. Lieutenant Grimes, top gun fighter pilot, sat at the controls... and with ample available seats, two more SEALs joined Billy. The rest of the assault team sat toward the back of the ship. Jason rode shotgun and watched Grimes familiarize herself with the cockpit.

Ricket stood in the aisle at Grimes' shoulder and continued to point out particulars.

"It does seem pretty similar to how *Epcot's* cockpit is laid out. Okay, let's see if I've got it." Grimes brought up the holo-display and, one at a time, initiated the multiple semitransparent layers: "Nav controls here... tactical weaponry here... phase-shift functionality is here... and wait... what's this, Ricket?"

"I have not had sufficient time to examine the true nature of that command layer. I believe, and this is purely a guess... it has something to do with accessing the Multiverse. On the underside of the inner hull, running the entire length of the ship, are devices that have similar properties to what we call the *zip farm* on *The Minian*. As I said, I'll need more time to investigate that aspect. Leave it for now."

"I think she's got it, Ricket. You can open the portal," Jason instructed.

Ricket stepped behind them and a moment later was seen at the front of the ship. At the access panel, he entered the long sequence and as soon as the portal window opened, he hurried back inside. Grimes made several more adjustments to the controls and then looked over to Jason.

"Let's go."

She pulled back on the controls and *The Streamline* rose several inches off the Zoo's deck. The holo-display changed orientation, providing a top-down view of the ship as it hovered within the confined space along the Zoo corridor. With practiced finesse, Grimes edged the ship forward, missing the right edge of the portal by no more than an inch. The ship's stern crossed over into the portal window of HAB 76—missing that edge by inches, as well. Slowly, the ship maneuvered to where it was perpendicular to the corridor. Grimes goosed the ship's dual drives, one mid-ship and one at the stern, forward.

Jason leaned back, craning his neck to look straight up, and saw nothing but blue skies. No sign of any flying Serapins. Relieved, he relaxed and sat back in his seat.

Grimes let the ship completely clear the portal, then set her down on the ground. Five men, armed with multi-guns, took up defensive perimeter positions around the pole that had the access panel mounted on it. Ricket went over to it and again entered the long sequence of Caldurian alphanumeric digits. *It's crazy only one person has this code.* Jason contacted Ricket via their NanoCom.

"Don't you think I should have that code, Ricket? What if something happens to you?"

Jason saw Ricket turn his attention away from what he was

doing and look back to the front window of *The Streamline*. "Captain, this same code is also available to you anytime. As Captain of the ship, it's already integrated into your nano-device's accessible memory. You simply haven't tried to remember it."

As Ricket finished up, Jason searched his memory. From past experience, accessing information from his nano-devices was somewhat different than simply remembering things or events from his past. There was a structure to it—not unlike how one accessed files on a computer hard drive—although a far more intuitive and automatic kind of process. And there it was: the digits appeared right before his eyes. More like symbols, the Caldurian alphanumeric characters progressively sped by, faster and faster, hundreds of them. "Huh, I guess I do already know the code."

"Cap?" Grimes asked.

"Nothing, just talking to myself."

Ricket hurried back from the access panel. The assault team quickly followed behind him—three of the men kept their weapons high, walking backward into the ship.

"All are onboard, Cap," Grimes reported.

"Head on out. Keep an eye out for anything that flies."

"Aye, Sir." She brought the ship straight up vertically several hundred feet before accelerating forward. They headed roughly along the same route Jason and his team had navigated the previous year. Below, the desert-like terrain gradually morphed from sandy dunes into a rockier landscape, and then there were towering cliffs, jutting high into the sky, at their left. Deep within one of those rock faces were the enshrined remains of fallen SEALs and rhino-warriors. Jason silently acknowledged each one—acknowledged their ultimate sacrifice.

"Aerial movement, Captain," Grimes said, pointing straight ahead.

Jason leaned forward in his seat. "Yeah, that's a feeding drone. No worries... they lumber along harmlessly."

Several miles ahead a volcanic river, snake-like, wound back and forth until it disappeared into the distant horizon. Encroaching on the scene below, beneath plumes of steam and smoke, Jason could see patches of bright red lava slowly moving deep within jagged crevices.

Rocky terrain below turned into lush green meadows. Gently rolling hills continued mile after mile until a distant line of trees grew in stature before them.

A small purple rectangular-shaped icon flashed on Grimes' nav holo-display. "We're closing in on the portal, Cap."

Grimes brought the ship down, about a mile in from the tree line, into an area far more sparse that led up to a steep sloping ridge. The cave entrance was fifty yards in front of them.

Jason marveled at how quickly they'd made it here, considering it had taken seven long days for their previous mission on foot.

Billy crouched down between Jason and Grimes. "Oh yeah. The cave with the bugs."

"The very same," Jason replied.

Grimes turned all the way around and looked at Billy. "What do you mean bugs?"

He shrugged. "Bugs... like seven feet long and three or four feet tall. Like cockroaches."

Jason nodded but kept quiet.

"This is one of your jokes. Oh, right. You do this... always the kidder." She was smiling until she glanced toward Jason and saw him stone-faced serious. "Oh God... Really?"

Both Jason and Billy nodded.

"That tunnel is way too tight for this ship, Cap," Billy said.

"Not going in that way. We'll need to phase-shift to where the tunnel opens up into a cavern. Lieutenant, can you bring up a cross-section of that ridge on the holo-display? Show us at least a mile deep inside."

It took several moments for Grimes to get things situated before the display showed a three-dimensional representation, a cross-section of the ridge line before them, and of the below-ground level terrain.

"There you go, perfect," Jason said. He gestured toward a hollow gap that traversed deep into the hillside. "This is the cave... it veers to the right here, and the area here is the cavern I was referring to. Plenty of room to phase-shift into and get *The Streamline* adequately positioned to exit the portal, which is here, along this back wall."

"You should sit down, Billy," Grimes said.

She brought up the phase-shift layer on the holo-display and locked on to the cavern area they'd pinpointed.

"Go ahead, Lieutenant."

Everything flashed white first and then there was nothing but darkness beyond the outer hull. Grimes found the *On* setting for the outside running lights and then for the forward spotlight. The cavern came alive with movement. From wall to ceiling, familiar, beastly-looking cockroaches scurried around—more than a few climbed over each other in a rush to get away from the powerful illumination.

Grimes's jaw dropped. She sat motionless, transfixed.

"You okay?"

"That's just about the most disgusting thing I've ever seen. To think I volunteered for this mission."

"You'll need to reposition the ship."

"I see it, Captain." Grimes ever so slowly brought the long ship forward and several degrees to port. She brought the ship down until it settled onto the floor of the cavern. A distinctive crackle and crunch emanated behind them. Grimes looked sideways. "I may have landed on a few of those things."

"Uh-huh. Try not to lose too much sleep over it." Jason got to his feet. "Time to get out there and open the portal."

"Don't look at me. I'd rather you just shoot me and be done with it."

That made him chuckle as he left the cockpit. Jason moved down the aisle until he found Gaddy. Jason patted Sergeant Jackson's shoulder. "How about you give me a moment to talk with Gaddy."

"Sure thing, Captain." Jackson got up and let Jason take his seat.

Gaddy was dressed in a battlesuit with her helmet retracted. "Hello, Captain. I see we're ready to enter onto Halimar."

"We're here. I need to talk to you about what will happen next. We talked earlier about the possibility of you reconnecting with your dissident friends."

"I told you, most of them died in HAB 12."

"So who's left?"

Gaddy nodded her head. "There's Zay. Zay-Lee. He was supposed to come with us into HAB 12 but got arrested. If he's been released, freed, he'd definitely help me."

"Would he have access to the kind of information we're looking for?"

"What Zay doesn't know; he can find out. He's a coder, a hacker. Lives and breathes anything and everything subversive."

"Good. That'll be your first order of business once we arrive on Halimar. I can't tell you how much we're counting on you. We're entering a hostile world, and without friends, we won't get far."

"I understand, Captain. First thing, I'll need is a pocket com."

Jason shook his head, not understanding.

"That's what we call our version of a cellphone. Only ours lets us talk to people on all our worlds."

Chapter 33

Two were dead. Perhaps they'd suffocated or they'd simply died from fright. Nan didn't know and she tried to shake the image of their ashen, open-eyed faces from her thoughts. The other six had been successfully extricated from their cocoons and were now sitting on the sectional couch, back in the truck bed. Seemingly fine.

Nan and Mollie sat next to Gus in the cab. At first light, Reese was tasked with doing an inspection of the truck. Without a heavy layer of grease covering the truck's exposed metal and tires, the molt weevils would have no trouble climbing onboard. She pushed that image from her thoughts too.

Gus brought the truck's speed up to forty mph while they continued down the last of the Broadmoor's fairways.

"Trees!" Mollie pointed at the windshield.

"I see them... I see them. There's not a lot I can do about that... to get off the golf course we'll need to pass under a few trees. Why don't you use that walkie and give Reese a heads up?"

Prior to getting behind the wheel, Gus had handed out six new, still in their manufacturer's cartons, walkie-talkies. It wasn't long before Mollie was banned from using hers. She'd driven everyone crazy with constant annoying chatter and talking like a big-rig trucker on a CB radio.

Nan pressed the talk button and said, "Reese, we're coming up on some trees. Heads up for any uninvited guests."

"I'm right above you on the overhang. Anything even twitches above me is going to get a load of buckshot in its ass."

Mollie leaned in and spoke in a country twang, "That's a big ten-four, good buddy."

Nan pulled the radio away from her and rolled her eyes.

Gus brought the big 797F down to twenty, then ten miles per hour. They'd reached the trees that marked the end of the golf course and paralleled the two-lane road on the other side. Instinctively, all three looked up as they passed beneath several tall oaks. Sure enough, a black, multi-legged molt weevil dropped from high above. Both barrels of Reese's shotgun boomed close by and caught the creature mid-flight, propelling it forward, beyond the front of the truck.

Gus eased the truck over the curb and turned left. "This is going to be a bit tight."

"What are you doing? You're going to hit that car, Gus!" Mollie shouted, standing up from Nan's knee.

"What do you want me to do? It's not like we can turn around and go the other way."

Three abandoned cars were pulled over to the right-hand curve, leaving less than adequate room for the huge truck to pass. Gus dropped into the lowest gear and let the truck climb over the obstacles one at a time. Each car was nearly flattened under the weight of hundreds of tons of steel. Mollie covered her mouth but soon was laughing hysterically. Nan shook her head but soon laughed too. Gus didn't see the humor in it but seemed to be enjoying himself.

"They sure have a surprise waiting for them when they get back to their cars," Mollie said.

Nan smiled but didn't think that would be the biggest surprise they'd probably encountered.

"You know where we're at, Gus?" Nan asked.

"Of course, I do. I've lived out here all my life. The problem's going to be what's up ahead: very rough terrain after this neighborhood ends." He veered the truck right at a fork in the road, and immediately the truck started to climb.

"I just saw a sign. This is the way to the zoo!" Mollie said excitedly.

"A slight detour," Gus said.

Nan didn't want to think about what the molt weevils would do to all those poor animals—most of which wouldn't be able to run away, escape from their enclosures. Just then a very large orange, white, and black tiger crossed the road directly in front of them. Clenched in its jaws was what remained of a molt weevil's carcass. *So much for the poor defenseless animals*, she thought.

It took ten minutes to crest the hill. Nan saw the zoo off to the right, built into the side of the hillside. They drove through the nearly empty parking lot and stopped at the public entrance, with multiple ticket booths and a high metal gate. The gate was ripped off its hinges in some areas, bent and distorted in others. But that wasn't what Nan, Mollie, and Gus were interested in, because a twelve-foot-tall African elephant stood right before the truck. The back half of the animal was partially covered in the greenish cocoon material. One of the majestic beast's tusks had the remnants of a molt weevil dangling from it.

"Its back legs are tied," Mollie said.

Nan had already noticed but didn't want to bring attention to it. "That's a dangerous animal, Mollie."

Reese was awkwardly coming down the rope ladder, still

holding the barrel of the twelve- gauge grasped in one hand. He jumped down the last three feet onto the metal deck. Nan got up, squeezed by Mollie, and opened the cab's door. "What are you doing?"

"I'm going to help that elephant." He handed Nan the shotgun. "This is for molt weevils, not the elephant."

The elephant still hadn't moved. Reese stopped at the metal stairway leading down to the ground. "Mollie, can you go back into the bed and find a rope?"

Mollie scampered up the ladder and emerged less than a minute later with a coiled rope in her hand. "Will this work?"

"Perfect... Toss it down."

She did as he asked, climbed back down, and joined Nan on the deck. Reese tied one end of the rope around the deck-top banister and kept the rest of the rope coiled in his hand. He turned around and walked down the slippery, grease-coated steps backward. He fed out the rope from its coil as he went. He smiled up at Nan. "I've had to do this a few times now... think I'm getting the hang of it." But his feet slipped out from under him and he landed hard on his backside. "I guess I spoke too soon." He got to his feet and carefully resumed his backward trek down the steps. Once on solid ground, he fished through his pockets and came out with a pocketknife.

Nan saw movement in her peripheral vision. A handful of molt weevils were at the far side of the parking lot. "Hurry up, Reese," she said, in as calm a voice as she could muster.

Reese tentatively approached the elephant head-on. Five feet out he stopped and looked at the animal. The elephant huffed and tried to take a step backward. More huffing sounds. Reese took several more steps until he was close enough to touch his long, hanging trunk. He gently patted it. He was saying something, but Nan couldn't make out his words. The elephant seemed to calm down a bit as Reese continued to talk in a soothing voice.

"Mom!" Mollie said under her breath. She used her wide eyes to gesture toward the other end of the parking lot. "They... are... coming!" she said through clenched teeth.

"I see them. Just keep still while Reese helps the elephant. She looks terrified, we don't want it to try to charge away." Nan moved slowly, bringing up and supporting the shotgun with both hands.

Reese was patting the elephant's thick front left leg, and now, ever so slowly, moved along the animal's side. Never losing contact, he petted the elephant's mid-section, and then its hind legs.

Both Mollie and Nan had their attention on the molt weevils. All five of them were up on two tentacle appendages and running. Nan thought they almost looked like people when they moved like that—people without heads.

"Reese! Hurry!"

He'd gotten grease on his hands from the rope hitting the greasy steps. He was having trouble getting a solid enough grip to pull the blade free on his pocketknife.

"Reese!" Nan said, this time with more volume.

He glanced up to Nan and she said the words louder this time, *molt weevils!*

The elephant also sensed the approaching creatures and became agitated. His trunk pointed upward, and a loud desperate honk filled the air.

"Damn it!" Reese said, still wrestling with the knife.

"They're coming... fifty yards, Reese!" Nan yelled, no longer concerned with upsetting the near-frantic elephant.

Reese resorted to using his teeth and finally got the blade separated from the handle. He locked the blade open and didn't waste a second before slicing at the thick cocoon wrappings binding the elephant's two hind legs.

"Reese... Now!" Nan screamed. She brought the shotgun up and aimed it in the direction of the sprinting molt weevils. She couldn't fire. She knew the spread of buckshot would hit both Reese and the elephant. Nan almost dropped the gun as Gus pushed his way past her. He had a handgun leveled in both outstretched hands and fired. The closest of the molt weevils fell, its legs continuing to gyrate and twitch. Two more shots rang out, but both missed their target.

Gus cursed, widened his stance, and took aim again. All four of the molt weevils were almost upon them. With one final pull of the knife, the elephant's legs were free. Reese and the elephant ran—Reese toward the truck—the elephant back toward the zoo.

With ten feet to go, a molt weevil dove toward Reese. Two of the creature's tentacles reached out stretching, catching his left ankle, and wrapping around it. The agent went down onto the pavement. Gus ran to the furthest end of the platform and pointed the gun nearly straight down. He fired once, twice, three times. Reese scrambled to his feet and darted to the steps. The other three molt weevils came at him: one from the left, one from the right, and one from directly behind.

Nan knew she had time for one word... she screamed, "Catch!"

Even before he'd looked up, the twelve-gauge was flying through the air in his direction. He caught it with one hand, flipped it around, and blew the closest of the molt weevils in half. Gus continued to fire until his magazine was empty, and the slide locked open. One molt weevil remained alive. It hesitated, then abruptly rushed after the elephant.

Reese got to the steps, retrieved the end of the rope, and pulled himself up to safety.

Chapter 34

rimes was back in the pilot's seat with Jason sitting next to her. Their visibility was zero. One or two of the big bugs had climbed on top of *The Streamline*'s sweeping nose section and hadn't moved in five minutes. What they did have was a perfect view of the underbelly of a seven-foot-long cockroach. Jason noticed Grimes purposely avert her eyes—first, by making repeated, unnecessary, setting adjustments to the holo-display and, eventually, turning completely around in her seat to speak with Dira, who was seated in the first row behind the cockpit.

They were waiting for a small security team to clear the area so Ricket could get to the access panel and open the portal window. Grimes nearly jumped out of her skin as three plasma bursts blasted the big bug in front of them. Charred and clearly dead, it fell away from the ship. Rizzo gave Grimes and Jason a casual two-fingered salute from below and then fired several more bursts at what, undoubtedly, were more out-of-view bugs. Ricket hurried to the cavern's back wall and wasted no time entering the access code. Rizzo, Billy, and Jackson provided assault cover against any lurking creatures daring to approach.

The portal opened and Ricket and the security team ran back into the ship.

Grimes used the holo-display to position and navigate *The Streamline* through the portal, just as she'd done back at *The Lilly*'s Zoo. They entered Halimar in the dead of night, which suited Jason just fine. Jason called back for Gaddy to join them in the cockpit.

Several moments later she stood at their shoulders, and as she looked past them, out to Halimar, Jason could see by her face she was happy to be home. Grimes set the ship down on a somewhat level area of hillside. Jason estimated they were several thousand feet above the open plains below, which were primarily farmland.

"You mentioned something about getting hold of a pocket com. Is this something you can buy, like at a store?" Jason asked.

Gaddy smiled and shook her head. "No. This isn't Earth. The government issues anything related to communications equipment or devices. We'll need to steal one."

Jason turned to look through the forward windshield. In the distance, past the farmland, were clusters of lights. "What do you suggest?"

Gaddy continued to stare straight ahead and then pointed. "That's the university. Get me in close to the area there and I can grab us a PoCom... that's what we call pocket communicators."

Grimes looked at Jason, who nodded his approval. "Don't run off, Gaddy; we need you to tell us where to go, once we get in close."

Grimes kept *The Streamline* close to the ground, but away from homes, buildings, or other structures. By the time they'd reached the school, the sun was just coming up. At a half mile out, Jason thought the university didn't look much different from any one of hundreds you'd find on Earth: imposing stone structures, grassy open areas, and tall buildings that were probably student dorms. When Jason turned to Gaddy, he saw she'd clasped a hand over her mouth and tears were streaming down her cheeks.

"What is it? What's wrong, Gaddy?"

"Can't you see what's happened here?"

Jason looked again and, indeed, now he did see. The walls of the university were pocked with blackened blast marks and what he'd first thought was early morning mist was actually sooty dark smoke. Student bodies lay prone on the ground. Scores of handmade signs, mostly torn and trampled, were strewn around like trash.

"Put us down in the quad area over there," Gaddy said angrily.

It took Grimes several moments to find an area that was sufficiently clear of the dead before setting the ship down.

By the time Jason got to his feet, Gaddy was already running down the aisle toward the mid-ship hatch. "Gaddy... wait!"

She opened the hatch and sprinted off the ship. Jason tapped Billy's shoulder as he ran by him: "Bring a team."

Jason triggered his SuitPac device and followed in the direction Gaddy had run. He saw her twenty yards ahead, bent over a body. It looked as if she were checking for a pulse—a sign of life—then she moved on to another body, and then another.

He approached but kept his distance. Jason had seen death countless times—he didn't need to check any of these bodies for life signs. They'd been dead for days. But Gaddy checked them all. Her deep, primal, mournful sobs kept him from moving closer. She gently turned the bodies over, one after another... the sobs continued. Billy, Rizzo, Jackson, and Traveler joined him, standing several steps back. Only Dira rushed forward, willing to encroach into Gaddy's now desperate quest to find someone, anyone, still alive.

Jason wanted to tell Dira she needed to activate her own SuitPac, but he knew she wouldn't listen. She would want to connect with Gaddy on a more personal level. She crouched at Gaddy's side and checked one young student's carotid artery for a pulse. She put an arm around Gaddy's shoulders and pulled her close. They clung together while Dira spoke softly to her—helping to soothe the pain of what had happened here. Eventually, they stood and slowly moved back toward Jason and the team. Gaddy stopped in front of him and reached for his hand. She placed a square device in his palm. "This is what a PoCom looks like," she said, sounding resigned to the catastrophic situation on the campus.

An abrupt sound brought everyone to attention. Jason checked his HUD and saw a moving life icon in the building to their right.

Traveler stayed put, while Billy, Rizzo, and Jackson spread out and headed for the building. Then desperate screams stopped them in their tracks. Jason's nano-devices translated the words: Gaddy! Gaddy! Gaddy!

Multi-guns came up, poised to fire, as a student burst through the first-floor doorway. Gaddy ran toward her. "Oh my God... Chala!"

A young female Craing about the same age as Gaddy ran across the quad and right into Gaddy's open, outstretched arms.

"I saw you from the second-floor window. I knew it was you the first second I saw you," Chala said, sounding out of breath.

"What happened here? Chala, who did this?"

"You know who did this! The Emperor's forces came two days ago... they didn't even ask the students to disassemble. They just started shooting... students, professors, anyone on campus, shot down without a second thought."

"How did you survive?"

"I hid. I cowered in a closet until they left last night. When I saw your ship, I thought they'd returned... that they'd come back to kill me, too."

Jason asked, "Are there any other survivors, Chala?"

She looked up at Jason but didn't answer.

"Chala, this is Captain Reynolds. He's a friend. They're from Earth... they're here to help us."

Jason saw the fear in her eyes. She looked so young, a child, not that much older than Mollie and Boomer.

"I don't know. Not that I know of." She turned toward Gaddy. "Can you take me home? I don't want to stay here by myself."

Gaddy brought her into a hug. Looking up at Jason, she silently asked him Chala's question.

"You can come with us, Chala, but I can't guarantee you'll be any safer. Truth is, you probably won't be. As for getting you home, we have a mission to accomplish first."

"I don't care... please just get me out of here."

Dira brought Chala into the Medical cubicle onboard *The Streamline* and gave her something to calm her nerves. Gaddy sat next to her on the gurney, while Jason sat on a stool across from them.

"Talk to me about what's happening here, Chala."

"Here on Halimar?"

"Yes, and the other worlds."

"You don't know?"

Jason shook his head. "No, other than that there have been protests—"

"Oh, it's gone far beyond that," she said incredulously. "It's a revolution, Mr. Reynolds."

"It's Captain, and a revolution typically involves weapons, a military response..."

"I don't know anything about that kind of stuff. Why don't you just turn on the news? I'm only a student."

Gaddy made an apologetic expression for her friend's snarky attitude.

As if on cue, Ricket arrived with a virtual notepad. He pulled at a three-dimensional video image until it was several feet wide and was hovering between them. It was a Halimar news report that looked surprisingly similar to a national news report from NBC, CBS, ABC, CNN or FOX, back on Earth.

Jason watched as a montage of dramatic videos provided a clearer example of what was happening on each of the seven Craing worlds. Chala was right to use the word revolution. The Craing masses were armed and, to some extent, even organized. Two separate clips showed government installations set afire, while another one showed government-deployed aircraft firing down on a charging mob of revolutionaries.

Both Gaddy and Chala were instantly captivated by the reports. They leaned in and wore the same expression... *they were proud to be part of the revolt.*

"We're looking at GAX-News, one of the few non-government-controlled stations," Gaddy volunteered.

Jason's attention was pulled back to the holographic display. A two-dimensional black and white video clip appeared, showing a triumphant-looking Martin Luther King striding in front of a crowd of people. Just one of his many civil disobedience marches.

"Earth's media transmissions continue to be an important influence on our society, Captain," Gaddy said. "High priest overlords tried to ban such *subversive* Earth media decades ago, but that only increased our demand for them. Earth remains an important example, an inspiration, to the Craing populace."

"We only want what you have on Earth," Chala added. "The basic freedoms your own people experience on a daily basis."

"Those freedoms came at a heavy price for our people. In some places they're still paying that price," Jason said, now viewing miscellaneous images of bare-chested African slaves, bound in chains; battle sketches from the American Civil War; and then sobering World War II photographs of emaciated prisoners held in Nazi concentration camps. More Craing three-dimensional clips then appeared, no less horrific, showing Craing men, women, and children slaves, being beaten by uniformed Craing soldiers. Next, alien beings were being led up a Craing heavy cruiser's gangway at gunpoint.

Jason shook his head as he watched the next series of video shots. Five elderly smug-looking High Priests were gathered around a large round table. Flames rose from a center caldron. The next shot was a close-up of fire dancing up from a metal grate and what looked like partial human remains—an upper leg and a man's open filleted chest—being roasted. The final images were wide-angle shots from somewhere in space. Jason recognized the cube-like shapes of a Craing dreadnought warship formation.

Seven massive vessels were converging around a singularly beautiful pink planet. It slowly rotated on its axis, with near-transparent white clouds above its surface. It looked like a painting... a watercolor of varying subtle hues. Simultaneously, bright amber plasma blasts shot out from the warships. Within moments the pretty pink hues changed to dark red and then to dark charcoal gray as all life ceased to exist on that pretty world. Jason flinched when the planet exploded, atomized into nothingness. The seven warships then moved into a V-formation, leaving only empty black space behind.

"At least for us, Captain, our fates have been tied together for many years," Chala went on. "The Emperor... the acting Emperor needs to be stopped. *The Great Space* initiative is the last straw, so to speak. It disgusts all of us. It cannot be allowed to continue."

Jason and Dira's eyes met. He saw her holding back tears. Only a few days ago, her own planet nearly succumbed to the same fate they'd just viewed on the video clip... and how close had Earth, too, come to being destroyed at Ot-Mul's hands?

Gaddy continued, "The Craing people have looked to Earth as a world example of what can be accomplished when the people unite. It's a beacon of hope. Right now, this is our time. We need your help, Captain."

Jason saw pleading in both Gaddy's and Chala's eyes. But helping the rebelling Craing citizenry while his own planet lay under siege, infested by creatures that could very well kill his ex-wife, daughter, and everyone else, wasn't his top priority. Although he certainly felt for the Craing people, his priorities were simple—do everything humanly possible to save Earth—his family. No, joining in the Craing's revolution was not going to happen.

Jason spoke softly, "Then help us find Ot-Mul. He still controls the most powerful military force in the known Universe. Destroying him, along with the high priest overlords, will be of mutual benefit to both our people."

Chapter 35

"You mentioned someone named Zay-Lee," Jason said.

Gaddy nervously glanced to Chala as if she wasn't sure how to respond.

"Why would you have anything to do with Zay?" Chala asked her friend, looking confused.

Gaddy gave Jason an accusatory look and then let out a slow, deliberate, breath. "Zay is Chala's boyfriend."

Recognition of an awkward situation crossed both Dira's and Jason's faces.

"This goes way beyond boyfriend troubles, Gaddy. Whatever you've got going on in your personal life needs to take a backseat."

"I'll need that PoCom back," Gaddy said in a flat voice.

Jason held out the cell phone-sized device Gaddy had handed him earlier.

She took the PoCom from his open palm and without looking at Chala, accessed a small display screen, which Jason assumed was some kind of directory assistance. She used the tip of one finger to make virtual connections, one tap after another, until the device clicked several times. Gaddy held the PoCom up to her ear and waited.

Jason heard a muffled voice answer on the other end. Gaddy gave Chala another quick glance and answered, "This is Gaddy."

His actual words were indecipherable but the excitement in the male's voice was clearly evident. It seemed Chala too could hear him because her eyes widened and her expression of curiosity quickly changed to one of fury.

Before Gaddy could say another word, Chala was screaming what Jason assumed were Craing curse words. Chala was up on her feet, inches from Gaddy's face. "How long?"

Gaddy avoided Chala's eyes and said, "Hold on, Zay..." She covered the device with her other palm and finally looked at Chala. "Almost a year. Sorry... It just happened. We were both getting more and more interested in political causes. At that time you didn't want to... or were too afraid to get involved. I'm sorry... but I need to talk to Zay." She brought her attention back to the PoCom and spoke quickly. Several times she had to tell him to stay on the subject at hand, and that she'd tell him everything later.

Chala sat back down on the gurney, looking dejected. As Gaddy finished up her conversation, she quietly whispered something to Zay before ending the call.

"So does he know where Ot-Mul is hiding out?" Jason asked.

"He thinks so. Zay-Lee told me that since I've been gone, he has been elevated to one of the leaders of the revolution. He said it's not safe to discuss this over the PoCom... he's on his way here now."

"Zay?" Chala blurted out. "Zay can't even make it to class half the time. The Zay I know has trouble deciding what to wear in the morning... how is he supposed to make the important decisions crucial to leading the resistance?"

Gaddy left Chala's comment unanswered.

Jason kept Gaddy on task: "How long before Zay gets here?"

"Not long. Maybe an hour."

"In the meantime, we need to get out of sight. Chala, is there a gymnasium on campus?"

Chala shrugged her shoulders, apparently not in the mood to have anything to do with him, or anyone else.

"There's an indoor Gallopy court," Gaddy answered for her. Seeing Jason's blank expression, she said, "It's similar to your game of tennis... only we use live intelligent interaction instead of a dumb yellow ball."

THE GALLOPY COURT WAS MORE SIMILAR TO A basketball court than to a tennis court, but in terms of being an adequate size to phase-shift *The Streamline* into, it was fine. It was a dimly lit arena of sorts; Jason guessed it could seat several thousand spectators. While waiting for Zay to arrive, Jason and Billy explored the surroundings.

Both wore battlesuits and carried a multi-gun.

"Funny... here we have an alien culture millions of miles from Earth, and life isn't all that different," Billy noted as they entered what appeared to be a locker room. "No separate men and women dressing and showering facilities, though."

"I'm not so sure female Craing have the same rights to play athletics. Or maybe only males play Gallopy." Jason shrugged his shoulders in response.

"You hear that?" Billy asked.

Not only did he hear the same distant flittering sounds—like tiny feet running—that Billy did, but Jason saw perhaps hundreds of life-sign icons pop up on his HUD. Sensitivity settings kept small organisms from typically showing up, but as they left the locker room and entered a smaller, adjoining area, the life icons came to life.

Jason's and Billy's helmeted spotlights provided just enough light to see the area was about twenty feet by thirty. There were four long tables, with ten stools positioned around each one, holding a collection of tools, and bundles in varying lengths of leather straps. It seemed the life icons, along with the loud skittering sounds, were coming from the back of the room. Billy and Jason approached the back wall. The size of standard mouse or hamster cages, hundreds of clear enclosures were stacked, row upon row, all the way to the ceiling ten feet above.

They moved in closer, bringing their visors within several inches of a cage. Expecting to see a small mouse, or perhaps some kind of reptilian creature, Jason and Billy both took a quick step backward.

"Holy shit!" Billy exclaimed. He looked from the interior of the enclosure over to Jason and then back. "This is messed up, man."

Jason had a queasy feeling in his stomach. The enclosure directly in front of him, in fact, all the enclosures, held small beings that, with the exception of their four- or five-inch statures, were human in every other sense of the word.

"I'm sure they only look... human," Billy said. "I mean, how—"

Billy's own words were cut short by two simple ones... "Help me."

JASON HAD BROUGHT A SINGLE ENCLOSURE OUT, where it currently rested on the gurney next to Dira. Gaddy and Chala had gone quiet. Eventually, Gaddy spoke up: "Yes, they're human. But we didn't do this to them."

"We?" Billy asked.

"The Craing. And it happened well over ten years ago. It was a space anomaly that affected an area of space... not a black hole, but something similar... not sure. Everything within hundreds of thousands of miles was altered... reduced to a fraction of normal size. The inhabitants of the space station didn't even realize what had happened to them until a Craing freighter discovered them."

"How many people are we talking about?" Jason asked.

Gaddy held Jason's stare for several long seconds before answering, "Thousands."

Billy was on the verge of going ballistic. "So... how do these unfortunate sons of bitches end up in cages at a Gallopy arena?"

"They were brought back here... to the Craing worlds. Everyone wanted one. You have to understand; they were prized... valued. These incredibly unique little beings were like nothing else in the Universe."

"So prized they were treated like caged rodents?"

"It wasn't like that!" Gaddy spat back.

No one spoke.

Chala, wedged in at the far end of the gurney, fidgeted with the hem of her shirt.

"So what's with this game? How are they used?"

Guilt spread across Gaddy's face. "You have to understand there were thousands of them. I don't know who exactly, but someone came up with a game, which then turned into a competitive sport. The small beings, we call them Gallos, are placed into spheres that they themselves can control... sort of navigate."

"Go on," Dira said.

"I don't want to talk about this anymore."

"Let me see if I can paint this picture," Billy said with a smile, but the smile didn't reach his eyes. "You've basically come up with a sport where a small ball is batted around a court. Right?"

Gaddy looked exasperated, "Not me personally, but yeah."

"And to make things interesting, you've added another element. Tiny, defenseless, people... people whose very survival depends on their ability to maneuver these balls... these spheres. What an exciting aspect... seeing if the little humans can stay alive long enough to make it to the end of the game."

Gaddy stayed quiet.

"So what happens when you've killed them all off? Certainly, a thousand people put through this kind of treatment across your seven worlds, in all your schools and universities, wouldn't survive all that long," Jason asked.

Gaddy's lips compressed into a line and her eyes stayed locked on the deck. She looked small and vulnerable like she wanted to disappear. The long silence was deafening.

Chala finally yelled the answer for her: "We breed them, okay? We breed the little fuckers!"

Chapter 36

E ight hours had passed since they'd embarked on their mission, leaving *The Lilly* for *The Streamline*, and Jason was already feeling a pull to get back there—to defend Earth... to rescue Nan and Mollie. Sure, from a tactical and academic standpoint, their mission to find Ot-Mul was imperative for Earth's ultimate survival. Jason knew that... but it was hard to think in universal terms when real-life emotions were at play. Jason's inner monologue was interrupted when Traveler passed by, carrying a stack of little enclosures.

Prior to Zay's arrival, Jason asked his team to help transport the hundreds of enclosures containing the tiny humans from the back room of the Gallopy arena building into *The Streamline*. Ricket informed Jason of an available storage cubicle about the same size as the one allocated to Medical. As happy as the miniature humans were to see fellow humans, they weren't happy they still were required to stay in cages. In fact, they were fairly adamant they should be freed right away. But from a safety standpoint, there were too many chances of them being stepped on—or sat upon. As the stack of cages filled every inch of the small cubicle space, the chattering and yelling of the confined humans increased exponentially. Jason attempted to calm them down, let them know their concerns would be addressed, all in good time, but soon found his patience stretched beyond limits and, against her clear objections, handed the new job of *small-people ambassador* over to Dira.

Zay-Lee arrived two hours later. The approach of his small, dilapidated ship was picked up by Grimes on *The Streamline's* sensors. Everyone, except a now over-extended Dira, moved outside, into the quad's quieter atmosphere, and waited to greet him as he exited from a rickety gangway at the rear of a military-modified cargo vessel. He was accompanied by three young Craing males near Gaddy's and Chala's age. In an Earth-like, urban bad-boy style, he wore a brown long-sleeve T-shirt, torn green trousers, and a knit skullcap pulled all the way down to his eyes.

A holstered pistol hung loosely around his hips. Zay was the first to approach and seemed genuinely excited when he saw Gaddy, giving her a long, affectionate hug, followed by an extended kiss on the mouth. Surprised, he noticed Chala standing nearby and awkwardly moved to embrace her as well. She held up both palms and rapidly shook her head, letting him know the thought of touching him was revolting. Embarrassed, he took a step backward. The tension between Gaddy and Chala could be cut with a knife, and Zay was not oblivious to that, either. Gaddy introduced Zay to Jason and his team, and then let Zay introduce his friends. Zay and his cohorts eyed Traveler warily, apparently unsure what to make of the seven-foot-tall rhino-warrior.

"We have a lot to talk about, Zay," Jason said. "I'd like to hear about the revolution... your successes as well as your failures. But right now, finding Ot-Mul is paramount to us."

"Didn't Gaddy tell you?"

"Tell me what?" Jason asked, glancing in her direction.

"Oh... sorry, I forgot to mention it."

"Anyway," Zay continued, "we've determined he's not on any of the Craing worlds. We suspect he's being harbored on Itimus-four."

Jason shook his head and waited for Zay to continue, having no idea what Itimus-four was.

"That's one of Terplin's five moons. Highly secluded, it is home and refuge to the high priest overlords. Reports are he's within the walls of Chrimguard, an ancient and highly fortified Grand Sacellum. Since the average Craing is not allowed to set foot on that particular moon, there's little intel for us to go on."

Zay and his rebel friends were having a hard time focusing on something other than the scattered bodies of dead students. And with the rising sun and its accompanying morning heat, there was the ever-increasing aroma of decomposing flesh. Jason gestured with both hands for everyone to move away from the quad and to follow him in the direction of the Gallopy arena.

"The reports you're referring to, where are they coming from?"

"From our counterparts on Terplin. Let me be clear, Captain Reynolds, no one's actually seen the acting Emperor. What we do have are encrypted interstellar communications, all now being generated out of Itimus-four."

"What's so important about that?" Jason asked.

"It's gone from zero transmissions to totally off the charts. There's no reason for a religious compound to be transmitting at that magnitude. But if you factor it from a command standpoint, *The Great Space* initiative requires tremendous logistical administrative support and coordination. We're fairly certain Ot-Mul has set himself up there to oversee his military assets in outer space, while still managing the rebellion locally, here within Craing space."

Jason saw the logic in what Zay was saying. In fact, he was sure the young Craing rebel leader was right on target.

They approached the Gallopy arena where both large doorways had been propped open. There was now adequate light streaming in to see inside the arena and see Dira standing by *The Streamline*, casually leaning against the ship's outer hull.

The four Craing men slowed, and Jason heard them commenting in hushed tones. Even in the semi-darkness, *The Streamline* was an impressive little ship. But Jason was mistaken; it wasn't the ship they were enamored with—it was Dira. As if on stage, she was cast in a rectangular beam of sunlight. Her violet skin seemed to glow, and when she smiled, her contrasting perfect white teeth brought all to a standstill.

She caught Jason's eye and pointed in the general direction behind her. "Sorry... I should be in there, but they never shut up. Perhaps it's being so small that makes their voices become... I don't know, more high-pitched?"

Jason saw Zay and his friends looking confused, but Jason didn't want to go into the whole *tiny-human-thing* again. He also no longer wanted to go inside the ship. If Dira couldn't take the noise he certainly couldn't either.

Jason addressed Zay: "Tell me what resources the rebellion has at their disposal."

"Resources?"

"Other rebels, such as yourselves; weapons; ships?"

The four looked at each other uneasily. "You saw the ship we came in. We have a handful of crafts similar to that. We also have an old, broken-down light-cruiser hidden away on Halimar, but it's not operational yet. No one knows how to repair it. As for rebels..." Zay smiled. "We have tens of thousands of citizens ready—wanting to fight. Weapons are another issue. There's not enough to go around."

Jason shook his head; theirs really was a grassroots rebellion.

He was surprised they'd stayed alive this long, considering the superior resources available to the Emperor.

Billy, his head enveloped in a cloud of white cigar smoke, cleared his throat. "It's not a game, kid. Going to war is a serious business. Do it wrong, not using proper discrimination, and all you'll accomplish is getting your people killed."

"We were hoping you could provide us with the kind of resources you're talking about."

Jason looked at the young Craing and tried to disassociate him from the actions of the ruling Craing, who had enslaved and tormented thousands of captive humans—some stacked in small cages mere feet behind him. Was theirs an evolving society, ready for change? He didn't know.

Ricket exited *The Streamline* and stood next to Jason.

"You're the one called Ricket?" one of Zay's cohorts said.

"I am Ricket."

"Why aren't you a part of this? We... everyone... know who you are... who you were. You're famous."

Jason saw an incoming NanoText request come in from Ricket. Jason read the message and looked down at his Craing friend. He thought about what was being asked and eventually nodded his assent.

Ricket removed a small rucksack from his shoulder and handed it to Zay. "Ensure these do not get into the hands of the Emperor's forces."

Zay opened the top of the rucksack, reached a hand inside, and came out holding a SuitPac device. He flipped it around between his fingers several times before looking over to Ricket. "What are they?"

Ricket took a step backward and triggered the small metallic device hanging from his belt. Within three seconds his battlesuit expanded out, one segmented section at a time, until he was fully encased in the advanced Caldurain technology of a hardened armored suit. Jason saw Zay's wide-eyed reflection staring back into Ricket's amber visor.

Ricket said, "These suits can propel you into space... have integrated weaponry... and will protect you from almost anything the Craing forces will fire at you. There are twenty-five of these SuitPacs in that rucksack. Instructions on the suit's usage are accessible via the HUD readouts."

Zay continued to look into the open sack as if he'd discovered a pot of gold. Perhaps he had, Jason thought. "Outfitted with those suits, Zay, you can board a Craing cruiser or storm a military compound. But as Billy, here, said so eloquently: it's not a game. Going to war is serious business. Do it wrong, or indiscriminately, and all you'll accomplish is getting your people killed. So do it right... build an organization; train yourselves in the ways of combat. If you can, align yourselves only with those who would join your fight. That won't be us. At least not today."

"Thank you, Captain Reynolds."

"Don't thank me. Those are a gift from Ricket."

Chapter 37

Chala chose to stay on Halimar with Zay; he'd promised to get her home. The way things were left, there was still a rift between Gaddy and Chala. Jason, although he didn't say anything, was glad to leave the drama behind. Within minutes of reentering *The Streamline*, Jason was ready to rethink his rescue of the small humans. Their chattering was constant and, as Dira had mentioned, their higher-pitched voices were beyond grating.

Before Grimes would receive orders to take *The Streamline* into space, that situation needed to be dealt with—one way or another.

Dira and Jason stood at the narrow entrance to the storage cubicle. He looked at the stacks of enclosures, all positioned to face in the same outward direction, and he could see most of the tiny humans in the closest deck-to-ceiling stack. Although they were humanlike in every sense of the word, they were not from Earth, and they did not speak English or any of Earth's languages. It was only through his internal nano-tech that Jason was able to understand what they were saying and for them, too, to understand what he was saying.

As Jason stood near the containers, their chattering increased. He glanced down the aisle and saw annoyed crew faces turned toward him. Traveler looked as if he was imminently close to killing someone. Jason brought his attention back to the enclosures.

"Can everyone hear me?" Jason heard too many responses back to keep track of, but the gist of their replies wasn't friendly. "I am Captain Reynolds. Let me be perfectly clear from the start. If you don't settle down and shut up, I'm going to leave you here... where it's back to being batted around in some future Gallopy match. It's entirely up to you."

The noise level diminished by half. Jason waited and, within the course of a minute, the ship became quiet.

"Thank you. Over the next few minutes, I want you to pick one person, an emissary, who can speak on behalf of all of you. We can't have you all screaming out at once, willy-nilly... it's way too disruptive." Jason gestured toward Dira. "This is Dira. She is the officer who will work with your newly assigned emissary. Keep in mind, she will inform me if things get out of hand again, prompting me to return you to Halimar and the Gallopy arena."

Dira leaned in close to Jason and whispered in his ear: "Am I supposed to feed them? Clean their cages too? Is that in my job description?"

She didn't look happy and, truthfully, it really wasn't fair to her. Jason turned to look down the aisle again and came to a decision. "As *Ambassador of the Little People*, Dira, you have the power to enlist as many subordinates as you deem necessary in accommodating our new guests. Maybe make up a revolving roster... I'll leave that up to you."

Dira chuckled, "That works. I know exactly who to start with."

"As long as it's not me, have at it."

. . .

JASON JOINED GRIMES IN THE COCKPIT. "Get us out of here, Grimes."

The words had no sooner left his lips before she phase-shifted *The Streamline* into open space.

"We're now in a low orbit around Halimar, Captain," Grimes said, "but it won't be long before we're noticed."

"That's not likely," Ricket said, coming up the aisle behind them. "Like both *The Minian* and *The Lilly*, Craing sensors will not detect *The Streamline*. The ship would need to be visually observed and... as small as she is, that is highly unlikely."

"Then let's keep as far away from other ships as possible," Jason said. His attention focused on the holo-display before them. "Let's take a look at the logistical layer."

She brought up a wide, bird's-eye view of the seven Craing worlds' Solar System, and then zoomed in on Halimar, and its neighboring planet, Terplin. Even though Ot-Mul's *Great Space* initiative had begun in earnest, there were still thousands of Craing warships about, either waiting to be deployed or permanently stationed on Halimar to provide ongoing security for the Craing worlds. In either case, *The Streamline* was far outmatched.

"Set a course for Itimus-four." Jason turned toward Ricket. "What can you tell me about the Chrimguard compound? I know it was another life... but you've undoubtedly been there before."

"Memories of a lifetime... prior to being a cyborgenic being... back before your father discovered me buried beneath the scrapyard, are almost non-existent... but not completely."

Jason saw Ricket's eyes lose focus as he mentally went *some-where* else. When he finally looked back at Jason, he had a somewhat bemused expression. "I do remember magnificent

232

surroundings, and an intensely bright orb, like a sun, hanging suspended from high up vaulted rafters. An important ceremony was in progress... there were priests in colorful robes wearing elaborate coned-shaped headdresses. I was very young... I was a different person."

Jason didn't see how that memory recall would be helpful to finding Ot-Mul, but nodded to his friend anyway. "Let me know if anything else comes to you, Ricket."

"I will, Captain," he said, turning away.

"Oh, Ricket?"

"Yes, Captain?"

"Is there any way to bring the small humans back to their original size? Perhaps in a MediPod?"

"Not in a MediPod... at least, not as they are configured presently. We would need to determine the exact conditions that brought about their transformation in the first place. Then I could explore a possible means to reproduce that same anomaly... but in reverse."

"Well, let me know if you come up with anything."

"Captain," Grimes interrupted, pointing to something ahead.

"Itimus-four?" Jason asked.

"That and a fleet of seven dreadnoughts in orbit."

"How soon before we're within range to phase-shift down to the surface?"

"We'll need to be in orbit first, Captain, as an intermediary step." Grimes brought up a surface relief view. "Chrimguard compound is here. As you can see, it's big... spanning several miles; I'm not able to get clear sensor readings on all of it."

Jason saw it for himself as he studied the holo-display. Dab smack in the middle of the compound was a gray, almost perfectly circular area that was blocked out.

Jason had never before seen the Caldurian's technology

bested by another culture. But that certainly seemed the case here. Not good.

Grimes continued, "Not only are we unable to get clear sensor readings—perhaps they're being blocked—I'm not sure but there doesn't seem to be a way to establish phase-shift coordinates. There are just no reference points, nothing, to lock on to."

The implications were not lost on Jason. Whatever this new technology was, it could be a game changer in other ways. The ability to phase-shift into a Craing warship was one of their few advantages. If this new blocking technology was integrated into a heavy cruiser or a dreadnought, they were in big trouble.

"Go ahead and get us into orbit. I want to get a better look at that compound... at least the aspects of it that are visible."

Within five minutes, Grimes phase-shifted *The Streamline* into a low orbit around Itimus-four. Their orbiting position was at a midway point between two dreadnoughts—thousands of miles from either ship. Jason had Billy enter the cockpit and become part of their conversation.

"We're above Chrimguard now, Captain."

Live, three-dimensional feeds of the compound filled the holo-display. With its near-white sandy terrain, surrounding what looked to be structures of stacked stone, Jason was reminded of the Middle East back on Earth. The architecture was simple but elegant. Large archways and towering obelisks set among three sprawling azure ponds characterized the grounds in a way one would expect of a spiritual epicenter. "So, the inner grounds to Chrimguard and the Grand Sacellum are hidden," Jason said.

"Looking at it now, it's as if there is a dome surrounding the inner compound. I originally thought it was some kind of energy force field, but it may be more than that. It's a force field, a shield, but it's also physical. Look here." Grimes zoomed in tight to one section of the compound. "See this area at the very edge of the dome? It's a kind of lattice mesh laid over a rigid, dome-shaped, superstructure."

Jason studied the dome and was pleased and concerned at the same time. Pleased, because the dome was not something easily retrofitted on a Craing warship, and concerned because there seemed no easy way to get into the Grand Sacellum.

Billy said, "It looks like there are only three separate ways to enter the inner compound. All three lead beneath the dome, though... what are those? Armed guard posts?"

"Exactly. And each is equipped with a monster-sized plasma turret."

Grimes brought up the logistical overlay, which indicated there were fifty or more red icons clustered around each of the three entrances. A large red icon passed over their zoomed-in area.

"What do we have here? Looks like they have airborne security. Yep, there are two gunships, crisscrossing the sky overhead. That makes things even more complicated," Billy said.

Jason wasn't looking at the gunships; something else caught his eye. "Can you zoom in closer here?"

Grimes did as she was asked, bringing the image on the holo-display in tight on what looked like a conveyor belt. "I'm not sure what that is, Captain."

"I think I know. Supplies. Not everything needs to enter through the three guard posts. Think about it... there'd be a constant roadblock of delivery vehicles blocking ingress and egress. No, this way small manageable items, like packaged goods, are placed on this conveyor belt and fed directly into the compound."

"What are you thinking, Cap?" Billy asked. "I'll guarantee they scan every box, every item, for explosive materials going into that place. So, if you're thinking about putting a bomb on that conveyor belt..."

"No... not a bomb. But if we could use this belt as a way inside to bring down whatever is powering that latticework dome..."

Both Grimes and Billy laughed out loud.

"Cap, sorry to burst your bubble of an idea, but there's no way any of us would fit on that conveyor belt, let alone through the opening into the dome."

"Are you sure about that?" Jason asked.

Billy's forehead folded into a scowl. Then the light came on and he looked back toward the stern of the ship and the cubicle housing several hundred small humans. "Seriously?"

Chapter 38

The huge truck continued on through the Cheyenne Mountain Zoo parking lot and got back on Cheyenne Mountain Highway, continuing to head south. Nan was keeping Mollie close to her, away from the truck bed—away from anyone who'd spent time inside a molt weevil cocoon. *Unreasonable?* she wondered. Probably. Especially since both she and Mollie had lived through that God-awful experience themselves.

"I need to go to the bathroom."

"You just went a half-hour ago."

"I drank a juice box," Mollie replied, fidgeting on her mother's knee.

"If she's got to go, she's got to go," Gus said, not taking his eyes off the road ahead.

"Go and come right back. I don't want you playing up there."

"You think they're going to turn into zombies... don't you?"

"I don't know what I think, but it's just safer if you do what I say."

"But Reese is up there. Wouldn't he protect me?"

Nan didn't have a ready answer for that. "Just go... do your business and come right back."

Mollie made a face and stood to leave.

"Bring me back one of those juice boxes on your way back... that is, if you don't get eaten by a zombie," said Gus.

"That's not funny," Mollie said.

Mollie was out the door and climbing the ladder when Gus glanced at Nan. "You know, there's not much chance of that happening."

"Who would have thought there was much of a chance any of this would happen? Have you taken a look at Cindy lately?"

"When we stopped a while back, I went up to take a leak. Yeah, she's definitely caught a bug or something."

"Bug is right. Maybe I've seen too many old movies, but a part of me thinks there could be thousands of little molt weevils gestating inside her... when we least expect it, she'll split open like an overripe cantaloupe, and they'll all come pouring out."

"Now I know where Mollie gets her over-imagination from."

Nan heard the familiar melodic tone in her head, indicating she was being hailed. She wanted it to be from Jason but saw it was from her father-in-law, instead. She brought two fingers up to her ear. "Admiral?"

"Hello, Nan. How are you? How is Mollie?"

"We're fine. We expect to reach the entrance to Cheyenne Mountain within the next hour. How are things in space? Is Boomer okay?"

"Boomer's fine. Listen, I have something important to tell you."

Nan sat up straighter in her seat. She hated it when someone said things like *I have something important to tell you...* like they were preparing you for terribly bad news—the worst news imaginable. Like Jason was injured, or even dead.

"It's been confirmed. The President of the United States has been taken by the alien creatures."

"Taken? What do you mean taken?"

"Washington has been completely overtaken. It's been verified; the most recent underground bunker they moved the President to was breached late last night."

"Verified how?"

"Video feeds. I saw them myself. Someone, an aide perhaps, opened the vault door and didn't notice a molt weevil waiting high above. Anyway... it dropped down and got its tentacles in and around the door. It was inside the vault within two seconds. One by one, it went after everyone... the President, his family, several cabinet members... soon they were all wrapped up in those cocoon things."

"You said he was taken."

"That's the other thing. Before, the cocoons were pretty much strewn about all over the place, but that's not the case anymore. The creatures are now collecting them, organizing them into stacks... then bundling the cocoons together in mostly confined, dark areas. Hell, the Jefferson Memorial alone must have five hundred cocoons, all tightly packed together in there," the Admiral added.

"That doesn't mean the President's dead, Admiral. I have first-hand experience in that regard. Some people survive when extricated. Mollie and I did. Others too."

"I've heard the same reports. The problem is, nobody has any idea where the President, or Vice-President, or any of the cabinet members, other than you, have been taken."

"What about the speaker of the house?"

"No clue."

Nan knew what the Admiral was alluding to—even without coming right out and saying the words. As of then, as ludicrous as it sounded, she was the acting President of the United States.

"So what do I do?"

Nan heard the Admiral laugh. "Staying alive, for one thing, would be good. Avoiding being trapped in another cocoon would be good too."

"This isn't funny, Perry," she said, reverting to his first name.

"Maybe not, but you have to admit, things couldn't get much crazier."

"I'm sure we'll be safe once we reach the entrance to Cheyenne Mountain. Talk to me about space. The three Craing fleets and Jason's mission to the Craing worlds."

"Haven't gotten an update from Jason in some time, but I'm taking that as *no news is good news*. As for the approaching fleets... they're still coming and we're still waiting for them. The good news is we have *The Minian*, which may not even the score, but it certainly gives us a fighting chance."

"That's good to hear."

"Nan. I'll be back in touch with you within the next few hours. There'll be a packet of information waiting for you at Cheyenne Mountain. When I do make contact... you need to be real clear about what our orders are."

"Your orders?"

"Our orders. Not so long ago, with Jason's help, our remaining Allied forces in space were moved under the purview of the United States government. Be prepared to make some uncomfortable decisions."

Nan wrapped up her NanoCom communication with the Admiral and cut the connection. She took in a long, slow breath and let it back out between pursed lips.

"Let me know if you need a potty break, Madam President," Gus said with a grin.

"You heard?"

"Enough. Albeit only one side of the conversation. I was

wondering... since there's an Air Force One for the President, would this be Dump Truck One?"

She offered Gus a courtesy smile and pressed the talk button on the walkie-talkie. "Reese, is Mollie still up there?"

"Um... yeah, looks like she's just hanging out with Calvin on the couch."

Nan's first reaction was to have him send her back down. "Tell me something. Any of the people we've extricated from cocoons look sick?"

"With the exception of you and Mollie, they all do. Cindy's been barfing over the back of the truck bed off and on for the last hour."

"Terrific." She hesitated before she told Reese the latest news. "There's something you should be aware of. The President and his family, all Washington, has pretty much been taken."

"So you're telling me you're the acting President?"

"That I am."

"Having sick people—potential carriers of who knows what —on this truck is a bad idea."

"Probably. Throwing them overboard isn't an option. I won't do that," Nan said. She waited for him to respond but only heard muffled sounds through the radio. "Reese?"

"Yes, ma'am. I'm getting Mollie away from the others. She's not too happy with me; you should see her coming down the ladder now."

Sure enough, Mollie was climbing down to her right. Nan opened the cab door and patted her knee. "She's here with me now... thank you, Reese."

"I'll be watching the others closely. Anyone who comes up here needs to notify me first and I'll escort them to the bathroom."

"Thank you, Reese. It's too bad it's come to this."

"Better safe than sorry."

She put the radio back on the dashboard and put an arm around Mollie.

Mollie squirmed her mother's arm away and continued to pout.

"Don't be mad, sweetie. Things are complicated. We need to be extra, extra careful from now on."

"I'm sick of this stupid truck. I want to go back to *The Lilly*. I want to stay with my dad." She stomped her foot and turned her face away from her mother.

"Hey, Mollie," Gus said, "You should try to cut your mother some slack." Mollie continued to silently stare out the side window. "How about we cause some trouble?"

Mollie turned her scowl toward Gus.

Then, both Nan and Mollie yelped as the big front tires went up and over a Cadillac Escalade, a Prius, and then a Ford Econovan. As the truck's tires began to *further* flatten the vehicles, sounds of metal and glass crunched loudly below. Mollie and Nan laughed out loud, and seeing Gus maintain a blank expression throughout the demolition made it all the more hilarious to them.

Chapter 39

At a half mile out from the entrance to Cheyenne Mountain, the NORAD and USNORTHCOM Alternate Command Center, Nan heard Reese on the walkie-talkie.

"What is it, Reese?"

"You wanted to know if anything's changed up here with those we released from the cocoons."

"What's happening?"

"Out of eight, half are sick and barfing off the back of the truck bed. The other half seems perfectly fine. Cindy, Calvin's mother, is... I want to say unconscious, but her eyes are open... unblinking."

Nan's mind reverted back to their earlier comments about zombies. She pushed those thoughts away, feeling silly. "What about her vitals? Heart rate, temperature, that sort of thing."

"Um, that's not really my area, but I'll check and get back to you in a few minutes."

Nan brought her attention to the road ahead. She didn't say anything aloud, but she'd noticed they hadn't passed any cocoons for the last hour. She thought maybe Teardrop and

Dewdrop had simply moved them out of the way, off the road, but why weren't any lying on the sidewalks or atop cars as they'd seen earlier?

Nan wondered if these molt weevils were following similar actions to those back in Washington—collecting the cocoons and stacking them into dark, confined places where they could be returned to later, for whatever purpose— maybe for food... or incubating pods for their offspring. Again, Nan had to mentally admonish herself for letting her imagination run wild.

The radio crackled and Nan grabbed it off the dashboard. "What's happening, Reese?"

"Some weird shit. Can you send those two robots, those drones, up here? Oh, and have them follow orders... directly from me."

Nan and Mollie swapped places. "Stay here, Mollie. Don't go up there unless I say it's okay. You understand?"

Mollie nodded. "I've contacted the drones."

As soon as Mollie said the words, Nan saw the two drones pass overhead and lower into the truck bed. "Gus, probably best if you hold up here for a while."

"I should go up there with you—" he offered.

"No, you stay here with Mollie. I'll call down on the radio to give you an update."

Nan made her way up to the truck bed and found Reese sitting on a pile of equipment, the shotgun lying across his lap. The sectional couch was broken into two separate seatings. Near the back, the sick were either throwing up off the back of the truck or lying down on the couch. The two drones were by the back couch, hovering over two of them... one was Cindy.

When Calvin saw Nan arrive, he got up from the healthy-human couch section and came over to where Reese was perched—in between the two groups.

"Why can't I be with my mom? Why do we have to be separated from the others?" he asked, clearly emotional about the situation.

"I'm sorry, kid... but I already told you. Your mother's sick. We need to determine if she's contagious."

"I don't care if she's contagious!"

Nan put a hand on the boy's shoulder and crouched down so she could look at him, eye-to-eye. "I know you want to be with her, Calvin. This is a difficult situation for you and for everyone else."

Calvin looked to the back of the truck, where his mother was lying on a sleeping bag. She wasn't moving and, to Nan's untrained eye, looked to be in bad shape. One of the drones, Teardrop, hovered above her and then silently moved where Nan, Reese, and Calvin were huddled together.

"What's Cindy's condition, Teardrop?" Nan asked.

"She is alive, Nan Reynolds. But her brain activity levels are below human guidelines."

Nan quickly wished she hadn't asked the question in front of Cindy's son; but, then again, he'd have to face his mother's prognosis soon, one way or another. Perhaps this was best.

"Why have some folks gotten sick, but not others?" Reese asked the drone. "Tell us in terms we can understand."

"Special Agent Nathan Reese, the only differentiating factor is blood type. Each one of the sick has either blood type A or blood type B. Approximately one-half of this planet's inhabitants have blood type A or B... the rest, predominately, have blood type O. The prognosis for those with blood type A or B, placed within a molt weevil cocoon, is that they will ultimately undergo five stages of metamorphosis... cellular conversion, embryo, larva, pupa, and imago. Each of those sick here has entered the cellular conversion stage."

"And next they will enter into the other stages?" Nan asked.

"No. That would not be possible."

Nan had always found communicating with the two droids frustrating. "Why not?"

"The other stages of metamorphosis require the organism to be shrouded within a cocoon. Survival past the cellular conversion stage, outside of the cocoon, is not possible."

Calvin was listening, but that last bit of information didn't seem to register on him—or he didn't understand.

Nan put an arm around the boy. "I'm so sorry, Calvin. I don't think your mom's going to get any better."

He looked confused, his eyes moving back and forth between her and Reese and then to Teardrop. "I don't believe you. You're lying!" He broke away from Nan's arm and sprinted toward the back of the truck. "Mom! Wake up... Mom!" He dropped down next to her, pulling her rigid upper torso into his arms, and cried.

The radio lying next to Reese crackled. "We've got company!" came Gus's baritone voice, followed by gunfire below.

Nan spun to see Teardrop and Dewdrop already in the air and engaging what seemed to be attacks from all sides. Plasma bolts erupted from the two drones as they spun around, darting up and down, while maneuvering around the outer perimeter of the truck bed.

How many of them are there? To her left, she spotted multiple long, tentacle-like legs coming over the edge of the truck. A molt weevil's torso flopped down into the truck bed. Reese brushed past her, leveled both barrels of the twelve-gauge, and fired. Nan looked away from the gory mess, lowering herself down onto hands and knees and spinning around, one way then the other, in case more creatures were landing around them.

As quickly as the attack came, it ended. The drones ceased firing and were silently circling the truck.

"That was close," Nan said, sounding relieved. But Reese wasn't listening to her. He stood staring toward the back of the truck. Turning, she saw where he was looking. More precisely, what he wasn't looking at. Both Cindy and Calvin were gone. "Oh my God... how did the damn things even get up here?"

"How do you think?" he snapped. "We obviously needed to add some grease to the sides of the truck." His voice sounded hollow.

She grabbed for the radio. "Gus! Gus! Is Mollie okay?" Nan waited—hearing only background hiss from the radio. "Damn it, Gus, will you answer me?"

"Mom, Gus can't hear you. He's outside kicking molt weevil carcasses off the deck."

"Mollie! You're okay?"

"I'm okay. I stayed in the cab."

Nan let out a breath and held the radio to her chest, saying a silent *thank you*. "I'll be down soon. Stay in the cab." She looked over to Reese. He was taking the loss of Cindy and Calvin hard. She knew it was guilt that had driven him to snap at her.

"Reese?"

"Yes, ma'am."

"There's no way you can go down there and grease the sides of the truck. Can you work with the drones, have them do it?"

He looked at her for several beats before nodding. "That's actually a really good idea. I'll take care of it."

Nan turned to see the four survivors nestled together on the couch. All were women and they looked terrified. She sat down next to them and did her best to appear calm.

"We're going to be all right."

A middle-aged, gray-haired woman wearing a floral print shirt was the first to speak up: "I heard what that robot thing said... about the blood types. I'm blood type O. We all are. Does that mean we're safe? Not going to get sick?"

The other three women waited for Nan's reply with anticipation.

"I think so. I think you're all going to be fine." Nan smiled and tried to look as confident as possible, but the truth was, she had no idea. No idea if they would be fine; if they would make it to safety—or anything else, for that matter. "The best thing for all of us is to stay busy. Why don't the four of you get lunch going?"

The gray-haired woman glanced toward the body of the dead molt weevil with a disgusted expression. "You can think about lunch right now?"

Nan shrugged. "Maybe we'll wait a bit. Um, I'll have Teardrop take care of... that."

She stood and joined Reese, who was transferring two five-gallon buckets filled with grease from a large drum container. "Hey. You going to be all right there, Special Agent Reese?"

"I'm fine." He stopped what he was doing and looked over to Nan. "Listen... I'm blood type B negative. If one of those things gets a hold of me, gets me wrapped up in a cocoon, don't hesitate to shoot me in the head."

Chapter 40

Ot-Mul had just settled in for the night, crawled beneath the covers of his bed, when a knock came at his chamber door. Irritated at being disturbed, he padded over to the door and opened it just enough to see who was there.

"I have urgent news, my Lord."

"I'm sure it can wait until morning," Ot-Mul said dismissively and began to shut the door. "It's regarding the destruction of the Vanguard fleet, my Lord."

Ot-Mul's first reaction was one of disbelief. "You're mistaken... that's simply not possible," he admonished the nervous high priest bowing before him in his ridiculous robe and tall pointy hat.

"It is true, my Lord. I am sorry."

Ot-Mul let the information sink in as he glared at the priest and his pasted-on smile. The stupid old coot obviously didn't get the gravity of this news. He should know that Ot-Mul's crew was the elite of the elite. That they shared a superior bloodline, a unique heritage, that reached back more than a thousand years. Besting his mighty Vanguard in battle was unfathomable.

"Tell me what happened... exactly," Ot-Mul ordered, his voice cold and stern.

"The details are still unclear. What we do know is that one of the dreadnoughts was subversively boarded, yet all Allied ships were too far a distance away. It's a mystery, my Lord."

"Which vessel was boarded?"

"Which one?"

"Which dreadnought was boarded, you idiot. Are you always this thick?"

"It was the replacement ship."

Of course! The replacement dreadnought was not Vanguard and it wasn't crewed by his Vanguard brethren. This had been nothing more than incompetence, by those of inferior breeding. That's what caused this new, devastating, personal defeat to him and the Craing.

Ot-Mul stared at the priest and felt his anger, his rage, continue to build. He knew exactly who had destroyed his fleet and how they'd done it. Captain Jason Reynolds. Reynolds, and that Caldurian phase-shift technology. Fists clenched, Ot-Mul screamed into the night. Without a second thought, he brought his right leg back, then quickly—and far more forcibly—kicked his bare foot up into the still-bowing priest's face.

The old man went down like a bag of rocks, his cone head-dress miraculously perched, if off-kilter, on his head. Ot-Mul closed the door to his suite. There'd be no time for sleeping this night. There was much to do.

Ot-Mul, now showered and dressed in an ornate flowing robe, walked quickly down the ancient, candle-lit stone passageway. His mind reeled. How could he have gotten so caught up in his newly appointed duties as Emperor, the least of which was dealing with a populace on the verge of revolution, that he had underestimated his enemies in space? Fortunately, he'd had the forethought to hide their new headquarters.

A commander doesn't survive, and certainly doesn't become a great conqueror of worlds, without learning from those defeated in battle. For the most part, Ot-Mul's enemies had fallen fast—quickly cowed into pathetic submission. Those who'd put up a valiant fight, showed some grit, at least earned some small measure of his respect. They'd still die, or be enslaved, but they had conducted themselves with honor. Ot-Mul had recently fought an adversary that nearly got the best of him. Their technology was inferior, their numbers few, but they'd hid their forces like none other. It was that same technology, one that emits a highly effective shield against attack, but also it's a signal suppression mesh, which now made Ot-Mul's new headquarters impossible to see and impossible to breach. Even phase-shift technology would not penetrate the dome barrier, for they had nothing to scan visually and nothing to lock on to.

He turned down another, nearly identical, candle-lit passageway. His eyes took in one ornate inset alcove after another—each framing an ancient Craing warrior or high priest overlord, from centuries—maybe millennia, past. The vastness of Chrimguard, with its six, high-reaching obelisks, massive sand-colored stone walls, and cobble-stone floors, was breathtaking. It was a hallowed, peaceful place, one Ot-Mul was unaccustomed to—one where he wasn't sure he rightfully belonged.

He heard distant chanting coming from the Grand Sacellum ahead. *Maybe this is a blessing in disguise,* he thought. It was time to go on the offensive. Time to finally take Captain Reynolds out of the equation—once and for all. To do that he'd need to be, for once, a step ahead. A smile spread across Ot-Mul's face. When they came... and of course they would come... the trap would be set.

Chapter 41

Via NanoCom, Dira let Jason know they'd gathered in the back to speak with the small humans. He left Grimes in the cockpit and made his way down the aisle, stopping when he reached Traveler. Because of his sheer girth, the rhino was the only one sitting alone, taking up two seats side-by-side. Even with the extra seating, he looked scrunched and uncomfortable.

"How you holdin' up, Traveler?"

"I am fine. How much more of this mission involves me sitting on my ass?"

Jason smiled at Traveler's way of saying things exactly as they were. "We're working out the details now. Shouldn't be too much longer."

Jason proceeded on, joining Billy, Dira, and Ricket, who were seated on the deck, near the stern of *The Streamline*. Without seats, storage, or cubicles at this semi-circular section, the area was easily the most open interior space on the ship. Dira had taken six now empty enclosures and stacked them high, one atop the other, in front of them. Six of the small humans, the most vocal ones of all, stood approximately at Jason's eye level upon the top enclosure.

"Why should we help you? We're just as much prisoners here as we were before."

Jason didn't answer their designated leader, Tadd, for a full minute. Answer the question wrong, or continue to piss off the little humans, and it was game over. The tiny man looked to be about Jason's age, shy of forty, and would probably be close in size and stature to Jason as well, prior to the events that shrunk him, and the other captives, to half the size of a G.I. Joe doll.

They'd learned the small humans were called the Rallm. Their planet was situated beyond the outer fringe of Allied space. Similar to humans on Earth, the Rallm had a diverse range of ethnicities and multiple races. From a technological standpoint, they were somewhat ahead of Earth, having progressed to FTL travel over one hundred years earlier.

Jason wanted to get things started on a positive note. He said, "What if I told you there was a possibility you and the others could be transformed back to your normal size? No guarantees... and first we'll need more information... more details on what exactly happened. But it's a distinct possibility."

All six of the rowdy ones excitedly responded with raised voices. Eventually, Tadd held up a hand, shushing them to be quiet. He took a step closer to Jason. "From what we've been able to piece together it was some kind of space anomaly. There were two ships... both appeared at the same time in Rallm space, close to the environ-station where we lived. It was as if two competing wormholes tried to occupy the same physical space. Truth is, at the time we didn't realize what had happened to us... to everything around us. That our area of space had *somehow* contracted. Over time we've come to accept our situation as irreversible."

Jason looked at Ricket and raised his eyebrows.

Mark Wayne McGinnis

Ricket said, "That piece of information helps... provides clues as to what happened. I have scanned your biometric readings and, while you are a fraction of your customary sizes, you look normal in every other way. The truth is, you shouldn't be able to exist here. I've detected that the very atoms that comprise your bodies, your clothes, and everything that encountered that space anomaly, are out of place in this realm of physicality. Atoms are a fixed size, bound by the laws of physics... but your atoms are on a scale of their own... which means your molecular structure does not fit within this plane of existence.

So, it is my hypothesis that you have traded places with another version of yourselves. Somewhere within the vastness of the Multiverse, there are virtual giants living amongst a world of tiny people. In essence, by some amazing fluke, you've swapped existences. What makes the situation worse is that your mere existence here, in this realm, causes problems... the very fabric of space and time here is affected in numerous ways. You must be returned to your own corner of the Multiverse for your own sake as well as ours."

Tadd stood with his hands on his hips, taking it all in. One of the men behind Tadd, a head shorter and totally bald, pointed a finger directly at Ricket. "You're one of them. You're a Craing, like the ones who strapped us into those wretched spheres and made us play your ridiculous games. One by one we were senselessly slaughtered. Do you know how many of us were crushed with the wide end of a Gallopy bat? And you seriously think we would offer to help you?"

Jason was quickly losing patience and it took more than a little willpower to maintain an outwardly calm facade. "Hold on... It would be a mistake to judge Ricket by his appearance. Something I would think you'd be sensitive to also. Understand, we, including Ricket, are at war with the Craing Empire. Ricket is not one of *them*. If anyone can help you with your current situation, it's our science officer, Ricket."

Tadd turned and looked to the others in his group and then back toward Jason: "If you release the rest of us from these cages, we will discuss helping you."

Jason thought about it and the inevitable problem resulting from doing that... little people getting in the way—getting stepped on.

Dira leaned in close, and he felt her breath on his ear. "Perhaps if they stay within one cubicle area," Dira suggested, "we could open things up for them, get rid of the enclosures."

Jason didn't much like that idea, but a concession was needed, and that was a possible alternative. "Fine, we'll go ahead and release you all from your enclosures, but you'll be required to stay in one section of the ship only. Would that be acceptable?"

Tadd considered this for a moment and eventually said, "Yes, that would be acceptable. But we'll want that concession made first... only then will we talk about this mission of yours."

THE NEXT ORDER OF BUSINESS WAS GETTING THE Rallm temporarily situated into their new environment. *The Streamline*'s onboard replicator took care of meal preparation for the Rallm. Dira prepared the tiny portions and distributed them on small, pre-cut pieces of paper. With the storage cubicle cleared out, the Rallm went to work setting up what was, in essence, a camp-like habitat. This immediately brought up new challenges. Previously, bathroom necessities took place inside each enclosure and were handled in the most rudimentary fashion. Basically, a corner was selected to piss and crap in with the hope their Craing captors would get around to cleaning up their mess every few days. Bathing wasn't even an offered option, although most used their water bowls once or twice a week to keep themselves at least partially clean.

Dira suggested one of the two onboard lavatories, the one right next door to the Rallm cubicle, be exclusively available for the small humans. Dira worked with Tadd to provide ramps and to fashion makeshift toilet seats over the toilet; for showering, they would keep a trickle of warm water running in the sink. Not a perfect setup by any means, but the newly dedicated bathroom was welcomed with exuberance by each of the small humans.

JASON WAS SEATED NEXT TO GRIMES IN THE cockpit when Dira crouched down between them. To his surprise, when she opened her hand, Tadd was standing on her palm. "You've kept your end of the bargain, Captain. Thank you." Noticing Grimes in the pilot's seat, he seemed momentarily to lose his concentration, then he looked back to Jason. "Tell me about this plan of yours. How we can help you fight the Craing."

"Let me bring you up to speed on the situation at hand. Due to the recent Allied attacks on Craing military and their government installations nearby on Terplin, as well as on other Craing worlds, their infrastructure has been seriously disrupted. Disrupted, but not destroyed. The Craing's true power lies in their far-reaching military apparatus. In space, the Craing dominate the known Universe.

As part of a new Craing initiative called *The Great Space*, they will further protect and isolate themselves. It's already begun, and they are systematically destroying any and all-star systems in any sector that could potentially pose a threat to them, either now or in the future. My planet, Earth, has been the focus of several recent attacks and, as we speak, five thousand Craing warships are closing in to annihilate my home world."

Tadd said, "We are well aware of the Craing... we have been since even before we were abducted. I'm sorry to hear about Earth."

Jason continued, gesturing toward the holo-display, "What you're looking at is the suspected secret hideout of the newly appointed Craing Emperor, Ot-Mul. We suspect the Craing Empire's government and military headquarters have been re-established there. Once a large religious compound, it was used exclusively by Craing high priest overlords. As you can see, our sensors cannot penetrate the area here, where we know there are sprawling city structures as well as their Grand Sacellum. As we zoom in, you can see there's a latticework dome, miles in circumference, which exercises some kind of advanced signal-blocking technology. As long as that dome is activated, we're blind to what's inside it and unable to lock on to anything tangible. Phase-shifting, how we transport ourselves, would be impossible."

"So, basically, you need to infiltrate the domed area and our unique size could help you achieve that," said Tadd.

Jason knew it wasn't that simple—what he was asking, especially after what the Rallm had already endured, was huge and could very well be a suicide mission for them. He began having second thoughts and considered scrapping the idea in its entirety.

Tadd must have seen the indecision on Jason's face. "For centuries, we've narrowly avoided the Craing and their overt hostilities. If what you're saying about *The Great Space* plan is true, then certainly the Rallm's days are numbered as well."

"You need to understand this could be very dangerous. Truth is... we don't know what you'll encounter down there."

"Why don't you tell me exactly what it is you need us to accomplish?" Tadd asked.

"If all goes according to plan, it shouldn't take more than a few minutes. You and your team will infiltrate the dome at one of its delivery depot entrances. You'll be transporting what is called a SuitPac device. Once you've gotten yourselves far enough into the complex, you'll activate the device. After that, we'll have the necessary, actual, coordinates we can lock on to. In seconds the rest of us will phase-shift in."

Tadd mulled that over for several beats and said, "If you're confident you can get us onto that conveyor belt undetected, it sounds acceptable. Can you show me what one of the SuitPac devices looks like?"

Jason removed the two-by three-inch device hanging from his belt and held it out.

Tadd looked concerned. "To you, that thing is small and insignificant. To us, it's pretty big and probably too heavy for us to carry individually." He continued to examine the SuitPac. "Get one we can work with, and I'll put a team together. We'll go from there."

Chapter 42

Nan heard the blare of a horn and felt the big dump truck slow before coming to a complete stop. "I should check on Gus; see what's going on down there." She put a hand on Reese's shoulder. "You going to be okay up here for a while longer?"

His eyes moved to the two bodies lying motionless at the back of the truck bed, then over to the four healthy women sitting together on the couch. "Sure. Turns out our passengers are an entertaining lot. We all get along pretty well. Just tell Gus to keep away from tall trees and, for God's sake, warn us first if he's going to start running over cars again."

"Will do." Nan gave a quick wave to the ladies and headed toward the front of the truck. She climbed the rope ladder, as she'd done numerous times before, and as she crested the bed's overhang she saw a welcome sight. To her left was a small square guard station and, farther up the road, the tunnel entrance to Cheyenne Mountain—the NORAD and USNORTHCOM Alternate Command Center.

Nan climbed down to the deck, opened the cab door, and scooted in close to Mollie.

"So where is everybody, Gus?"

"Not sure. This guard station is supposed to be manned 24/7. Other than a shitload of dead molt weevil carcasses strewn about, place seems pretty deserted."

"Maybe try the horn again," Mollie suggested, quickly covering her ears.

Gus honked the horn several more times and waited for something, anything, to happen.

Nan leaned forward, squinting her eyes. "What's that?" she asked, pointing toward the guard station. "Looks like there's a note taped to the door."

One of the drones was coming around the front of the truck. Nan opened the door and yelled out, "Teardrop... can you bring me back that note?"

Teardrop moved over to the guard station and hovered in front of the door for several seconds. When it returned it held the torn-off note in one of its outstretched, articulating claws. Nan took the handwritten note.

"What does it say, Mom?"

"It's addressed to me. Says that because of the molt weevil attacks, they had to abandon the guard station. We're to proceed up the road to the entrance and they'll let us in. I'm guessing there's a video camera," Nan said, adding a shrug.

Gus put the truck in gear and got the big Caterpillar 797F powering forward up the hill toward the arched entrance at the face of the mountain. He brought the vehicle right up to the entrance and killed the engine. "Entrance is too tight for us to drive into... we'll have to hoof it in the rest of the way."

Nan looked straight ahead through the windshield into what seemed a dark and unwelcoming tunnel. She was relieved to see Teardrop and Dewdrop proceed forward on their own volition. "Sitting here won't accomplish anything," she said. The three of them moved out of the cab and stood on the deck.

On the pavement below were hundreds of dead molt weevils.

"Looks like there was quite a fight here. And there's something else..." Gus said, walking to the far end of the deck and looking back around the truck's other side.

"What's that?" Nan asked.

"Look around here. See anything moving?"

"There aren't any molt weevils trying to climb up the sides of the truck, like usual, Mom," Mollie said.

"Yeah, that's all well and good, but I'm not going anywhere near that dark tunnel until I'm sure the coast is clear."

"Me neither," Mollie seconded, making an exaggerated, wide-eyed expression.

Both drones emerged from the tunnel. Dewdrop rose and hovered several feet directly in front of the deck.

"What did you find in there? Are you picking up any life signs of the military personnel that run this place?"

"Nan Reynolds, there are no other human life signs within the proximity of this facility," Dewdrop said, completely void of emotion.

"I don't understand. This was supposed to be the most secure location on the planet. What the hell happened?"

Both drones said nothing.

Reese stood up, now standing on the overhang behind them. He held the shotgun casually pointing toward the sky. "Ask them if they detect more of those creatures hiding in there. I think that would explain it."

Teardrop said, "There are no living molt weevils within this facility."

Gus and Nan glanced at each other—obviously taken aback by that answer.

"You're saying the molt weevils... specifically those here in this tunnel, are dead?" Nan reiterated.

"All the molt weevils on this planet are now deceased," Teardrop said.

Mollie clapped her hands together. "Good! I hated every one of them."

"Wait, how is that even possible? How could... probably many millions of molt weevils suddenly die off? Just like that? I don't get it."

Neither drone responded.

Nan looked back over her shoulder. "Stay here with our passengers, Reese. We'll go take a look."

"Um, ma'am... I'd feel a lot more comfortable if you stayed close, where I can protect you," Reese said nervously.

"The drones say it's safe... I think you can take that to the bank. Gus and both drones are armed. Keep an eye on our women friends up there... make sure no one comes near the truck."

"I'm coming with you, Mom," Molly said.

Gus was the first to climb down the stairs, using the attached rope to keep his balance on the slippery steps. Once he was on the ground, Mollie, and then Nan, followed.

"Hold up!" Reese said from above them. A small satchel descended down from another rope. "You'll need these... radios, flashlights, and a few other things you might find useful."

Mollie ran to the satchel, untied it, and started to rifle through the contents.

"Just bring it back here, Mollie," Nan ordered.

Mollie did as she was asked, handing the bag over to her mother. Nan gave a wave to Reese and distributed the contents between the three of them.

"Radio check," came Reese's voice from the radio.

Mollie was the first to answer: "Read you loud and clear."

Gus ejected the magazine on his handgun, checked it, and reinserted it. "Let's go."

The three proceeded deeper into the tunnel, with Mollie the first to turn on her flashlight.

"So not only is this place deserted, but the electricity is also out?" Nan asked, looking over to Gus.

"The facility has its own power station; everything here is self-contained... doesn't make any sense," Gus answered.

"Mom..."

"I see them, sweetie." Nan had her flashlight clicked on and was sweeping its beam from left to right as they walked. Cocoons. Neatly stacked like cords of wood.

Mollie scurried in closer to her mother. "Maybe I should have stayed with the truck."

There was something big and white up ahead. As they got closer it became more evident what was there.

"I've read about this," Gus said. "We'll pass through three of these big blast doors before we reach the NORAD Alternate Command Center."

Both Nan and Mollie looked at Gus and then at the ten-foot-high metal door.

"Three feet thick and solid steel," Gus added.

"Probably doesn't do a whole lot of good if it's left open like that," Nan said.

First, the drones, followed by the three humans, stepped through the partially open door. On the other side, the road continued on until it was swallowed up in absolute darkness beyond.

Nan was wondering if they should even keep going. She felt Mollie reach for her hand and grasp it tight.

Mollie spoke in a near whisper: "There's even more of them now, Mom." Her flashlight beam illuminated what was on their right side.

She was right. Cocooned bodies were stacked all the way up to the rocky ceiling, some twenty feet above. "Let's just ignore them, okay?" Nan said, pulling Mollie in closer as they walked.

Dewdrop, in the lead, was now less than ten feet in front of Gus. Teardrop was the same distance behind Nan and Mollie. They continued on for another mile before they spotted the second blast door ahead. Five minutes later they could see that this one too had been left partially open. Passing through the opening Nan saw the fleshy remnants of a dead molt weevil up above—perhaps cut in half as the door was closing. She was glad Mollie hadn't noticed it.

Immediately after passing through the second door, Nan felt, more than heard, *something*. The drones were acting strange as well, and when they stopped and began to slowly encircle them, she knew they had gone into protection mode.

"What's happening?" Mollie asked.

With a series of clicks, Gus chambered a round.

Flashlight beams swept both sides of the road. Nan looked at the ever-present stacks of cocoons. *Something isn't right.* She heard Mollie take in a short breath. "What is it?" Nan asked.

"Look!"

"I don't see it... what do you see, Mollie?"

"Right there! On the ground."

Nan moved the beam of her flashlight to the pavement at the side of the road. "It's just more of the cocoon material... wrappings."

Gus's baritone echoed off the rock walls: "Well, that's the problem. Looks like quite a few of these cocoon things have been unraveled."

Nan played her flashlight over the green stacks and saw what Gus was referring to. Easily half of the cocoon wrappings were misshapen, split open, and empty.

Chapter 43

"Let me do it."

Jason hadn't noticed that Gaddy had wedged herself forward and joined the conversation. Too many people were huddled behind the cockpit—he missed *The Lilly*. Before he could respond, she continued: "I'm small and I'm fast. You send a clumsy, big human down there and he'll be noticed... stick out like a rhino-warrior... the whole plan will turn to shit."

Billy, standing in his battlesuit and poised to go, shrugged. "Maybe she's right. In this particular instance, a smaller-sized person is probably better."

Gaddy shook her head, looking bewildered: "What's the big deal? It's sixty seconds; I'll get in and get out."

Jason turned back to the holo-display and the close-up view of one of the delivery depot posts outside the dome. They'd waited for nightfall and deliveries to slow down. Although there were small cargo vehicles still pulling up every few minutes, it seemed safe enough to phase-shift in and out without being noticed.

"You're comfortable using the suit... setting phase-shift coordinates?"

Gaddy made a face that conveyed it was a stupid question.

"I will pre-set the coordinates for you," Ricket volunteered.

"No... I'll do that myself, thank you," Gaddy replied irritably.

"All right... fine, then," Jason said.

Gaddy smiled and darted toward the rear of the ship.

"You know this is a half-baked Hail Mary of an idea, don't you? Maybe we should get our asses back to Earth," Billy said, searching first one and then a second battlesuit pocket for what, Jason guessed, was a cigar.

"How many worlds, billions of people, in this sector alone, are being atomized even while we stand here? So, no," Jason told him. "I want Ot-Mul: He's the key to bringing the Craing's systematic sector annihilations to an end."

Jason hadn't seen the Rallm's cubicle encampment for several hours and was surprised to see how it had been transformed. What he assumed were things primarily made of paper—tents and other structures—now filled the cubicle's open space. He saw Dira crouched in the far corner using a pair of scissors, cutting out a pattern on a sheet of paper. She continued to work without looking up, and said, "It's actually kinda fun. Like making little dollhouses."

Tadd and three other Rallm men were standing below Jason's left foot. He could so easily have stepped on them accidentally. Jason knelt and took a closer look at what they had come up with. Two of the men wore what looked like harnesses made from fabric. More strips of fabric tied together, like ropes, were tethered to the SuitPac.

Jason leaned down closer. "Is that a rubber band?"

"Yep," Dira said.

Tadd signaled to the two men wearing the harnesses. Like two plow horses, they dug in and pulled the SuitPac. Their progress was slow at first, but once they'd picked up a little momentum, they were able to drag the thing all around the cubicle with relative ease.

"Is there a way we can affix some wheels to it?"

"Ricket's working on that aspect."

In typical fashion, Ricket showed up, as if on cue, by Jason's side, holding something in his hand. "This should help."

Ricket waited for the two Rallm men to make their way back to Tadd. "Can you have them take off their harnesses?" Ricket asked. He placed what looked like a small jury-rigged cart, wheels and all, on the deck. He then positioned the SuitPac on top of it and reattached the two tethers to the rubber band. "Let's try that out," Ricket said, looking pleased with his handiwork.

Again, the two men slipped on their harnesses. This time, though, they had little trouble getting the SuitPac to roll easily behind them. Jason and Ricket watched them run from one side of the cubicle to the other. The irony wasn't lost on Jason that they would be transporting one of the most advanced technological devices in the Universe by means maybe a mere step above what cavemen would have used.

The Rallm team consisted of Tadd and three other small men. Only Grimes, of *The Streamline*'s crew, would remain onboard.

Gaddy carried a small backpack prepared by Ricket. She opened the flap and looked inside. The SuitPac device, the little handmade cart, and the four Rallm men all sat in a cardboard box. Several of the men gave a cursory wave. She closed the pack's flap and slipped it over one shoulder. Gaddy and the others deployed their battlesuits.

"You know what to do... I want you back here within sixty seconds," Jason said.

"I got it. I know what to do." Gaddy returned Jason's fist bump and phase-shifted away.

In that very same instant, she was transported to the surface of the Terplin moon, Itimus-four. Immediately, she went down on one knee and surveyed her surroundings. She was crouched behind one of the massive rock obelisks and, looking up, she saw there was something affixed to the rocks three-quarters of the way up... a netting or mesh of some kind, stretching horizontally out over the city, and affixed to the many other obelisks positioned around the walls of Chrimguard. The same mesh netting hung down vertically, revealing that it really wasn't so much a dome as it was a tent.

Gaddy checked her HUD. No other life icons in the vicinity. She moved forward, staying low, and approached the mesh curtain. It wasn't what she'd expected; in fact, she could almost see right through the crisscrossed latticework. She slid her gloved hand down the mesh and was able to poke a finger inside. She grabbed and pulled at it. It didn't move or give way in the slightest. She didn't know what the material was, but she guessed it was incredibly strong.

A sound to her left brought her back to the mission at hand. Two sentry guards had appeared out of the darkness onto a stone stairway not far behind her. They were in what seemed to be a heated discussion and didn't look up. She admonished herself to be more vigilant. She waited for them to pass before heading off in the opposite direction—toward the delivery depot.

She reached a cobblestone road, a smaller offshoot of the

main road, which led into Chrimguard. In the distance, several large vehicles were being inspected by four armed guards. And there, too, was the gargantuan, turret-mounted plasma weapon she'd seen on the holo-display. Positioned forty or fifty feet high up on the city wall, she saw that it was constantly panning—left and right—always tracking for potential threats. Keeping to the shadows along the shoulder, she followed the smaller delivery road until it opened up into a small parking lot, where there were delivery vehicles.

Most were parked in several rows, apparently out of service for the night. Gaddy then saw where she needed to go. Beneath a well-lit cantilevered awning was a busy group of four uniformed Craing workers. Two were moving back and forth between a delivery vehicle and a wide countertop, while the other two were placing packages and envelopes onto a moving conveyor belt that led into Chrimguard. Gaddy used the zoom function on her HUD to get a better look at the conveyor belt. The packages moved no more than ten feet before disappearing into a small opening—an opening with a flap. Gaddy guessed it was made of the same mesh material that surrounded the rest of the inner city of Chrimguard.

Zooming in close on the conveyor belt provided her a view of something else. Almost imperceptible, behind the vertical mesh curtain, she noticed the protruding muzzle of a pulse weapon. Then she saw there were others. At twenty-foot intervals, armed guards were watching the depot. Even phase-shifting closer, there was no way she could get close enough in to get the Rallm team onto that conveyor belt.

One of the workers got into the small delivery truck and drove over to where the other trucks were parked. He hopped out, strode over to an identical-looking vehicle in the adjacent row, and drove it over to some waiting workers beneath the awning. Ah! There was her answer.

Contrary to the confidence she'd shown Ricket concerning her ability to set phase-shift coordinates, she needed a few moments to get things right. Gaddy took in a deep breath and let it out slowly. Then phase-shifted.

Now inside the truck, in the semi-darkness, she saw the cargo section of the delivery vehicle was practically full. She activated her helmet light and saw that both sides had floor-to-ceiling shelves. Small packages and envelopes were stacked up all around her. Gaddy wondered how long before the back door would open, and the transfer process begin again. Without wasting a second, she removed her backpack and took out the small open box containing the Rallm men. As her helmet light shone down on them, they used their hands to cover their eyes against the brightness.

"Sorry."

She held up the box and mentally assessed its size. Maybe eight inches by eight... a perfect square. Most of the boxes on the shelves were smaller than that. She found the largest one, nearly the same size, on the top shelf. She set the box of Rallm men down on the floor and, on tiptoes, stretched for the *just-out-of-reach* package. It was then she noticed a step stool on the floor nearby. Gaddy got the stool repositioned and easily grabbed the package off the top shelf. It seemed heavy for its size. Hanging from a cord was a small box cutter. She quickly flicked the razor-type blade out from its protective housing. As she began to slice open the bottom of the box, she heard voices coming closer from outside.

Following the edges of the box, she made three slices— enough to pry open a lid and dump out the box's inside contents. Whatever it was, it clanged when it hit the metal flooring. In the beam of her helmet light, she saw it was a heavy, gold-chained necklace.

Out of the corner of her eye, Gaddy saw the back door latch

turn and the cargo door begin to open. Holding both boxes side by side, three of the Rallm men squirmed free from one box and entered the other one. Though they moved quickly, she silently cursed them for taking so long.

The Craing worker stood in the now-open doorway but was still facing the other worker. Not really tracking their conversation, Gaddy did hear something about his shift being over and needing to clock out. With all four Rallm men finally transferred, and knowing she was out of time, she shook the SuitPac device, along with the cart, into their package. There were several audible groans from within and she hoped she hadn't inadvertently crushed any of them. The cargo door opened wider as the worker finished saying whatever it was he was saying. Gaddy did her best to reposition the flap, but it wasn't perfect. Under even the most casual inspection, it would be evident the package had been tampered with. Gaddy tossed the package of Rallm men onto the floor, turning off her helmet light, just as the cargo door opened up the rest of the way.

Chapter 44

They'd watched Gaddy's movements—from the drop location to an area next to the dome, then down the narrow road leading to the delivery depot, and then into the cargo vehicle.

"So much for only taking sixty seconds," Billy commented.

Jason was thinking the same thing as he watched the Craing worker mosey over to the back of the delivery vehicle and stop. "What's taking her so long?" he asked aloud. "She must be in trouble... let's get down there. Ricket, phase-shift the team—"

In a flash of white light, she was back, standing in the stern of the ship in the same spot she'd left seven minutes earlier.

"That was cutting it close," Jason said, relief in his voice that she'd returned unharmed.

"Captain... the SuitPac."

Jason turned back and leaned over Grimes' shoulder.

She gestured to the holo-display that was zoomed in on the delivery depot canopy. Sure enough, there was a highlighted blue icon moving beneath the awning. "I'm tracking the Suit-Pac. It's left the back of the vehicle and been moved to what, I'm assuming, is the conveyor belt."

Five seconds later the icon disappeared.

"It just went beneath the dome."

"It's a tent."

Jason turned to see Gaddy standing behind them.

"It's actually more like a tent than a dome," she said.

TADD WAS FURIOUS. BOTH BRUN AND LARCMORE were injured, and it was a miracle neither had been killed. He pulled his legs in as the cart slid around, close to where the four of them huddled. It was now lighter outside since the side of the box with the flap was opening up wider with every jostle and bump.

"How's it feel?" Tadd asked, looking down at Larcmore's outstretched leg.

"I won't know if I'll be able to put any weight on it until we get out of here. Hurts a bit."

Tadd felt the carton tumble forward and then everything went weightless for several seconds. "Hold on!"

In a sickening end-over-end drop, Tadd grabbed Larcmore, keeping his eyes locked on the makeshift cart with the heavy SuitPac strapped to it. The box landed and something smashed into the side of his head. Everything went black.

Tadd regained consciousness, upside down, with his head throbbing. There was more light entering now.

"Tadd!" came Dorland's hushed voice.

"Yeah, I'm... okay. What's our situation?"

"Larcmore's dead."

Tadd looked over to the other side of the box and saw Larcmore's still body lying beneath one of the cart's wheels. "You and Brun?"

They both answered at the same time: "Good... still alive."

Tadd slowly got himself turned around and carefully got to

his feet. Both Dorland and Brun were doing the same. Tadd noticed Dorland was holding his arm.

"Is it broken?"

"No. I don't think so."

Tadd steadied himself as his world continued to spin around him.

"Your head's bleeding. Maybe you should wait—"

"I'll be fine." Tadd crossed over to the cart. It had landed right side up. He stepped onto the cart and then, on hands and knees, used the ramp-like SuitPac to climb up to the semi-open box flap. He grabbed the edge of the box with one hand and used his other hand to push up on the flap.

"What do you see?" Brun asked.

"We're on the floor with a hundred other boxes. I don't see any movement." He let the flap fall back and looked down at Brun and Dorland. "If we're going to do this, now's the time."

"You did hear me tell you Larcmore's dead, right?" Brun said irritably. "Four people are needed to activate that SuitPac-thing. We're totally screwed."

"One thing at a time. Right now, we need to get this box flipped onto its side... hopefully, without killing any more of us."

It took far longer than Tadd thought it would. Once the three men had the box flap pushed all the way open they used their combined bodyweight to tip the box onto its side. That accomplished, the cart with the attached SuitPac now lay on its side. Getting both repositioned took more time to correct. Tadd had purposely kept his eyes averted from Larcmore's mangled body since discovering him dead. Now, as he and Brun carried his body to the other side of the box, he took in the damage to the younger man's crushed head. Whatever it took, they needed to return to being normal-sized men... being this small totally sucked.

Wearing the two harnesses, Tadd and Brun strode forward,

until the pull ropes went taut. Tadd looked over to Brun. "You ready?"

"Ready."

Tadd looked to the back of the cart. "You ready to push us, Dorland?"

"I guess."

Tadd leaned forward and pulled. The wheels on the cart started to turn—slowly at first and then faster. Tadd and Brun emerged from the box at the same time and kept pulling as the cart gained forward momentum behind them. But as soon as the cart's makeshift wheels encountered the first of many gaps that separated floor cobblestones, the left wheel began to wobble on its axle. Tadd and Brun continued to pull but both kept a leery eye on the wheel.

Earlier, standing at the top of the box, Tadd had noticed an alcove off to the side. It wouldn't provide much in the way of concealment, but it was better than being out in the open. They soon had a good rhythm going and, like a team of horses, quickly maneuvered the cart around one fallen package after another. By the time they'd reached the alcove, all three were drenched in sweat. It was only then that Tadd heard voices—Craing voices.

Tadd scurried over to the wall they'd just passed and looked around the corner. More workers. They were picking up the strewn packages and putting them back on the conveyor belt. He ran back to the cart.

"We need to do this... right now!"

Brun and Dorland stared back at him blank-faced. "How?" Brun asked incredulously. "The thing's still on the cart. Don't we have to put it on the ground first?"

"No time," Tadd answered. "You two stand on the top edge of the cart, on this side. I'll do the same on the other. Go!"

Tadd moved to the far side of the cart and got himself positioned in front of the right-hand side spring tab on the SuitPac. He then noticed two Craing workers coming into view; bending over, they picked up boxes as they moved along. Once they turned back the way they'd come, there was a good chance Tadd and the others would be spotted in their little alcove.

Both tabs were slightly inset, halfway down the side of the SuitPac. They'd practiced the routine on *The Streamline* and even then, with four able-bodied Rallm men, it was no easy feat getting the two tabs compressed at the same time.

Tadd saw the tops of Brun's and Dorland's heads duck as they got set. "Push!" Tadd urged, his arms outstretched and leaning into the tab. He pushed. The tab receded about halfway into the case. *Crap!* Tadd let it spring back out. He repositioned his hands and got a little better footing. *This is never going to work... it barely worked when we were four and uninjured,* he thought, but *he* readied himself for another try anyway. He saw Brun's and Dorland's heads duck down again. Tadd took a deep breath and felt his heart skip a beat; a Craing worker, opened-mouthed, was looking directly at them.

"Push! Push! Push!"

Tadd gave it everything he could—he pushed until his arms and legs began to shake. What started out as a low groan in his throat quickly grew into something akin to a battle cry, "AHH-HH!" The tab moved all the way into a locked position with a resounding *Click*. Tadd waited for the other side to lock... *Come on!*

The Craing worker was yelling something now. Others came into view. Although the workers were approaching slowly, cautiously—they were nearly upon them now.

Click!

Chapter 45

Tadd didn't know what was happening. This never happened while practicing back on *The Streamline*. His first reaction was to run, get away from the damn thing before it exploded, or imploded, or whatever the hell it was doing, over the course of several seconds. What he didn't expect was to see the SuitPac, a device nearly as large as himself, not only reduce in size but systematically, section by section, cover his entire body in a fitted battlesuit.

He stood there, frozen in place, not knowing what to do. Then he saw the bodies of Brun and Dorland, lying dead, beneath the scattered pieces of the broken cart.

Tadd was so caught up in what was happening, he'd forgotten about the Craing workers. It was only when a huge hand swept down, multiple fingers enfolding him, that he remembered them.

He waited for the pain—what surely would be the excruciating, bone-crushing, last moments of his life. But the pain didn't come. In fact, he felt... fine. The hand gripping him released and Tadd fell back onto two open palms. A face stared down at him from above. The Craing worker was talking, speaking in Terplin. Tadd had picked up some of their language during his time as a captive, back at the arena. The worker wanted to know who Tadd was. Who had sent him here? But then another voice came—not the workers'—but Captain Reynolds'.

"Tadd?"

"Um, hello? Yes, Captain Reynolds, it's me, Tadd... I'm here."

"So... you're wearing the battlesuit?"

"Yes, but I don't know how... we got the SuitPac device initialized, just as you told us to do. I didn't expect—"

"The others? Where are the others in your team?"

"All three are dead."

"I'm very sorry, Tadd." Jason wasn't expecting to hear that. "Can you tell me what's around you? Are you alone?"

"No. I'm presently being held in the hands of one of the Craing workers. There are three of them looking down at me—they are all talking at once."

"Okay. Hang on—we have a lock on you. Stand by."

JASON PHASE-SHIFTED THE ENTIRE TEN-MAN TEAM into the depot together. It wasn't a particularly pretty phase-shift. Having Tadd's coordinates was one thing, but the mesh dome—the tent—had kept details of what lay in surrounding areas hidden from sensor scans. The subsequent result was their battlesuit-matter displaced any other *matter* that happened to be in the way. Two SEALs, Thomason and Gomez, found themselves standing, waist-deep, within the conveyor belt itself. Dira had displaced the front edge of a metal table, and Rizzo's left arm was hidden inside a block wall. Everyone else stood in the clear, including Traveler.

Jason gestured toward Rizzo. "Billy, can you give Rizzo and the stuck SEALs a hand?"

The three Craing depot workers, doing their best not to move, were wide-eyed and looked terrified. Jason figured they were harmless. He noticed one of the workers had his hands held out in front, palms up. Sure enough, Tadd, wearing a tiny battlesuit identical in every other way to his own, was standing up and waving toward him.

"Dira, can you get Tadd? Find a place to keep him safe."

She moved in between the three Craing and held out an open palm for Tadd to jump across to.

Jason turned and found Gaddy standing to his right. "Let's try the nice approach first. Can you ask our friends here where we can find the Emperor?"

Gaddy nodded and approached the three Craing. She retracted her helmet and smiled. "Hello, my name is Gaddy. I am from Halimar. We are not here to hurt you."

"You are with the resistance. I have seen your picture."

Gaddy glanced over at Jason, then back to the one who'd spoken. "Yes, I am Gaddy. Can you help me... help us?"

All three workers shook their heads no at the same time. "No. We would be tortured or executed. Our families too. As much as we believe in your cause, the revolution, we cannot jeopardize our lives."

Jason was curious to see how Gaddy was going to handle this mostly-expected reaction.

"Do you see that member of our team? He is what you call a rhino-warrior: seven feet tall and well over one thousand pounds. And that thing he carries... the hammer? He uses it to crush his enemies." Gaddy turned to face Traveler and raised her eyebrows. Traveler grunted but played along. He approached them, raised his hammer over his head, and let it come crashing down on the cobblestone flooring mere inches from their feet. Everything shook at the impact, and the resulting hole in the ground was several feet wide and a foot deep. Cracks spidered out from the crater in all directions.

"Now imagine what that hammer can do to each of your heads... the mess that would make," Gaddy said. "I'm going to ask you one more time, then I'm going to ask my friend Traveler to use his hammer *three* more times."

The workers kept staring at the broken stone floor until one of them answered: "We can tell you where the Emperor's quarters are. It is late. In all likelihood, he is asleep in his bed."

Ricket brought out his virtual notepad. Now that they stood beneath the disrupting mesh, he was able to scan the surrounding area of Chrimguard, including the Grand Sacellum, and project it into a hovering, three-dimensional representation.

"Show us," Jason commanded the workers. "Lie to us and we'll come back with Traveler, looking for you."

All three pointed to the same location on the display. "It is here. Near the Grand Sacellum. But many soldiers are present, and something else too." Two of the Craing workers glared at the third: "Silence. You must not!"

He kept going: "Two days ago twenty shimmering mechanical soldiers were brought in."

"Shimmering mechanical soldiers?" Jason repeated.

All three nodded.

Jason felt a cold chill come over his body. Jason and Billy looked at each other. Billy said, "We're in trouble... Shit, I thought we'd destroyed those things."

Ricket was busy making selections on the virtual notepad. The display changed to a slowly- revolving image of a Caldurian-designed battle droid. The droid was no taller than the average man, but much wider, with four squatty-looking legs, a barrel-like torso, four arms, and a circular turret of a head.

Every surface was covered with thin, razor-sharp plates that constantly moved, not unlike old-fashioned push-mower blades.

"This what you're talking about?" Jason asked.

Again, all three nodded in unison.

"And they guard the Emperor's quarters?"

"Yes. For two days they have been here, at Chrimguard; they are always on patrol."

"This changes everything," Jason said, the dread at their situation sinking in. "These things are as close to unstoppable as you can find. They utilize *The Minian*'s same advanced phase-shift tech. Individual sections, as well as the whole construct, can phase-shift into the Multiverse and back at will. Fire a plasma bolt, or a micro-missile, or throw a rock at it, and it will phase-shift away. And it possesses a wide array of offensive weaponry. Try to touch the thing anywhere, and you'd be sliced into bits by its constantly moving mower blades. It has three small integrated plasma cannons on its torso, and the equivalent of a turret-mounted railgun right there, on that thing that looks like its head. Oh, and this battle droid is completely autonomous, with its own highly advanced AI."

Billy shook his head. "Bringing in that kind of firepower... sounds to me like we were expected, Cap. Maybe it's a trap."

Jason thought back to events that had taken place above Terplin, on the space platform, the Ion Station. In the process of recapturing *The Minian*, five of those highly advanced and incredibly lethal battle droids had nearly defeated them. Jason looked at his team. How many more would be sacrificed in this mission... Billy? Traveler? Dira? What price would they have to pay to take out Ot-Mul?

"Ricket, can you verify he's even here?"

"I was just verifying that, Captain. He most definitely is. He's currently within the walls of the Grand Sacellum, far below ground, along with seventy-five other Craing."

"That must be a counsel convened of their High Priest Overlords. I'm sure of it... this is the most highly secret, most important, of all their meetings."

"Our lord Ot-Mul is being confirmed," the chattiest of the workers said.

"Confirmed?" Jason asked.

Gaddy and Ricket wore the same troubled expression. "As in going from an acting Emperor to becoming *the ruling Emperor*," Gaddy explained. "It's a twenty-four-hour ceremony, where the ruling overlords transfer all governing and military power over to Ot-Mul."

"Captain," Ricket said, "through this induction ceremony, Ot-Mul will also undergo the *transformation of eternity*."

"Just as Emperor Quorp underwent previously, and Emperor Reechet before that," Gaddy added. "Lom would have been a part of that mix too, but he was killed prior to being *confirmed*."

"So Ot-Mul will be a cyborg, just as you once were, Ricket?" Jason asked.

The three Craing workers were now looking at Ricket with renewed interest.

"The technology today is far more advanced. The resulting outcome will provide for a much more natural, more organic, body. But yes, it is still a cyborg," Ricket answered.

"Wait... so we basically have the entire Craing ruling body, including Ot-Mul, right here... right now."

The three workers, as well as Ricket and Gaddy, nodded.

Billy's typical smile disappeared from his lips. "Wait a minute. So... we end them... there's actually a chance we can end *The Great Space* bullshit?"

"That and the Craing people have a real chance to gain their independence," Gaddy added.

Jason let that sink in. After more than a year of fighting the

Craing, could they really hope for an end of it all? He thought of Earth, and what remained of the Allied fleet, now preparing for the approach of five thousand Craing warships—could that dreaded onslaught be halted too?

Dira retracted her helmet and stepped in front of Jason. There was pain in her eyes. "Win or lose today, we have to try. I... have to try... for all those who died on Jhardon."

"And for two rhino-worlds that no longer exist," came Traveler's deep voice.

Jason's mind turned to Mollie and Nan... were they even alive? Was Earth even a home to return to?

Jason made eye contact with each and every one of his team. One by one they nodded their assent.

"Two teams. Rizzo, find something we can use to tie these three up with."

Chapter 46

Nan pulled Mollie in closer as they steadily moved deeper into Cheyenne Mountain and the NORAD Alternate Command Center.

"Mom, I'm scared."

"Don't be scared. You heard what Teardrop said, *all the molt weevils are dead.*" Nan hoped her casual smile successfully covered up how she was actually feeling.

They'd been walking the better part of an hour since they passed the second blast door. With the exception of their narrow flashlight beams, the dark was oppressive and absolute. To compensate, Nan had to strain to hear any unnatural or strange sounds over Gus's rhythmic wheezing.

"Gus, any idea how far it is to the next blast door?" Nan asked.

"No idea. The good news is it's impossible for us to get lost in here."

They continued on in silence for another fifteen minutes and then the radio crackled. Nan brought it close to her ear and strained to hear. "We ra... sta... al ... ov... kil... nee... help"

It was faint but there was no doubt it was Reese's voice. He was excited, yelling something mostly unintelligible. He definitely needed help. The three stopped walking—waiting to hear if there was more coming.

"Reese, please repeat... did not hear what you said. Are you okay?"

Nan turned up the volume but only radio *hiss* filled the confined space around them.

"This far in... it's amazing any signal got through at all," Gus commented.

"We should go back," Mollie said, looking back in the direction they'd come. "They might be in trouble and need our help."

"That's not going to happen," Gus responded, his tone probably a bit more prickly than he intended. "Your mother's the acting President of the United States and *trouble* is something we need to keep her safe from. A whole lot of people will be counting on her in the days ahead."

Gus was right, Nan thought. She was still having difficulty coming to terms with the fact she was presently the highest-level government official and *de facto* U.S. President.

"Well, we have to do something. I'm sending the drones back."

"Not sure that's a good idea," Gus said flatly.

Nan shrugged. "Teardrop... Dewdrop... I want both of you to return to the entrance. Do what you can to help Agent Reese and the others. Do whatever you have to do to protect them. Get back here as soon as possible. Do you understand?"

The two drones hesitated. Teardrop said, "We are to protect Agent Reese and the others and return." They turned and moved quickly back in the direction they'd all come. Nan noticed the fear on Mollie's face as she watched the two drones speed off.

"It'll be all right, Mollie. They'll be back before you know it," Nan said.

Nan's attention was instantly brought to the road ahead. Something skittered by, just beyond the beam of Gus's flashlight. She brought the beam of her light up higher. Had she really seen something or was it merely her now wildly overactive imagination?

Her mental doubts were quickly answered. "I saw it," Gus said. He slowed his pace and slowly moved the beam of his flashlight from one side of the tunnel to the other. He shook his head and shrugged, moving forward. But Mollie stayed firmly where she stood. Nan glanced down at her and saw an expression of total fright. Mollie wasn't looking ahead or to either side of the road. She was looking up, where countless pipes and cables of varying sizes hugged the very top of the rocky tunnel thirty feet above them, now exposed in her flashlight beam.

"Holy shit," Gus said, his voice several octaves higher than normal.

Three flashlight beams were now aimed at the ceiling: They were all naked—Men, women, children—hanging from either one or both arms. Several hung upside down, their legs securely wrapped over pipes. Nan felt Mollie rapidly inhale—ready to scream. Placing her palm over her daughter's mouth, she bent down so her own face was mere inches away. "Don't scream," she whispered. "We need to stay quiet... very quiet."

Mollie closed her eyes and nodded she understood. Tears were welling out from her clenched-closed eyes.

Gus was still staring up at them, examining them. "Look at the way their heads are tilted to the side and their eyes are closed." He looked back at Nan. "They're asleep. Every last one of the sons of bitches."

With reluctance, Nan looked back up. *How many of them are there?* She aimed her light high in the air, back the way they'd come. *Oh my God.* People had been lying up there all along—at least since they'd passed the second blast door. There were hundreds of them—maybe more.

"Gus, we need to pick up the pace."

The three of them half-jogged, half-ran into the darkness ahead.

Gus was soon winded, his wheezing getting worse. A cacophony of wet, rattling coughs erupted. He brought the inside of his arm up to cover his mouth, but the sound was... *loud enough to wake the dead.*

Gus slowed and staggered as he ran with Nan and Mollie fast upon him. Nan gently patted his broad back, if for no other reason than to give him assurance he was cared about. He seemed to get ahold of himself and his coughing subsided, though he continued walking with his arm hugged tight across his bright red face.

"That's it... you're okay. Just keep on walking... take deep breaths." Nan really wanted to tell him to hurry up, to move his ass. As if reading her thoughts, Gus did somewhat pick up his pace.

"Stop looking at them!" Nan scolded, pulling Mollie's arm and flashlight down. "Pretend they're not there."

Mollie gave her mother the *'you're absolutely crazy'* look but did her best to keep her attention forward.

Off in the distance, something reflected back their flashlight beams. It was white and large. It was the third blast door. Mollie and Nan looked at each other but neither went quite so far as to smile. The thought that kept creeping back into Nan's mind was she was fairly certain whatever she'd seen earlier, what she had discounted as her eyes playing tricks on her—was one of those *people*—one who was awake and moving around down here on the same road... *somewhere.*

As they approached the blast door, there was something

significantly different about it, compared to the other two... this door was closed.

Nan pushed back the despair that wanted to rush into her consciousness. Sure, they'd made it this far, but what now? Turn around and go back? She doubted Gus could make it. He looked, and sounded, terrible.

Gus was the first to reach the gargantuan door. He pulled on it. "Twenty-five tons of steel and it's closed up tight."

Mollie said, "Maybe you're not pulling hard enough."

"Maybe it's a good thing it's closed," said Nan. "Think about it. Wouldn't you close it too with these things hanging around outside?"

"You could knock," Mollie said.

Nan involuntarily glanced up and shook her head. "Try to do it... quietly."

Gus flipped his flashlight around in his grip and gently gave the steel door several consecutive taps.

Nan said, "Didn't you say the door's like three feet thick and weighs twenty-five tons? Do you think those little taps registered on the other side?"

Gus tried again, only louder this time. They waited. Mollie went back to looking upward, staring at the many bodies hanging there. They waited and listened.

"They're like zombies, huh?" Mollie whispered.

Nan really didn't want to go there; had purposely not gone there. She shook her head. "Whoever heard of sleeping zombies?" she asked with a straight face. Apparently, it struck Mollie funny. Perhaps it was the tension—the seeming hopelessness of their situation, but Mollie started to giggle.

Nan glared down at her and whispered "No!" That seemed to push Mollie over the edge. Both hands covered her mouth as her giggles quickly erupted into laughter. As irritation flared on Gus's face, Mollie completely lost it. She had to sit down to catch her breath between howls that echoed around and around —off stone, steel, and concrete.

Nan bit the inside of her cheek and waited. She knew, from experience, a nine-year-old would, in good time, settle down. Anything she'd say now to reprimand her would only set her off again. Irritated, she looked at Gus. "Well, if that didn't wake them up, nothing will. Knock on the door like you mean it."

Gus shrugged and turned toward the closed door. He hesitated and then brought the flashlight way back and slammed its long handle onto the cold, flat metal as though he was pounding in a nail. The sound reverberated all around them. Four more times he hammered his flashlight at the door. On the fifth strike, the flashlight went dark—the bulb shattered. He turned away from the door and let his weight lean against it. "If they didn't hear that, I'm not real sure what we can do." He held out a hand for Mollie and she pulled herself back to her feet. She wasn't laughing anymore, although a smile was still there.

Mollie bit her bottom lip and quickly pointed her flashlight upward. Already more than a little irritated with her, Nan was about to admonish her again when she noticed something. She'd only glanced up for a fraction of a second before looking down at Mollie. Something registered at an unconscious level. *Eyes open.* She looked again. The man, hanging twenty feet above them, his head still cocked off to the side, was no longer sleeping. His eyes were open, and he was looking straight back at her.

Chapter 47

J ason took Ricket aside. "Look, you and I both know we're not prepared to go up against twenty battle droids. We need to find a way to take them out... another way. Outsmart them."

"The weaponry on *The Streamline* is highly capable—"

Jason cut Ricket off. "It's the same damn problem. One, they emit protective shields against plasma-fire attacks, and two, getting a lock on anything is impossible as long as that dome or mesh, or whatever the hell it is, blocks signals."

Ricket simply raised his almost non-existent eyebrows.

"What?" Jason felt the seconds ticking by. Their two teams were waiting to move out. Five thousand warships were headed for Earth, and planets throughout the sector were being fucking annihilated. Then the obvious hit him like a ton of bricks. "Of course! We bring down the tent."

Jason brought everyone back around him. "Listen up! New plan. How many obelisks are supporting that tent mesh, Ricket?"

"Five around the perimeter of Chrimguard and one, much taller, in the middle." Ricket had his virtual notepad up and was looking at a zoomed-in view of the mesh and obelisks. "It appears the mesh utilizes a thick cable, which is secured about three-quarters of the way up on each obelisk."

"Why don't we just blow the obelisks into dust from *The Streamline*?" Billy asked.

Jason shook his head. "Nope, that won't work. Gravity would drop the mesh back down on top of the compound, and we'd be no better off."

Jason had a thought but quickly dismissed it... *too crazy... too dangerous.* The problem was, nothing else was coming to mind. He turned his attention to Traveler. After all he'd gone through over the last year, he hated putting him in harm's way again.

Traveler raised his hammer and did that thing Jason had come to recognize as a smile. Jason closed his eyes and let out a long breath. When he opened them again, he spoke aloud: "Traveler, you're not afraid of heights, are you?"

THE FIRST PART OF THE PLAN WOULD BE TRICKY, over-the-top dangerous. Jason would have to take Ricket's word on the capabilities of *The Streamline*'s weaponry. He was also making an assumption that the mesh tent would be as much a disruptive shield to weapons fired from beneath it as it was from those fired above it. He contacted Grimes and went over the plan. She was immediately onboard with it with one caveat: Could she make the precision shots Jason was asking for from her current, high orbit, location? There was no way Jason was going to put *The Streamline*, their only ticket home, in any more jeopardy than necessary. They'd have to move forward and hope Grimes could make the necessary shots.

"Traveler, you ready? You know what to do?"

"I am ready. I... will need help with the phase-shift coordinates."

"Any of us would. Since we're putting you on top of that mesh surface, Grimes will be calculating them for you. Check your HUD."

Jason heard Traveler's snort beneath his helmet, which somehow compensated for the hot bursts of steamy snot rhino-warriors often expelled throughout their day.

"You just have to keep the mesh continually rolled back as Grimes takes out the obelisks, one by one."

"I understand. I will not let the mesh fall onto the compound."

"Good. Now the Craing aren't going to be sitting around, their thumbs up their ass, while all this is going on. Jackson and Thomason will be on Billy's team. Rizzo and Gomez will be on mine. Ricket and Dira will phase-shift wherever they are needed. I want to be perfectly clear here... we are not going to defeat the battle droids by going head-to-head against them."

Rizzo looked confused. "So how do we... destroy them?"

"We don't, Grimes does. More specifically, Grimes *and The Streamline*. Once Traveler has peeled the overhead mesh tent back, Grimes can fire right into the compound and destroy the battle droids with her big plasma gun. That, or we'll provide the coordinates for her."

"I like it," Jackson said. "One problem—at least half the droids are deep underground, protecting the Emperor and the High Priests. There's no way *The Streamline*'s plasma fire can penetrate down to that depth."

"That's right," Jason replied. "And that's where we'll need to be smart, fast, and agile. Our job will be simple... antagonize and infuriate the droids however possible, to the point they pursue us—chase us up to the higher levels. Then Grimes takes them out... like shooting ducks on a lake."

Dira rolled her eyes at Jason's analogy. She raised a hand.

"You don't have to raise your hand. What's on your mind, Dira?"

"So, let's say we do all that. Take down the droids. What's the plan for the Emperor and the High Priests?"

"You don't have to be a part of that. War is ugly. But they are harbingers of mass killings... destruction throughout the Universe—"

"You don't understand. I want to be there. If those monsters are going to die... today... I'm going to be there too!"

Oт-Mul sat and listened to the old fart drone on and on about only God knew what. Mor-Crik was speaking *Kalpin*, an ancient Terplin dialect that he didn't understand, and suspected half the priests sitting there didn't either. How old was the reigning high priest overlord? Hunched over and supported by a walking stick, he had to be well over one hundred years if he was a day.

Ot-Mul was now eighteen hours into the ceremony and seriously wondered if he could last the remaining six—that is, if the proceedings didn't run over, and they always did. That sober realization had only come to him within the last few minutes. He hated this shit. The pomp and circumstance... the religious mumbo-jumbo. *What am I doing here?* He was a decorated and admired Fleet Commander. Was he to spend the rest of his life sitting in council meetings, dressed up in frilly robes? He didn't want to think about the ridiculous headdress he'd be required to wear.

His attention was pulled back to the speaker. He was smiling and pointing the end of his walking stick in Ot-Mul's direction. Applause filled the five-hundred-seat chamber of the Grand Sacellum. Soft illumination glowed from an immense translucent orb, carved from some kind of stone or mineral that hung from high above the proceedings. Ot-Mul stood and bowed—first, to the high priest overlord at the podium, and then to those on both his left and right within the chamber. The old coot continued on, but he'd changed gears, delving now into a familiar theme of ensuring the continued, enduring, Craing legacy. Ot-Mul sat up a bit straighter when he heard the words *transformation of eternity*. So there it was. He was to basically hand over his *Crainganity* to become... what... some freak of nature? *Immortality, sure, but at what price?*

High Priest Overlord Mor-Crik made his way back to the raised dais, where he would once again join Ot-Mul, sitting to his right. All eyes turned to the empty podium. *Well, what's next?* Ot-Mul thought. *Can we move this along?*

Ot-Mul watched as the next speaker finally made his way to the podium. Wearing the uniform of a decorated Fleet Commander, a royal-blue medallion hanging around his neck, Ot-Mul knew exactly who the officer was: Vigil-Kin—his replacement-to-be as supreme Craing Fleet Commander. Vigil-Kin shared the same bloodline as Ot-Mul, evident by the small tuft of black hair at the top of his head.

Ot-Mul smiled as the officer began to speak. Inside, though, he seethed, hating his arrogant distant cousin. Especially now, for his cousin would soon hold the one position, Ot-Mul realized, he wanted to keep for himself. Was it too late? Was it even possible to halt such proceedings? He did not want to be Emperor... he knew that now. Ot-Mul looked to his right and saw one of the Caldurian battle droids standing guard. As if reading Ot-Mul's thoughts, it turned in his direction. Its shimmering, constantly spinning, blades of armor gave the droid an almost ethereal presence within the hallowed chamber. He could only blame himself—he'd produced the menacing droids on the Ion Station and then had them stockpiled on the surface of Terplin. He recognized the irony in that: his ultimate means of protection were also his captors.

Two more battle droids entered and held positions in the back two corners of the chamber. It was at that moment that Ot-Mul had an epiphany. He was not the first acting Emperor to have second thoughts, but the proper time to change his mind had long gone... if he'd ever even had that option.

The sound of a heavy stone moving—sliding over another— brought the proceedings to a hush. Ot-Mul hadn't paid notice to it earlier, but he now saw that the front wall of the chamber, flat and unremarkable as it was, was slowly descending into the floor. At some point, a rhythmic chanting had begun. All faces were now turned toward Ot-Mul. The wall descended the final few feet, exposing an entirely hidden room behind it. At the room's center was a beautiful, ornately carved, raised pedestal. The chanting got louder as a group of priests entered the once-hidden chamber, pushing forward various types of technical and medical equipment within close proximity of the raised pedestal.

It was time... time for the transformation of eternity.

Chapter 48

Nan, momentarily paralyzed, watched in horror. They didn't all fall at once. But three did. One man and two women, each one naked, weathered the fall from twenty feet above, dropping into low crouches with no apparent injuries. Then they moved with lightning speed.

Mollie let out a scream and Nan stifled her own. There was something familiar about the way they moved. They didn't so much walk as they did skitter, moving from side to side. And then, in the split second, she had time to think, she had it... *they move like molt weevils.*

The three beings darted and circled about them, coming in and out of the darkness. Their faces were blank—expressionless. Nan pushed Mollie behind her and together they backed up close to the blast door. Gus had his gun raised and was tracking whichever one came in closest.

"Get away from us!" he yelled. The authority in his deep voice seemed to have an effect on them.

One of the women started to make a sound. It was guttural and nonsensical, as if she was trying to talk but didn't know how; *maybe she's mimicking Gus,* Nan thought.

Perhaps they aren't dangerous? Nan hoped. Then Gus took a wild slap in the face from the man. He'd struck him in an awkward, almost caveman-like, hitting motion. Stunned, Gus looked humiliated and shot the attacker.

Mollie shrieked as the dead man fell, lifeless, onto the concrete road several feet away. One by one more bodies fell down from above, but the gunshot did keep the attackers back for a minute.

"We have to do something, Gus."

"I thought I just did," he answered back.

More bodies fell from above.

"You don't have enough ammunition to kill them all." Nan began looking left and right, seeing them approach.

"I have five more magazines and I have this." He took out a second gun, one that looked identical to the first. "It's a Glock 19, same as mine. Take it." Without taking his eyes off the attackers, Gus passed his second gun back to Nan with the two magazines. "You have three mags, holding fifteen rounds each... plus, there's a round in the chamber. Between the two of us, we can do a lot of damage."

Before Nan could say anything more, Gus fired again, and a woman fell to the floor. Mollie covered her eyes and wedged herself closer into Nan's back. Nan knew how to shoot—knew how to eject a spent magazine and smack in a fresh one—but she didn't want to. *What? They were going to shoot them all just because Gus got bitch-slapped?* No. It didn't seem right. Maybe there was a way to help them. Bring their humanity back to them.

A tall black man rushed Nan and clubbed her with a closed fist to the cheek and then darted away left. It hurt and nearly knocked her off her feet. Before she could turn and look to her left, she felt Mollie moving from behind her. "Damn it, just stay where you are, Mollie!"

Spinning around, Nan discovered Mollie was no longer there. She spotted two blonde women, both middle-aged, dragging Mollie away by fistfuls of her hair.

Before Nan could think she charged after them. "Get your dirty hands off her you zombie freaks!" Nan took several blows to her head and back as she ran into the mayhem. The first one to block her progress was an elderly man with a wild, white mane; she pulled her trigger and he took a bullet in the chest and fell away. She got a glimpse of Mollie's feet as she was dragged away. Nan fired again and again and kept on firing till she'd cleared a path to the two blondes holding Mollie. Nan ran forward, placed the muzzle of the Glock to the back of one of the women's heads, and fired. The woman fell dead in a heap, still clutching Mollie's hair in a tight fist. In the split-second Nan took to bring her gun's aim around to the other woman, she was sent flying backward in the air by what easily could have been an NFL defensive tackle.

She landed on her back with enough force to knock the wind out of her lungs and cause the Glock to tumble loose into the hordes behind her. Gasping to catch her breath, she heard Mollie's muffled voice cry out, "Mommy!"

Again and again, Nan tried to sit up, but the countless strikes to her head and body, the weight of so many beings pressing in on her, made it impossible. Like a swarm of bees, they circled in and out, each taking a turn striking her before darting backward. Frantically she fought, kicking out with her feet, and punching anyone, anything, within striking distance.

Pain and fatigue quickly took its toll. Nan didn't want to die like this—didn't want her little girl to die like this. She covered her head with her hands, brought her legs in tight, and curled into a ball. *Why isn't Gus firing? Where the hell is he?*

Suddenly, three rapid gunshots were fired above her. The

mass of naked arms and legs withdrew several feet. Nan looked up, expecting to see Gus coming to her rescue. But it was Mollie, bloodied and bruised—her little girl! The NFL guy was approaching; a full head taller than anyone else, he came barreling through the throng of zombies without hesitation. Mollie fired once and the Glock's slide clicked open. She was out of bullets.

Nan, rising to her hands and knees, somehow managed to pull herself upright. Mollie rushed into her arms and together they backed away from the mountain-sized zombie. He too was uttering nonsensical guttural noise. He paused three paces away from them.

Frantic, Nan took the gun from Mollie. Her hands were shaking so uncontrollably it took several tries to eject the spent clip. Together, they continued to back away until there was nowhere to turn. There were too many of them and they were completely encircled. Desperately, she tried to retrieve a fresh mag from her pocket, but they'd run out of time and were rushed from all sides.

Nan felt Mollie burying her head in her chest and shaking in uncontrollable sobs. Together, they lowered to the floor and tried to make themselves smaller as fists hammered down on them. Nan saw Gus lying on his back, sprawled flat near the blast door. His face had taken an awful beating, blood pooling by his nose and mouth.

"Are we going to die, Mom?" Mollie asked, her lips trembling, terror in her voice. She looked around as if expecting another attack at any second.

Nan kicked out and missed a male teenager approaching on all fours, his teeth bared like a rabid dog's. "I don't know... maybe," Nan gasped. "I'm so sorry, Mollie. I'm sorry I couldn't protect you better. I'm sorry you had to endure such horror."

Mollie kicked out at the same teenager and connected to his lower jaw. He skittered away. "I wish I could have seen Dad again. I wish he was here."

"Me too, sweetie... me too."

A thunderous gunshot, louder than any Glock could produce, sent the attackers skittering away to huddle along the walls. Several, like spiders, no, like molt weevils, climbed up the walls and hung down from the ceiling pipes.

It was Mollie who saw him first. Seeing astonishment on her daughter's face, Nan turned and looked back in the direction they'd come.

"Reese!" Mollie cried out.

His suit jacket was gone, and his once stark white button-down shirt was stained with blood and dirt. He rushed to their sides and helped raise them to their feet.

"I thought you were dead. The radio. We heard you yelling," Nan told him. "We sent the drones back..." It was then she saw Teardrop and Dewdrop hovering nearby.

"I was trying to warn you. The bodies at the back of the truck came alive... came at me when I was asleep. I took a few fists to the face, so I kicked their asses overboard. That's when I noticed there were a lot more below, wandering around on the ground. If it wasn't for this shotgun—the noise it makes—I don't think I could have made it here. But it was really the drones that saved the day. Thank you for that."

"And the others? The four women on the truck?"

"Left them jammed in the cab. Uncomfortable, but safe." Pulling a couple of fresh shells from a satchel he wore over one shoulder, Reese reloaded. Nan did the same with the Glock. It was then she noticed the bites on Reese's arms.

"They bit you?"

"Oh yeah, the ones outside by the truck... all carnivores looking for a meal. Give it time and these will do the same."

Reese eyed the approaching NFL-sized guy. Even though he had a bullet hole in his upper left chest area, it hadn't slowed him down much. He rushed forward, both arms reaching. Reese and Nan shot him at the same time—propelling him backward several yards. He came down hard on the pavement, landing like a big slab of beef.

After that, the rest scurried off: either up the walls or back down the road into the darkness.

Reese turned and assessed Mollie's injuries first, then Nan's. "Sorry to say, but you both look like you've gone twelve rounds with Ali."

"Ali Babba?" Mollie asked.

"No. Muhammad Ali... the famous boxer." Nan smiled as she corrected her.

A deep rattling groan came from the direction of the blast door. Gus was trying to sit up. The three moved to his side and carefully helped him sit up. He coughed several times and spat blood onto the road. Leaning against the door, he used his tongue to check for missing teeth.

"Well, I still got my choppers... that's at least something." His gun was right where he'd dropped it and, with another groan, he leaned over and retrieved it. "What the hell are those things?"

Nan shook her head. "Something the molt weevils left behind for us."

"I hate molt weevils," Mollie volunteered.

"Why didn't you just signal them to open the door?" Reese asked.

"Ha, ha, that's not funny," Nan said with a pained half-smile.

"I'm serious." Reese took three steps to the far side of the door, where it opened out from the thick surrounding framework. Sure enough, they saw a large, bright red push button mounted onto a square electrical box. He looked back at the three stunned faces and slapped the button.

Nothing happened for several seconds. Then an alarm sounded, and the overhead lights came back on, lighting all the way back to the first blast door. In a mass exodus, the *human-ish* molt weevil-zombies fell down from above and skittered away—back down the road toward the other blast door.

The massive door began to open, causing Gus to scramble to his feet. All three—Reese, Gus, and Nan—raised their weapons and pointed them at the slowly expanding opening.

They took several more steps as the door opened wide enough to see inside. Six soldiers, pointing automatic weapons in their direction, stood ready to shoot. A man, dressed in navy-blue dress slacks and a pale blue shirt, tentatively approached from behind. When he saw the four standing there, his eyes widened and his mouth fell open. Composing himself, he rushed between the soldiers. "Oh my God... Lower your weapons! Oh my God, Madam President... We thought you were... Come in! All of you come in!"

In a matter of seconds, all sorts of people began to appear inside the wide-open blast door: three medical personnel, service men and women, as well as highly-ranked officers from every branch of the military.

Nan held up a hand, bringing the man in the blue shirt to a halt. "Please, just answer me this: Is Captain Reynolds still alive? We both need to know."

"I'm sorry, we don't know for sure. We think so. But there are other developments you need to be brought up to speed on. For one thing, the Craing fleet has entered our Solar System. Five thousand warships have amassed near Neptune."

"Let's get inside and you can bring me up to speed," Nan said.

"Hold on, ma'am," a medical attendant said, "you've got a pretty nasty bite on your shoulder that needs attending to."

Chapter 49

Traveler phase-shifted to the coordinates Grimes provided him. He stood on the mesh that spanned across and above the inside walls of Chrimguard, perhaps a good half-mile in diameter. Suddenly aware of how high up he was perched, he held out his arms as if to steady himself. He'd underestimated the size of the inner city below and, more importantly, the size of the black material that was toughly spread to the distant high obelisks in the distance.

He bounced his girth up and down a few times, testing the mesh material's support of his weight. There wasn't much give. It was still dark outside and the soft light coming up from inside Chrimguard was visible through the lattice-type material below his feet. He heard the Captain's voice in his helmet.

"Billy, you in position?"

"Aye, Cap. We're just now reaching the first floor. Battle droids are all over the place. Don't think they detect us."

Ricket's voice came on the line: "Not with the signal-suppression provided on our battlesuits."

"Copy that, Billy... thanks, Ricket. Traveler, you in position?"

"Yes, Captain, I am standing above Chrimguard."

"Copy that, Traveler. Hang tight. Grimes, my team's also in position. You ready?"

"Aye, Cap," Grimes replied. "Target in position... firing now."

Traveler watched as the obelisk directly in front of him received intense blue plasma fire. The stone pillar was turned to sand and dust within seconds. The mesh below his feet sagged as he moved forward, no longer attached to a structure. Traveler had to tread carefully; his footing along the edge was becoming difficult. He grabbed the loose mesh piece in both hands, pulling it into his arms.

He'd no sooner taken three steps back when the next obelisk was hit. As that one too crumbled, Traveler began rolling up the excess, detached, material; the weight on his arms had doubled.

For the plan to work, Traveler was told he'd have to move quickly. He'd have to keep up with Grimes' systematic destruction of the obelisks. He was trying his best. Now, with three stone pillars obliterated, the combined weight of the three rolls of mesh material on his arms was taking its toll. As obelisk number four fell away, Traveler was thrown off his feet and dragged several yards forward. Without letting go of the now substantially larger mesh roll, Traveler managed to find his footing and turn around in the right direction; by digging in his heels, he stopped his forward slide.

An alarm Klaxon shrieked from below. Traveler saw movement: small Craing beings moving into position—seconds later, their plasma fire came up from below.

"Are you all right, Traveler?" Grimes asked over comms. "Sorry, I'll slow it down... wait for you to get your balance back."

Like rolling up a circus tent, Traveler continued his laborious work of pulling and rolling, pulling and rolling. Then, awkwardly bent over, he told Grimes, "You can continue. I am ready."

As center obelisk number five came down, it became impossible for Traveler to stand upright. He fell again on his butt and was on the verge of falling into the city, hundreds of feet below.

"I think that will do it, Traveler," Grimes said. "If you can manage it, get all that mesh thrown over the far side of the city wall..."

But Traveler was already sliding uncontrollably down the sloped material. As he began to drop feet first, falling toward Chrimguard below, a white flash appeared, and he was instantly back onboard *The Streamline*.

"Good job down there, Traveler," Grimes said, looking back from the cockpit.

"I did not complete my mission."

"I'm looking at the compound now; with the exception of one small corner, the mesh is out of the way... no longer a problem."

Following behind Jason, Rizzo and Gomez moved down a narrow, curved stairway to the lowest elevation. Alarms had started blaring minutes earlier and Craing security forces were scurrying into position to defend the acting Emperor and the high priest overlords.

"Don't forget, prolonged plasma fire from a battle droid will end you. Use phase-shifting as a defense... be smart."

Rizzo and Gomez both answered, "Aye, Cap."

According to his HUD, there were five battle droids in relatively close proximity. All of them were on the move, patrolling.

Jason gestured down the hallway: "Okay, we've got one coming up the hallway to our left about forty feet out. Engage it when it comes into view. Keep its attention while ascending the stairs backward." Jason checked Chrimguard's layout on his HUD, plotted in new coordinates, and phase-shifted away.

He phase-shifted back into position in the same hallway, some twenty-five feet behind the battle droid. Just seeing the thing raised his heartbeat. *Damn, I never wanted to be anywhere near one of these things again.* And now they were facing twenty of them. Jason scrolled through the list of available multi-gun munitions on his HUD readout. He'd had luck with the rail-gun munitions option, but it was the *Expansion Gum* option that worked best before by causing a viscous stream of brown sludge to spew out in short squirt bursts—gumming up the droids' spinning mower blades.

Jason hung back and waited.

"Here it comes, Cap. Engaging now," said Rizzo.

The noise from Rizzo and Gomez's plasma bursts filled the hallway. The battle droid slowed, then compensated by phase-shifting sections of its body segments in and out of the Multiverse. As planned, Rizzo and Gomez backed their way up the stairway, maintaining a downward barrage on the big droid. Once it reached the foot of the stairs, Jason attacked it from behind.

Squirt squirt squirt. He shot the viscous liquid over every inch of the battle droid. Its shimmering spinning blades, now a gummy-brown mess, ground to a halt. In an instant, it changed direction and came for Jason, utilizing a combination of rail-type munitions and plasma fire. Jason felt himself being hammered backward. In the five seconds he'd been driven back, his HUD readings showed his phase-shift shields were already on the verge of failing. An alarm signal began strobing noisily inside his helmet, while three different warning messages flashed on his HUD.

I need to get the hell out of here! Jason phase-shifted around a corner, further down the hallway. He leaned against the wall to catch his breath. Most of the plasma fire he'd been hit with was to his chest. He recalled the eruption of painful heat blisters the last time he'd fought one of these things.

Plasma fire continued on the stairway. Jason phase-shifted to his last position and saw the battle droid advancing up the stairs. Changing to rail munitions, Jason joined the fight. Again, the battle droid slowed, and this time seemed to be faltering.

"Don't let up, guys," Jason said, now on the stairway. As he rounded the corner he could see the droid, Gomez, and Rizzo. Jason was being hailed by Ricket but focused on the droid; he ignored the hail.

Both Gomez's and Rizzo's battlesuits were glowing red. Jason knew from experience their skins were blistering underneath.

"Shift away, both of you!" Jason yelled.

Rizzo did as ordered but Gomez was already too far gone. He'd stopped firing and was trying to run up the remaining stairs. He stumbled and fell. The battle droid moved in for the kill—firing relentlessly until Gomez ignited into a raging ball of flame.

Jason found Rizzo's life icon and phase-shifted to his coordinates. He found him seated on the floor, his back to a wall. Jason knelt next to him. "You okay, Rizzo?"

"I'm okay... nothing the nanites won't repair over the next few hours. Gomez?"

Jason shook his head. "Sorry, he's gone. You need to be looked at just the same."

Again, Ricket was hailing him via his NanoCom.

"Go for Captain."

"Captain, I've been analyzing the structural elements of Chrimguard—"

Jason cut him off. "Ricket, I don't have time now... hold on for a second."

He hailed Dira.

"You need me there?" she asked.

"Yes, Rizzo's down... needs some medical attention. Gomez is dead."

Dira said, "I'm on my way."

Jason, keeping a close watch on his HUD, noted only one battle droid had been destroyed by Billy's team and that they'd lost Thomason. Both Dira and Ricket flashed into the hallway. Dira had already opened her medical satchel as she knelt next to Rizzo.

"Hold on. You'll need to wait until we're clear, Dira. We've got company coming: four battle droids."

"Captain, I need to speak with you..."

"What is it, Ricket?" Jason snapped.

"We can bring down the compound."

"What does that mean?"

"The obelisks were more than ornamental—they were significant structural elements. It wouldn't take much for the upper structure to fold in on itself and fall onto the lower floors. Bring everything down on their heads."

"Is this something we can do here, from within the compound?"

"No... Grimes can do it from *The Streamline*."

Jason wanted to pick up the little Craing man and kiss him. "You just saved our lives, Ricket. What would we do without you?"

Jason patched into his team's comms. "Listen up, everyone. We're getting the hell out of here... like right now. Grimes, standby, we're on our way back to you."

· · ·

Mark Wayne McGinnis

As the overlords carefully lowered Ot-Mul down onto the raised pedestal, his eyes took in the cacophony of strange, seemingly ancient, mechanical—as well as other, much more advanced—devices surrounding the platform. He felt his naked flesh come in contact with the cold, hard, surface, beneath him.

One of the high priest overlords approached. In his left hand, he held a metallic six-inch-long needle. A needle with a hose attached to its other end. Ot-Mul took in the priest's smile and then his ridiculous cone headdress. No less than six other overlords stepped in closer around the pedestal.

The high priest told Ot-Mul to relax. The others began to softly chant.

"Where are you putting that needle?" Ot-Mul asked, doing his best to sound indifferent.

The priest's eyes quickly darted to Ot-Mul's lower extremities. The old priest's smile wavered. "This will be... somewhat uncomfortable, my Lord."

The quiet stillness of the Grand Sacellum was suddenly shattered by an ear-piercing alarm. All of the High Priests stood upright, looking nervously all around them. Ot-Mul sat up. There was no doubt about it, Chrimguard was under attack.

Ot-Mul had been planning his escape from the *transformation of eternity* procedure, and that six-inch needle, even before he heard the thunderous plasma fire coming from above. He catapulted himself off the pedestal. It's amazing what a natural instinct for self-preservation does to a crowd of scared old priests, he thought, watching them frantically scuttle off in all directions. He found his robes and headed back into the main chamber. He motioned toward the back of the chamber and within moments he had four of his battle droids rapidly advancing.

"You will get me out of here, out of Chrimguard, even if you have to blast holes in the walls to do so. Go!"

With two in front and two behind, Ot-Mul and the battle droids quickly fled the chamber of the Grand Sacellum.

The End.

Thank you for reading The Great Space, Book 6 of the Scrapyard Ship series.

GOOD NEWS! The entire Scrapyard Series is available. Just go to Amazon.com

If you enjoyed this book, please leave a review on Amazon.com

To be notified of new books, please join my mailing list - I hate spam and will never share your information. Go to this link to subscribe:

http://eepurl.com/bs7M9r

Please check out all my books here: markwaynemcginnis.com

or go to the **Also by Mark Wayne McGinnis** page of this book.

Thank you, again, for joining me on these SciFi romps into space.

Cheers, Mark Wayne McGinnis

Acknowledgments

I am grateful for the ongoing support I receive for the Scrapyard Ship series books, as well as for the other books I've written. This book, number six in the Scrapyard Ship Series, came about through the assistance and combined contributions of others. First, I'd like to thank my wife and partner, Kim McGinnis, for her boundless love and unwavering support of my less-than-routine profession, with its crazy hours, demanding timely schedules, and putting up with my perpetual complaints about my ever-aching back.. None of this would be possible without her. Second, I would like to thank my mother, Lura Genz, for her tireless work as my first-phase creative editor and a staunch cheerleader of my writing. At 83, she's still a force to be reckoned with when it comes to editing the clunky, odd sentence. I'd like to thank Mia Manns for her phenomenal line and developmental editing ... she is an incredible resource. And Eren Arik produced another magnificent cover design. I think it's my favorite so far. I'd also like to thank those in my writer's group who have brought fresh ideas and perspectives to my creativity, elevating my writing as a whole. Others who provided fantastic support include Lura and James Fischer, Sue Parr, and Chris DeRrick.

About the Author

Mark grew up on both coasts, first in Westchester County, New York, and then in Westlake Village, California. Mark and his wife, Kim, now live in Castle Rock, Colorado, with their two dogs, Sammi, and Lilly.

Mark started as a corporate marketing manager and then fell into indie-filmmaking—Producing/Directing the popular Gaia docudrama, 'Openings — The Search For Harry'.

For the last eleven years, he's been writing full-time, and with over 40 top-selling novels under his belt, he has no plans on slowing down. Thanks for being part of his community!

Also by
Mark Wayne McGinnis

Scrapyard Ship Series

Scrapyard Ship: (Book 1)

Scrapyard Ship: Hab 12 (Book 2)

Scrapyard Ship: Space Vengeance (Book 3)

Scrapyard Ship: Realms of Time (Book 4)

Scrapyard Ship: Craing Dominion (Book 5)

Scrapyard Ship: The Great Space (Book 6)

Scrapyard Ship: Call to Battle (Book 7)

Scrapyard Ship: Uprising

Mad Powers Series

Mad Powers (Book 1)

Mad Powers: Deadly Powers (Book 2)

Lone Star Renegades

The Star Watch Series

Star Watch (Book 1)

Star Watch: Ricket (Book 2)

Star Watch: Boomer (Book 3)

Star Watch: Glory for Sea and Space (Book 4)

HOVER

Heroes and Zombies

The Test Pilot's Wife

The Fallen Ship Series

The Fallen Ship: Rise of the Gia Rebellion (Book 1)

The Fallen Ship II (Book 2)

Junket: Untamed Alien Worlds

USS Hamilton Series

USS Hamilton: Ironhold Station (Book 1)

USS Hamilton: Miasma Burn (Book 2)

USS Hamilton: Broadsides (Book 3)

USS Hamilton: USS Jefferson - Charge of the Symbios (Book 4)

USS Hamilton: Starship Oblivion - Sanctuary Outpost (Book 5)

USS Hamilton: USS Adams - No Escape (Book 6)

USS Hamilton: USS Lincoln - Mercy Kill (Book 7)

USS Hamilton: USS Franklin - When Worlds Collide (Book 8)

USS Hamilton: USS Washington - The Black Ship (Book 9)

ChronoBot Chronicles

Made in United States
Orlando, FL
22 January 2025

57605901R00176